The Adventures of Finn and Annie
Cozy Mystery Set Volume 1

FINNIAN CHURCH IS TRYING to piece his life back together. After losing his leg while in the Army, he is starting a new career as an insurance investigator. Joining him is newly hired videographer, Annie Summers — a woman who lost her hearing but is trying to make it as a single mother of two. The world might see them as broken and battered souls, but as they come together to solve mysteries, they discover they make a great team. Join this unlikely duo as they investigate their way through murder, arson, theft, embezzlement, and maybe even love, seeking to distinguish between truth and lies, scammers and victims.

The Adventure of Finn and Annie is a collection of 10 mini-mysteries that weave into one story filled with mystery, joy, humor and romance. As you join Finn and Annie in their adventures, you'll meet a loveable cast of characters while you follow two people grow together. In these clean, heartwarming short stories by Wall Street Journal bestselling author Christopher Greyson, join Finn and Annie as they team up to solve mysteries and just maybe fall in love!

Praise for Christopher Greyson's
Finn & Annie

Finn & Annie are amazing!

A really great, sweet mystery!

Enjoy the brilliance of Finn and Annie!

Finn & Annie on the surface seem "broken." Together, however, they are unstoppable!

Five Brilliant, Shiny Stars!

From multi-award-winning *Wall Street Journal* bestselling author Christopher Greyson comes this spellbinding tale with jaw-dropping secrets, a colorful ensemble of characters, and a protagonist you'll root for from the first page to the last. Christopher Greyson's novels have been read by millions of readers.

ALSO BY CHRISTOPHER GREYSON

The Girl Who Lived

One Little Lie

Pure of Heart

The Adventures of Finn and Annie

The Detective Jack Stratton Mystery-Thriller Series:

And Then She Was Gone

Girl Jacked

Jack Knifed

Jacks are Wild

Jack and the Giant Killer

Data Jack

Jack of Hearts

Jack Frost

Jack of Diamonds

Captain Jack

DEDICATION

This book is dedicated to my brother Ted. He has watched over me my whole life and I am very grateful for his continued inspiration.

A MINIMYSTERY SERIES

THE ADVENTURES OF
Finn &
Annie

COZY MYSTERY SET
VOLUME 1

WALL STREET JOURNAL BESTSELLING AUTHOR
CHRISTOPHER GREYSON

GREYSON MEDIA

CONTENTS

THE ADVENTURES OF FINN AND ANNIE-THE CASE OF THE ATTIC DOOR

THE ADVENTURES OF FINN AND ANNIE-THE CASE OF THE DROPPED GROCERIES

THE ADVENTURES OF FINN AND ANNIE-THE CASE OF THE WAYWARD RIDE

THE ADVENTURES OF FINN AND ANNIE-THE CASE OF THE PHANTOM PET

THE ADVENTURES OF FINN AND ANNIE-THE CASE OF THE DISAPPEARING DIAMOND

THE ADVENTURES OF FINN AND ANNIE-THE CASE OF RAINING NAILS

THE ADVENTURES OF FINN AND ANNIE-THE CASE OF A MOUSE IN MY SOUP

THE ADVENTURES OF FINN AND ANNIE-THE CASE OF THE MISSING GIFT

THE ADVENTURES OF FINN AND ANNIE-THE CASE OF THE SLIPPERY DOG

THE ADVENTURES OF FINN AND ANNIE-THE CASE OF LIGHTNING STRIKES TWICE

A MINIMYSTERY SERIES

THE ADVENTURES OF

Finn &
Annie

THE CASE OF THE ATTIC DOOR

CHRISTOPHER GREYSON

A MiniMystery Series

THE ADVENTURES OF
Finn &
Annie

THE CASE OF THE ATTIC DOOR

WALL STREET JOURNAL BESTSELLING AUTHOR
CHRISTOPHER GREYSON

GREYSON MEDIA

CHAPTER 1

F innian Church opened the door to the well-kept house and was greeted by silence and the faint stench of death. He glanced up and down the deserted street, frowned, lifted up the police tape as he maneuvered under it, and entered. The new videographer looked to be a no-show. So much for references from his mother. He should have known better. Finn's mom was perpetually trying to find him a girlfriend, and even though she swore that this wasn't the case, he didn't believe her.

He took out his smartphone and recorded a slow pan of the living room, making certain the date and time code were in the corner of the screen. Besides the odor of a corpse a few days past its expiration date, it was a nice house. The ME and his crew had taken the body, and the police had finally given Finn access to the crime scene.

From the report of a home invasion, he'd expected a chaotic scene, but the living room was neat and immaculate. There wasn't a spot of dust anywhere. Everything was meticulously placed and arranged. An enormous TV hung on the wall, and a large couch faced it, with a brown leather recliner to one side. A teak coffee table sat on a tan area rug in front of the couch. Oak flooring spread into the kitchen in the back. The only thing out of place was a medium-size cardboard box in front of a bookshelf, labeled with a large black X.

He moved to the hallway, turned around, and took another panning shot. Checking his watch again, he grimaced. He'd had high hopes for today, but with the videographer not here, his expectations of wearing just one hat on the job were quickly fading. He'd wanted to be free to think solely about the case, without the distraction of multitasking.

Weren't for bad luck, wouldn't have no luck at all. Finn's perpetually grumpy uncle's words came to mind, making him smile. But Finn didn't believe in luck. He believed in planning, and today his plan had gone wrong—simple as that.

Pushing aside his frustration, he kept the video rolling and he moved farther into the house.

A hallway extended to the right of the kitchen. To the left were two closed doors and a staircase leading up to where Ralph Evans had been found. Finn's shoes clicked off the steps. The dark hardwood was beautiful, but it only reminded him of the high number of slip-and-fall cases he'd covered that involved beautiful polished-wood stairs very similar to these.

A ski slope without the snow.

He shook the railing, but the stout wood spindles hardly vibrated.

Secure handrailing, check.

Two wall sconces provided ample illumination for the corridor.

Well-lit, check.

The upstairs hallway was lined with photographs on both sides. Some were of Ralph Evans and his wife in exotic places around the globe; others were professional prints. There were a lot of them. The floor in the hallway was bare oak, too.

No rug, check.

The tape outline of the body, only four feet away from the

top of the staircase, looked like one of those green army men Finn used to play with as a kid. Left leg pulled up and left arm stretching out. The outline was consistent with the detective's assumption that Evans had been crawling for the stairs when he died. As Finn walked around the outline, the click of his heels and the squeak of the floorboards echoed in the enclosed space.

He turned back to the pictures on the wall. They formed a timeline of Ralph's life. At one end was a picture of Ralph as a little boy on the first day of school, smiling from ear to ear and missing a couple of teeth. Then came a collage of pictures showing Ralph growing into a tall young man. A photograph of his college graduation was farther down the line, and next to that was his wedding day. Ralph was beaming and so was his bride. Mrs. Evans was a plain-looking woman, but her huge grin made Finn realize that the cliché was true: all brides were beautiful. The last picture was a framed photo of the couple. On the bottom of the frame were the words, *together forever.*

The faces of the friends and fellow soldiers that Finn had lost in the war slowly cycled through his mind. His therapist had taught him several techniques for stopping the morbid thoughts, but he merely closed his eyes and watched as the faces of his fallen friends paraded by. The pain of remembering their sacrifice was a small price to pay for what they had given. He prayed that someday he'd forget the horrors of war, but forget his friends...? Never.

The front door banged open, and a woman called out, "Hello?"

Finn loosened his tie and took a deep breath before shouting, "Upstairs!"

He was working on stress-reduction techniques. His therapist had encouraged him to perform little micro-rhythms: loosen tie, take a deep breath, long exhale, let the stress float away. It never worked, but he was still trying.

He retightened the knot in his tie and waited for the sound of approaching footsteps. Instead he was startled by the clatter of someone setting something down.

"Hello? Finn?" the woman called out again. "It's Annie Summers, the videographer."

Finn bristled at her informal manner, an infraction that he might have overlooked if she weren't also late.

"I'm upstairs, Ms. Summers," he shouted down, even louder. "Please come up." Though he said "please," his tone left no doubt that it wasn't a request.

His phone buzzed in his pocket. He pulled it out to check the incoming text message, but his attention was focused on the stairs. He could hear the videographer pacing back and forth. Why didn't she come upstairs?

"Ms. Summers, please..." His irritated voice trailed off as he read the text:

SRY LATE. WHERE R U?

It was from Annie Summers.

His patience gone, he shouted, *"Upstairs!"*

The front door opened and closed. *What in the world is she doing?*

His phone buzzed again. I'M DOWNSTAIRS.

Stuffing his phone in his pocket, he thundered down the steps. A bright-green duffel bag with painted yellow daisies sat beside the front door next to a tripod. He marched to the door, yanked it open, and stared straight into the prettiest blue eyes he'd ever seen.

CHAPTER 2

The woman didn't flinch. A broad smile spread across her heart-shaped face. "Finn?" Ducking underneath the police tape, she thrust a hand out, and he moved instinctively to shake it. "I'm your new videographer. Sorry I'm a bit late." Keeping hold of his hand, she stepped by him into the house, turning him as she went. She smiled as she awkwardly released her grip. "I brought my video camera and a still camera. Your call. Do you want a top-to-bottom?"

Finn straightened his tie and glanced at her jeans, ankle-high boots, and thick, gray, casual sweater. The faded jeans weren't ripped, but had a streak of what looked to be a mix of peanut butter and jelly near her hip and a pink sparkly smear on her thigh.

"Oh, darn it." Her eyes had followed his, and she started wiping at the stains with a cloth she produced from a front pocket.

Finn decided to shelve discussing her unprofessional appearance for a later time, if that would even be necessary. He was already planning to place an ad for another videographer.

"Sorry about that." She scrubbed at the stains. "I thought with a crime scene I might have to get dirty, so I hope you don't mind me wearing jeans. They started out clean, but I'm just a walking napkin for my kids." She pointed at the peanut butter. "Tommy's six. And this is glitter paint from my little artist, Tammy. She's five."

"So, you have kids?" He tugged the knot of his tie.

"Two. It's just us three musketeers at home." She cleared her throat and shifted under his gaze. "They won't interfere with my being on call. I have a friend who watches them."

"That's not an issue. Kids don't matter." Finn coughed. "I mean, as far as the work is concerned. I just..." He stepped past her and headed for the stairs. "Let's start upstairs and work our way back. My mother didn't know if you had done insurance investigation before. Have you?"

He glanced over his shoulder. Annie was still wiping at the stains and making no attempt to follow. He cleared his throat and reminded himself that he was no longer in the service. He no longer issued orders—he made requests.

"Ms. Summers, before we proceed, I need to know a little about your level of experience."

Stuffing the cloth back in her pocket, she turned to face him and smiled. She sure was pretty, and the grin seemed genuine, but it didn't win him over. That was twice he'd had to ask the same question, and now she not only refused to answer but had a big smile on her face.

"Ms. Summers—"

"Just Annie. Where do you want to start? I can use the tripod, freehand, or I have a body rig in my bag. I can do whatever you need." She crouched down and unzipped her bag.

"Have you worked an insurance investigation before?"

"If you want still pics, I can do that, too." She held up a digital camera with a lens as wide as the smile on her face.

Finn was about to explode. Why was she being coy about her insurance experience? He could show her the ropes, and he'd made it clear to his mother that he'd train any new hire. He was sure his exacting mother would have relayed that information. His temples were throbbing.

"I also want to thank you," Annie continued. "And I can assure you that you won't need to make any adjustments for me. Sometimes texting works best, but I have a gazillion speech-to-text apps. I won't slow you down, and I really, really appreciate this job." For the first time, he noticed that she spoke slowly and very carefully.

Finn felt a flush heat his entire face and neck, and he had to loosen his tie again. *I'm an idiot.* "You're hearing-impaired?"

"I'm deaf." She gave him another sunny smile. "Aurally, I get nothing—no sound. But like I said, it won't be a problem."

Finn pressed his lips together like they might reveal the sudden panic racing through his mind. Had he said anything offensive? He'd raised his voice, but he was upstairs. Satisfied he couldn't have offended her, he found a pang of doubt still kept his mouth closed. Could a deaf person function in this role?

Annie twisted a silver ring on her hand. "I can read lips like no one else. I assure you, I can do this job." Again, that impossibly sunny smile and those sparkly blue eyes.

The thought of her courage, her spirit, that smile that made her look like a five-year-old seeing her first butterfly, made Finn burn with shame. What a hypocrite he was. He of all people should be the last to put up a wall against someone with a physical challenge.

He held his head still and spoke directly to her. "Let's start upstairs. Still pictures are fine."

She nodded happily and picked out her gear from her daisy duffel.

When they reached the top of the stairs, her nose wrinkled at the odor, but Finn had to give her credit: her hands were as steady as a rock as she snapped a picture of the tape outline. Then she followed him down the hall five feet to the dried pool of blood, and the dark stain shone in the camera's flash.

He waited until she lowered the camera and was looking at him before speaking. "We're just going to document the scene and take some measurements. It's an active police investigation, and their guys have already been through here. Mrs. Evans will be back in town tomorrow."

"Where is she now?"

"Visiting relatives in Ireland. That's the reason no one discovered Ralph for nine days. A neighbor found him."

Annie brushed back an errant strand of blond hair that had flown loose from her messy bun. "It's very clean for a home invasion. Not that I have any experience of that." She lay down on the floor and snapped a picture of the hall. "What did they steal?" She stood up and dusted off her pants.

"Nothing that the police and neighbor could tell. They'll know more once Mrs. Evans looks the home over."

Finn blinked and turned away as the flash from Annie's camera blinded him.

"Sorry!" She looked embarrassed.

"Yeah," he muttered. "You don't need to take pictures of the ceiling."

"I wasn't." Annie pointed at a rope dangling from a panel in the ceiling. "Attic stairs. I thought you could use it for a distance reference."

Finn nodded. "That's right. So you've done insurance work before?"

Annie shook her head. "No, but I got my hands on everything the library had when your mother told me about the job."

She stood a little taller and flashed a smile as bright as the flash that had blinded him. Her proud grin made Finn's earlier worries that he may have offended her vanish in an instant.

"Why don't you get some video and I'll take measurements?" he said.

"Sure thing." Annie nodded, turned, and hurried downstairs.

"Careful on the stairs!" Finn called out to her as she heedlessly thundered down them. He rolled his eyes. It would take some effort to remember that he couldn't communicate with her unless she was facing him.

He took his laser measurer from his jacket pocket and started entering figures on his tablet. Annie came back up wearing what looked like a vest with a mechanical arm and camera attached. Even though she jogged up the stairs, the camera didn't bounce.

"Steady cam," she proudly announced. "I can get one continuous shot from upstairs and then move through the downstairs if you'd like."

"That would be great, once we're done. I still have to get some measurements. Why don't you start in the back bedroom and work your way toward me?"

Annie started recording, and Finn went back to his figures.

Several minutes later, squeaky floorboards announced Annie's arrival. She stopped in the hall and stared down at the bloodstain. "Hmmm."

He looked up at her. "Is something wrong?"

Annie shook her head. "Just thinking."

Finn studied her, suddenly fixated on trying to guess what thought was making her lips press together and her nose crinkle. With her hand on her hip, she looked like she was appraising a piece of modern art and confused by the artist's intentions. He glanced away when she looked at him and he realized he'd been staring.

"I'm done up here," he said. "Let's go downstairs."

"Sorry," Annie said, stepping forward and placing a hand gently on his shoulder. "I can't understand if you don't look at me."

"Right, I forgot." He pivoted back around, and his left foot slipped off the top stair. He fell—and the all-too-familiar sensation of dropping made his stomach lurch.

But he instinctively tightened his grip on the railing, holding the tablet safe in his other hand, and managed to keep the slide down to four stairs. Other than his butt, the biggest thing hurt was his pride.

Annie rushed over to him. Her look of concern was quickly replaced by a puzzled stare. He knew she had seen. His left pant leg was hiked up, revealing the prosthetic extending from just below his knee. Her eyes darted back to his face, and he saw in her features the expression he dreaded above all others.

Pity.

"I'm fine." He planted his right foot against the banister and pulled himself upright.

"The wood's slippery," Annie said, her voice even lower than usual.

Finn got up, readjusted his pant leg, and stomped down the stairs. He didn't intend to stomp, but the fall had thrown off his rhythm. It was one of the hardest parts of losing his leg. Part of his mind still thought it was there, and that made simple tasks like walking down the stairs a risk.

At the bottom of the stairs, he checked his tablet. It was fine, but he'd banged up his knuckles holding on to it when he crashed against the railing.

Annie stepped in front of him and peered into his face. "Are you sure you're all right?"

"I'm fine." He tried not to glare as he looked her in the eye and repeated, "Fine."

Seemingly satisfied, Annie resumed taking pictures.

Finn pulled up the police report and checked the attached

crime scene photos. He scrolled through two before he felt Annie looking over his shoulder. He turned so she could see his face. "These are the actual crime scene photos. They can be pretty graphic."

She nodded. "What happened?"

He scrolled over to the report summary. "The police suspect that someone broke in while Evans was home, and they surprised him. A robbery gone bad. The ME confirmed that cause of death was blunt force trauma to the back of the head."

Annie's mouth pulled to one side, and she raised an eyebrow.

Once again Finn found himself wishing he had psychic powers. "What?" He lowered his tablet.

"Nothing." She shook her head and started to turn away.

Finn stepped over to remain facing her. "Look, one of the reasons I hired you was to get another pair of eyes on this. If you have an opinion, I'd like to hear it."

Annie's skeptical look deepened. "It's probably nothing, but... isn't the hallway loud?"

Finn shook his head. "Loud? I don't understand."

"The boards up there are really squeaky. So how did someone surprise Ralph and hit him on the back of the head?"

Finn looked up at the ceiling like he had X-ray vision. He pictured Ralph walking out of the back bedroom and down the hall. A silent shadow slipped out of the other room, rushed up behind him, and struck him in the back of the head with a heavy object.

Finn replayed the scene, turning up the volume. This time, the man rushing down the hallway set the whole space ringing with squeaky floorboards and echoing footfalls, and Ralph, alarmed, turned to face his attacker.

The tablet flickered as Finn scrolled over to the autopsy photographs. "The ME is positive that the fatal blow was the one to the back of his head."

"I'm sure it was. I'm probably totally wrong. It just seemed odd that—"

"Wait a second." Finn lowered the tablet. "How do you know the upstairs floor squeaks?"

Annie swallowed. "I haven't always been deaf. I noticed that the floorboards have a lot of give when you walk on them. I remember that sound could be like fingers on a chalkboard, and since there's nothing up there like carpet or fabric to deaden the sound, I just figured it would be loud."

Finn nodded, impressed. So she could remember sounds. Interesting. Everything she said made sense. He took a deep breath and could feel himself finally calming down from his fall on the stairs.

"Maybe he heard the guy and tried to run," Annie said. "Then the guy hit him over the head from behind."

"That would work," Finn agreed. "And Evans got the bruise on his forehead from hitting the floor face-first."

Annie looked at the photo and nodded, but then started shaking her head. "How did he get those scratches?"

Finn scrolled back to the detective's summary. Ralph had four scratches running from the middle of his forehead to the top of his bald head. The scratches weren't deep, but they were hard enough to leave rough red lines.

"The detective thinks Ralph surprised the intruder in the hallway and they struggled. The intruder may have had something in his hand that caused the scratches. Ralph broke free and the intruder struck Ralph in the back of the head as he ran away."

"What struggle?" Annie turned her camera around so Finn could view the pictures she'd taken. "All the photographs on the wall are level. Can two men fight in a narrow hallway and not make a mess?"

Finn lowered the tablet and stared at Annie.

"Don't listen to me," she said. "What do I know? The police

are already looking for someone who's breaking into homes in the area, right?"

"Several break-ins. Two were on this street." Finn paused, trying to recall the information. "A neighbor said he heard a loud bang a couple of days earlier—before they found Ralph's body. He just thought it was Ralph doing some work, because there was a ladder on the side of the house."

Annie moved beside him to look at the tablet.

"I'm sorry I didn't get a chance to send you the report," Finn said. "They have to be encrypted and it's rather complicated. Next time I'll send you the report in advance." He clamped his mouth closed, mentally kicking himself for not choosing his words more carefully. He didn't know if there would be a next time.

Annie pointed to the summary. "It says the back door was unlocked and slightly ajar."

"The intruder could have come and gone that way."

Annie nodded and stepped away. "It's just so sad that someone gets killed putting up Christmas decorations."

"Why do you think Evans was putting up Christmas decorations?"

Annie pointed to the cardboard box with the big black X. "X is for Xmas."

Finn crossed the room and opened the box. Sure enough, it was filled with red and green place settings and table decorations.

"See?" Annie said over his shoulder. "But I was wrong about the decorations. He was setting the table."

Finn shook his head. "I don't know if you're wrong. Maybe Ralph was getting ready to hang decorations. That's why the ladder was against the house."

"Are there any other boxes around?" Annie scanned the living room. "It's a big house—I'd think they'd have more decorations."

"I didn't see any other boxes." Finn realized: "If Ralph took the ladder out in order to hang decorations, there should be other boxes."

"Is there a basement?"

Finn shook his head. "But there *is* an attic. Let's go up."

CHAPTER 3

F inn stepped carefully around the blood and stopped beneath the rope hanging from the upstairs ceiling. He pulled it, the trapdoor lowered, and folding stairs swung down and opened, stopping four inches off the floor. He had to push down on them in order for them to lower completely to the floor. When he took his foot off, they sprang up slightly, bouncing up and down and tapping against the wood.

Great, a moving staircase.

He grabbed both sides of the stairs and started to carefully make his way up them. Because of his prosthetic, he needed to lift his left leg far back so his shoe would clear the riser. He bristled when Annie moved over and reached out to support his arm.

"My bad. Sorry." She made a playful frown.

"It's... I... Don't worry about it." Finn hurried up the stairs as quickly as he could.

The unfinished attic had a plywood floor covering bare joists that stretched off into darkness. The floor bounced almost as much as the hanging stairs, and Finn grabbed a crossbeam for support.

Annie climbed up after him. "We need light."

He looked around for a switch, but Annie pressed a button on her phone to use it as a flashlight. Finn pointed, and Annie highlighted several boxes in the corner. Each had been labeled with a large black X.

"More decorations." Finn reached forward to open the nearest box.

Annie grabbed his arm. "Careful." She aimed her flashlight up at a thick ceiling joist that he had just narrowly avoided hitting his head against.

"Thanks, Annie. I would have..." His words trailed off as an idea began to form.

Annie's light reflected off an object on the floor. "What's that?" she asked.

Finn reached down into the shadows, grabbed the object, then held it up.

"It's a headlamp." Annie made a motion like she was putting on a hat. "Like bicyclists wear at night."

Finn turned it over. The device consisted of a cloth band with a plastic plate attached to it. Clamped onto the plate was an LED light. The power switch was set to ON, but the light was off.

Finn rubbed the four plastic tabs sticking out of the plate—and his eyes widened. It was as if he was putting the last pieces of a jigsaw puzzle together.

"Oh, no way," he said. "This *wasn't* a home invasion."

"Then how did Ralph get killed?"

He grinned. "You were the one who figured it out, Annie. Ralph was decorating the house for Christmas. There's no light up here, so he used this." Finn held up the headlamp. "He was getting the boxes of decorations out and smashed his head against the joist. Ralph was three inches taller than me."

"That's what made the scratches!" Annie yelled excitedly.

"Ralph smacked his head, and the lamp scratched his forehead as it came off. The lamp tumbled next to the box, and Ralph fell..." Finn looked down the stairs.

Annie shook her head. "But if Ralph fell into the hallway, the folding stairs would have still been down."

Finn's grin widened as he motioned for Annie to move away from the staircase. "I've got a theory about that." He peered down at the spring-loaded, wooden folding stairs that hovered four inches higher than the hallway floor when there was no weight on them. *It wasn't much bounce, but...*

Grabbing a joist to steady himself, he tried to press down on the stairs with his prosthetic leg and quickly pull it back up. The stairs bounced a little bit, but he wasn't able to really shove down hard with his leg.

Annie waved her hands. Her eyes sparkled, and he could see she realized what he was trying to do.

"Can I try?"

Finn moved aside, and she took a position like a gymnast on the parallel bars, holding on to a joist with both hands and standing on the edge of the floor. She hopped down, and landed directly in the middle of the folding staircase. The staircase banged off the hallway floor. Annie immediately hopped up, lifting herself off the stairs and landing back on the attic floor.

The staircase bounced, folded back up, and slammed shut with a bang.

Finn grinned broadly and wiggled a finger in his ringing ear. "That must have been the big bang the neighbor heard. Ralph hit his head on the beam, fell through the opening, bounced off the stairs, and hit his head again on the wood floor. The stairs folded back up into the ceiling. Case closed!"

For once, Annie wasn't smiling. "Please tell me you can open the stairs again."

Finn stood there blinking, unsure of the answer. To his surprise, he wasn't panicked. He would have expected that when facing the prospect of being trapped in an attic, his familiar symptoms of PTSD would blast into him with the same fiery intensity of the IED that ripped off his leg. But they didn't materialize. Instead he found himself staring into Annie's blue eyes. She was searching his face, praying that he'd rescue her from this trap of his own making, and like a schoolboy desperate to show off for the new girl in town, he was determined to find a way out.

"Of course I can get us out. No problem."

His boast made Annie's smile return—which only fanned the flames of his determination.

Finn scanned the attic, his gaze stopping on a broom leaning against the rafters. Seizing the potential key to their freedom, he moved to the end of the folding stairs, at the side where the door swung down, and motioned to Annie to move to the other side, where the stairs connected to the floor.

"When I push the stairs down with the broom, you flip the stairs the rest of the way open with your foot."

Annie gave him a thumbs-up, nodded rapidly, and got in position.

Finn couldn't stop grinning as they worked together to gain their freedom. He pushed the stairs down, Annie flipped them open, and they snapped into place, fully extended to the floor below.

Annie clapped her hands together and hurried down the stairs. When she reached the bottom, she planted one foot on the stairs and held them in place as she waited for Finn.

Finn looked down. His heart was thumping in his chest; he felt like he was about to jump out of an airplane. But he knew it wasn't because of the stairs. It was because of the woman who smiled up at him like bottled sunshine.

He started down. With each step, his hand tightened on the railing. And when Annie's hand at last took his, he felt like a conquering hero stepping onto the floor.

"I'm sorry I doubted that you had a way of opening the stairs when we were in the attic. I'm a little claustrophobic." Annie suddenly wrapped her arms around him.

Warmth. The slight scent of jasmine. Silky hair brushing his cheek. Her embrace was the briefest of gestures, but for Finn it was a breakthrough. With a simple hug, sweet Annie had managed to smash through his protective shell like a Sherman tank.

"Congratulations again on solving this case." Annie stepped back, her face aglow. "I think we'll make a good team."

"I have to disagree with you there, Annie," Finn said as his smile continued to grow. "I think we'll make a *great* team."

A MINIMYSTERY SERIES

THE ADVENTURES OF

Finn &
Annie

THE CASE OF THE DROPPED GROCERIES

WALL STREET JOURNAL BESTSELLING AUTHOR

CHRISTOPHER GREYSON

A MiniMystery Series

THE ADVENTURES OF

*Finn &
Annie*

THE CASE OF THE DROPPED GROCERIES

WALL STREET JOURNAL BESTSELLING AUTHOR
Christopher Greyson

GREYSON MEDIA

CHAPTER 1

Finnian Church sat parked in front of the big white house and double-checked the address against the insurance claim. The appointment time listed in his calendar was 2:00 p.m., but it was 1:58 and there was no sign of Annie. He was starting to text her when the sound of screeching tires behind him made him drop his phone, press his back into the seat, and brace for impact.

In the rearview mirror, a banged-up sedan, the color of a bruised banana a week past its prime, skidded to a stop, leaving just inches separating the vehicles. Finn's road rage short-circuited when he recognized Annie in the driver's seat.

Seemingly oblivious to how close she had come to making impact, she smiled, brushed her blond hair back, and bounded out of the car, her bright-green duffel bag slung over her shoulder.

As Finn stepped from his vehicle, she waved enthusiastically. "Made it on time." She grinned, apparently mighty proud of herself.

"Are you out of your mind?" Finn loosened his tie and tried

to take deep breaths. "Do you have any idea how close you came to hitting me?"

Annie waved a hand dismissively. "I didn't even come close. My dad was so freaked out about my being deaf and driving that he had me take a TVOC driving class. That's the *same one* the police take. Except I had a former NASCAR driver for an instructor. He was an experienced stunt man, too."

Finn nodded, but then shook his head when he saw the tiny sliver of space between the two bumpers. "You nearly turned me into a crash test dummy. While we're on the job, let's drive like insurance investigators and not daredevils."

"Okey-dokey, boss."

Again, that impossibly sunny smile and those sparkly blue eyes brought him up short. She had taken to calling him "boss," and though he technically was, he didn't much care for it as a nickname.

"Let's skip the 'boss' and stick with Finn. Did you receive my email?" He stood facing her so she could read his lips.

Annie nodded, her blonde, long, loose curls bobbing around her shoulders. She flashed her perfect smile, then made a circular motion in front of her teeth. "The insurance claim is for hurting his teeth. It looks like he bashed a hole through them."

"Sure did. That had to hurt."

Finn started down the cement walkway. The white colonial was well-maintained and boasted a manicured lawn. Four brick steps led up to a wide wooden porch.

Annie had already removed her camera before Finn even pointed to the steps. He nodded his approval, and she lit up as if he had just high-fived her. Maybe he should have. As his videographer, she was already exceeding his expectations. She had an intuitive feel for it, not only capturing just the right footage of the accident scene but always finding the perfect spot and angle.

Finn continued up the steps and rang the doorbell. It chimed, followed by the bark of a friendly-sounding dog.

Finn adjusted his tie. Since losing his left leg below the knee, his fight-or-flight instinct had sharpened, maybe because flight now consisted of awkwardly lurching away. His doctor was unsure why Finn, once an avid runner, still struggled so much with his gait, but anything beyond a fast walk usually resulted in him crashing to the ground in a frustrated heap.

"Can I help you?" a voice said. The homeowner stood in the open doorway, holding a large golden lab by its collar.

Finn had been so distracted by his own thoughts, it took him a moment to compose himself. "Good morning. We're the insurance investigators. I'm Finnian Church and this is Annie Summers." Finn held his hand low and motioned to Annie, who waved as she snapped another picture of the steps. "We need to take some measurements of the accident scene, and I need to ask you some follow-up questions, please."

"Certainly. I'm Jordan Miller. This is Molly." He patted the chubby dog, who wiggled from nose to tail, then pattered down the hallway and disappeared.

"I'll get the measurements, too." Annie pulled out a tape measure and started recording the data from the stairs.

"There's not much to tell, really." Jordan crossed his arms and leaned against the doorframe. He tilted his chin toward his chest so he was looking down at Finn. It was a bit of a power play, and Finn got the impression that Jordan was a wannabe alpha-male type.

"All the same," Finn said, "if you could walk me through what happened, I'd appreciate it."

"I came home from grocery shopping and I was bringing the bags up the front steps. I tripped and ended up going face-first into the doorknob." Jordan stepped out onto the porch, closed the door behind him, and pointed at the knob. "It busted a hole in my upper and lower teeth."

Jordan blinked as Annie's flash blinded him. She snapped two more pictures of him and then took out her measuring tape.

"What's she doing?" Jordan asked, blinking wildly.

"Measuring." Annie held the tape up to the tip of his head. "Five-ten."

Now that Jordan was off the threshold and on an equal level with him, Finn resisted the urge to look down his nose at the shorter man. But Finn didn't need to play games to prove his masculinity.

"I'm five-eleven, actually."

Jordan reopened the door and stepped back up onto the threshold. Molly suddenly reappeared, dashing down the hall. She skidded to a stop on the polished wood floor, a red ball in her mouth, and pushed against Jordan's leg, but he ignored her.

"The dental visits were a nightmare," he continued. "My dentist is the best in town, but he's still trying to get the color to match."

Finn's family pride bristled at hearing the claim that this man's dentist was the best dentist in town. Finn's brother was a local dentist as well, and he was confident Liam was the best. Liam would have had no trouble getting the color of Jordan's new teeth to match.

Receiving no attention from her owner, Molly pushed by Jordan and bowled into Finn. The heavy dog pressed herself just below Finn's knee and the top of his prosthetic. Finn stumbled back in an effort to right himself, quickly shifting his weight to his right leg, but it was too much, too fast. He hopped on his right leg, completely off balance, his left leg sliding out at an awkward angle.

With the fluid grace of a dancer, Annie stepped up next to him and wrapped a balancing arm around his waist. She stood firmly in place, her side pressed against his.

"Sorry about that." Jordan snapped his fingers, but Molly ignored him and trotted in front of Annie.

Finn glanced down at Annie, and she released her grip from around his waist. He fought down the flash of shame and cursed his own pride. He hated needing anyone's help. If Molly had crashed into him a year ago, it would have been the dog that stumbled backward, and Finn wouldn't have given it another thought.

"Why did you bring the groceries up the front steps?" Finn asked. The dog had hiked up his pant leg a bit, and he pulled it back down over his prosthetic.

"Excuse me?" Jordan snapped his fingers again. "Molly, get inside."

"You park your car in your garage. Why didn't you bring the groceries in from there?"

Molly stepped closer to Finn, and Annie grabbed the red ball from her mouth. She held it up, and the dog pranced. "Go get it!" She tossed the ball into the house and it flew down the hallway, bouncing off the polished wood and walls. It sounded like she'd flung a bowling ball into the house. Finn winced as the ball careened into the kitchen and thudded against the baseboard.

Molly took off after it, her nails making almost as much noise as the ball.

Jordan scowled at Annie, but she just smiled and started taking more pictures, completely unaware of the racket she had just created.

"Sorry about that," Finn muttered.

Molly came racing back toward them, the ball in her mouth once again. This time Finn braced himself and stopped the charging dog without losing his balance. She opened her mouth and dropped the slimy ball into his hand.

Gross.

The ball wasn't made from the squishy plastic he'd

expected; it was solid plastic, as hard as a bocce ball, and surprisingly heavy for its size.

No wonder it sounded like a cannonball when Annie threw it.

Finn held the ball out to Jordan, not wanting to give it back to the dog. "What kind of ball is that?"

"Street hockey. I used to play. College."

Annie looked up from her notepad. "Excuse me, what was your answer for why you brought the groceries in through the front door? Did I miss it?"

Jordan shuffled his feet. "The garage was... getting cleaned. Spring cleaning. So I parked in the driveway and brought the groceries up the front steps."

Annie cast a quick sidelong glance at Finn. The brief look let him know that she doubted Jordan's story too.

Jordan suddenly snapped his fingers and tapped his index finger against his temple. Finn cringed. Any first-year acting student knew not to use this clichéd movement to indicate they had just 'realized' something. Jordan might as well have twirled a handlebar mustache to show he was the villain in a story.

Finn folded his hands together and waited for the lie that was about to come.

"Maybe that's why I tripped." Jordan nodded at his own sudden revelation. "Since I never bring groceries in the front door, I wasn't used to doing it and... boom! I tripped." He glanced down at Finn's left leg. He'd seen the prosthetic. "You understand losing your balance, right?"

Finn wanted to knock the smirk off Jordan's face, but he swallowed his anger. "Thank you for your time, Mr. Miller." Finn shook Jordan's hand. "We'll be in touch."

"Great. Like I told you, it was just a simple misstep." Jordan looked as if he was about to say more, but thought better of it and clamped his mouth shut. He grabbed Molly's collar, waved at Annie, and closed the door.

Annie cast a quick puzzled look in Finn's direction before

putting her camera in her bag and following him down the walkway.

Once they were out of earshot and close to the cars, Annie said, "You didn't buy that story, did you?"

"Jordan's not winning any Oscars, that's for sure. But I want to go check something out before I talk to him again. And I need to swing by and speak with my brother about Jordan's teeth."

"Your brother?"

"He's a dentist."

Finn had five brothers and one sister. All of his siblings had gone on to professional careers. He was the only kid in the family who hadn't. He'd intended to make a career in the military and then law enforcement, but the IED that ripped off his leg changed all that.

Worse, since he was the baby of the family, his siblings had always watched out for him, and now that he'd lost his leg, they were all smothering him with offers of help. He didn't *want* their help, and he certainly didn't want their pity.

It wasn't a matter of pride—at least, that was what he kept telling himself. It wasn't even about the leg. It was simply that before the bomb he'd felt like his own man, fiercely independent. And now... the blast had done more damage than just his leg. It was like it had ripped a hole inside of him, and nothing he could do fixed it.

Finn's hand tightened into a fist. He didn't need anyone's help.

"Do you need me?" Annie stood facing him, and because she was whispering, the personal space rule was broken by at least six inches.

Finn stared into her blue eyes, and the double meaning of her question made him blush and question his earlier conviction. In the short time he'd known Annie, he'd found himself wanting to be around her the way a cat seeks out sunshine. But he pushed those thoughts out of his mind and focused on business.

He took a small step back to be sure she could see his mouth as he spoke, and hoped she wouldn't wonder about his reddened cheeks. "I'm heading to my brother's and then to the Ice Palace. I may need a picture, but it'll just be an exterior shot."

"The Ice Palace? I take the kids there all the time. I'll meet you there!" Annie nodded rapidly and hurried to her car.

Finn called after her, once again forgetting she couldn't understand him with her back to him. "I might not need photographs if I'm wrong!" He took out his phone and texted her. The last thing he wanted was to waste Annie's time on a wild goose chase.

Annie backed out and shifted into drive. Just before she zoomed off, she stretched her arm out the window and waved. The simple gesture made Finn smile. Annie gave off an effervescence, like sunshine in a bottle, just bursting to get free. Finn hit SEND and got into his car, still smiling. *Annie Summers.* As Annie's car rounded the corner and disappeared, he closed his eyes and hoped his theory about Jordan was right. Mostly because then he could call Annie and see her again.

CHAPTER 2

F inn stopped outside the white farmhouse that his brother
had converted into a dentist's office. Why most dentists
chose to convert old homes into office space was beyond him,
but he couldn't deny his brother had done a fabulous job.

The renovation had been a family affair. Everyone had
gotten involved—except for Finn. They'd all tried, repeatedly,
to convince him to chip in, but he just hadn't been able to
handle the "new normal" just yet. There was a time when Finn
would have been bounding all over a construction project,
climbing the structure like a sailor scurrying up a mast. But
now? Now everyone cringed and winced when he lifted a
power tool. It wasn't their fault. Nor was it his. He just needed
to relearn.

That was what his therapist, Dr. Rodgers, kept telling him.
The diminutive man would often fold his hands in his lap and
say, "You must unlearn what you have learned."

The first time Dr. Rodgers made the comment, it set Finn
off. He vented and swore for a full minute before demanding,
"Who came up with that garbage? Freud?"

Dr. Rodgers shook his head and smiled. "No. Yoda."

Finn chuckled at the memory as he got out of his car. Dr. Rodgers wasn't a typical therapist, and he appreciated that. The more he knew of the doctor, the more he liked the man.

Finn bypassed the ramp and held on to the railing as he climbed the four stairs to the front door of his brother's office. The converted waiting room still had the charm of a farmhouse living room, and the half dozen people sitting there appeared quite comfortable.

Liam's receptionist, Sandy, smiled as Finn approached the window.

"Hey, Finn. Do you want to wait in the office?"

"That'd be great. Tell him I only need a couple of minutes, tops."

Sandy's eyes rounded in concern. "Is everything okay?"

Finn forced the smile to remain on his face. "Everything's fine. I need his professional opinion on some teeth."

Sandy exhaled, but the look of pity on her face remained.

Finn gave her a polite nod and headed for his brother's office. He tried not to let Sandy's concern get under his skin—tried, and failed. It was understandable, if irritating, that his family continued to worry about how he was adapting to civilian life, but it was unacceptable that they expressed those concerns to everyone they knew. It made him feel like his disability was defining him to everyone in town—to the point that he was considering moving.

Liam wasn't in his office, so Finn stepped inside and closed the door. The room was furnished with a wooden desk, a leather chair behind it, and two matching leather chairs in front. Finn wondered how often any of these chairs were even used. Liam didn't really do any of the office work; his jewel of a wife, Mary, ran the office with an efficiency that would make a staff sergeant jealous. Truth be told, she made Finn jealous of Liam, too. Mary was the type of spouse who made her partner stronger and brought out his best qualities. Liam had turned

into a better husband than Finn had ever imagined his irre-
sponsible older brother could be.

No sooner had Finn walked to the desk than the door
opened and Liam entered.

"Hey, Finn. Everything okay? Why don't you sit down?"

Finn ignored his brother's motherly tone. Liam was staring
at him like he was a toddler unused to walking who could fall
over at any minute. Finn hated the look, even if he understood
it.

"I'm fine," he said. "I just have a quick question."

Liam shut the door, but not before casting a glance out
toward the waiting room.

"It'll only take two minutes," Finn said. "Can you take a look
at these teeth for me?" He turned on his tablet.

"Is this for work?" Liam's voice rose excitedly. "Sure. No
problem. Don't worry about me, little brother. I have all the
time in the world for you."

Finn forced a smile. It seemed wrong to be mad at someone
for being overly nice to him, but that was how he felt. He would
give anything to go back to the old days when Liam would
punch him in the arm and tell him he could only give him two
seconds because he was swamped.

"Check out this guy's mouth." Finn scrolled to the photo of
Jordan's teeth and enlarged it.

Liam grimaced. "What did the guy do, try to eat a
doorknob?"

Finn's hopes sank. He stared at his brother incredulously.
"When did you get psychic powers?"

Liam laughed. "Is that really what happened?"

Finn gave a one-shouldered shrug. "That's what I'm trying
to figure out. This guy claims he was carrying a bag of
groceries, tripped, and landed mouth-first on a doorknob."

Liam cringed. "That would do it."

"Could something else cause that type of injury? Like a street hockey puck? They're round."

Liam nodded. "Of course, it could be a number of things. There's no way for me to tell you exactly what caused that injury. All I can say is that it was something round. Someone could have jabbed the guy in the face with the butt of a pool cue."

"Perfect. That's what I wanted to know. Thanks, Liam."

Finn started for the door, but his brother stepped in front of him, blocking the way.

"Hey, I heard that you got a new partner." Liam waggled his eyebrows. "And I heard she's real cute."

"Not going there." Finn's lips pressed together. "And tell Mom to stop trying to play matchmaker."

"She wasn't." Liam raised his hands in mock surrender. "You were the one who said you needed a photographer. You can't blame Mom if she happened to get one who's kinda hot."

Finn grabbed the door handle. "It's purely business."

"Sometimes business and personal mix well. Look how it's worked for me."

Finn shook his head. "Asking your office manager for a date was beyond stupid. You know, I still think you married Mary just so she didn't sue you for sexual harassment."

Liam's face flushed, and he leveled an accusatory finger in front of Finn's nose. "That's a low blow, you—" His face turned even redder as he choked down whatever it was he had been about to say.

Finn punched his brother's arm. "I'm just razzing you. Seriously, it's work, and that's it. Thanks for the time."

Before Liam could say anything else, Finn slipped out of the office and limped toward the exit.

His brother meant well. So did his mother. But he wasn't ready to try another relationship yet. Losing Karen was still too fresh. Too raw.

Finn knew he was rushing, but he couldn't seem to force himself to slow down. As he got into the car, his prosthetic foot caught on the frame, and the door bounced off his shoe. Muttering and swearing, he lifted his leg into the car, closed the door, and stopped his fist an inch before it slammed down on the dashboard. He closed his eyes and slumped back against the seat.

His leg wasn't the only thing he'd lost in the explosion. He'd lost Karen too. His fiancée couldn't cope with the new Finn. The damaged Finn.

To her credit, she tried. They went to couples' counseling with Dr. Rodgers. But Karen was a fitness and outdoors buff, and she was frustrated that Finn could no longer do the things she enjoyed. Dr. Rodgers suggested alternative ways to spend time together, but Karen viewed that as "settling." Settling for something less than what she wanted.

Finn could still picture the Facebook post. Karen had thought she was messaging a friend, but instead she had posted it for all the world to see. Even now, her words still cut him to the core.

I'm leaving Finn. I've tried, but I need a whole man.

He sat there watching the cars go by. He wasn't angry with her. How could he be? It was how *he* felt, too.

He wasn't whole anymore.

CHAPTER 3

Finn walked through the front doors of the Ice Palace and shivered. Kids of all ages zoomed around the indoor ice-skating rink, and music blared over the speakers. At a large wooden desk, a crowd of people were getting skates. Finn waited patiently for them to finish, then stepped forward.

He found himself face to face with a woman who could double for Mrs. Claus. She was short and chubby, with white hair pulled back into a bun, and an enormous smile tucked between two rosy cheeks.

"How may I help you, young man? You look to be about a thirteen?"

It took Finn a second to register that she was asking for his skate size. "Actually," he said, "I'm an insurance investigator, and I'm doing some background investigation on a case."

Finn was surprised that the woman kept smiling. Most business owners reached for a figurative shotgun when he announced what he was doing. Some even reached for the real thing.

"How can I help?"

"I heard someone mention they played in a street hockey league here. Do you still host these leagues?"

"We sure do." She grinned proudly. "The championship is coming up in four weeks. The playoffs just started. They don't play in the main rink, but in the covered rink out back."

Finn took out his phone, brought up the picture of Jordan Miller, and showed it to her. "Have you ever seen him?"

"Jordan? I *know* him. He's on the Blue Devils." She leaned forward and made a face. "He tries. Not the most talented or personable player, but he's a decent forward. How's his mouth?"

"You know about him breaking his teeth?" Finn asked, amazed.

"Of course I do. He took a ball straight in the chops." She shook her head. "He'd taken his mouth guard out to trash-talk. Kind of ironic, huh?"

Finn swallowed down his growing excitement. "So you saw Jordan get hurt?"

She nodded. "But he'd better not have put in an insurance claim. He signed the waivers. We're in no way liable."

Finn's fingers danced excitedly on the counter. "You said he signed something. Can I get a copy of that, please? I'll also need to take a statement from you."

"Sure thing. Would you like the accident report?"

Finn wanted to do a happy dance. He felt like Mrs. Claus had just given him the best Christmas gift ever: his case all tied up with a red bow. "You have officially made my day."

Her smile grew even wider. "And that makes mine. Let me get someone to cover the desk, and I'll go getcha everything you need."

Finn held both fists up in a silent cheer.

A voice spoke behind him. "I take it things are going well?"

He jumped as Annie touched his shoulder.

Finn turned to face her. "They couldn't be better. I was

about to text you..." He trailed off as he noticed the two children standing beside her.

"I was hoping you'd be..." Annie began. "That is, I wanted to come see... I mean, the kids, uh, wanted to skate. This is Tommy." She placed a hand on her son's curly brown hair. He gave a big grin, revealing two missing teeth. "And this is Tammy." Tammy was a thin girl with blond hair in a pixie cut. She clung to Annie's leg and kept her blue eyes mostly on the floor. "And this," Annie said to her kids, "is Mommy's boss, Mr. Church."

Tammy and Tommy exchanged a quick look and snickered.

"Hello." Finn waved. "Did you come to skate?"

Tommy nodded, sending his curls bouncing. "Can we go now, Mom?" He signed to Annie as he spoke.

Annie smiled, and both kids took off like rockets.

Finn noticed they already had ice skates in hand, and they were more colorful than the rentals they had at the rink. "They have their own skates?" he asked.

"We come to the free skates. It's short money and they'll sleep well tonight." Annie's smile wavered. "Tommy's a natural. Tammy just started going onto the ice. She used to just run along the outside of the rink and watch her brother through the Plexiglas. She's still a little nervous."

"I'm sure she'll get the hang of it."

Annie placed her fingers on both sides of her mouth. "You sure look happy. I take it your hunch panned out?"

"It couldn't have gone better. You were right: Jordan's story was a fairy tale. The only things missing were a unicorn and a rainbow. He got hurt *here*, playing street hockey. They're getting the accident report for me now."

"That's awesome." She squeezed his hand.

Finn fought the urge to look down at her fingers. He wasn't sure if she was touchy-feely because she was deaf or if she was just that type of person. He also didn't want to draw attention to it, because he didn't want her to stop.

"But why didn't he just report that he got hurt here?" she asked.

"Because insurance wouldn't cover it. He signed liability waivers. That's why he made up the story about getting hurt at home, so his homeowner's policy would cover his dental bills."

Annie's eyes brightened in understanding. "I guess we'll need an outside photograph of this place after all. I'll do it before we leave. Great job figuring it out."

"The answer fell into my lap."

Annie shook her head and lightly touched the side of his head. "You figured it out, Finn. Take that in." She grinned impishly. "Since I'm rhyming, I'll finish with: it's Finn for the win!" She gave a little cheer.

Finn swallowed. Ever since he'd been back after his tour of duty, it had seemed like all he'd done was keep people at arm's length. But somehow Annie managed to wrap her warmth around him like a spring breeze.

Mrs. Claus reappeared with a folder and her ever-ready smile. "I've got your paperwork. Just let me know if you need anything else."

Finn took the folder. "Thanks again."

Annie nodded over to the rink. "Well, I'd better check on Tammy. Congratulations."

Finn followed along beside her. "Annie?" He tried to position himself slightly ahead so she could read his lips. "You did a great job today, too." He held the folder up. "This is a win for both of us. If you hadn't thrown Molly's ball, I'd never have thought of looking here."

Annie gave him a thumbs-up. "We're a good team. I—"

"*MOMMY!*" Tammy's pained cry rose above the music and chatter of the skaters. The little girl had been using a training aid that looked like a walker for the elderly, but now she sat on the ice and struggled to stand back up.

Annie whipped open the door to the rink, prepared to go to her daughter's rescue. But it was Finn who, surprising himself, charged out onto the ice. He instantly cursed his foolishness. He had been so determined to help the little girl that he didn't even think about what he was doing. As soon as his shoes touched the ice, he was about as graceful as a hippo on a bike. He held both hands out in front of himself and let momentum carry him toward Tammy.

The girl had managed to get up on her own, and she shuffled toward him with the training aid. "Don't be scared," she said, wiping away a tear. "Here. We can share."

Finn was about to object, but at that moment he slipped, and would have fallen had he not managed to grab hold of the training aid.

"Oh my gosh. Oh my gosh," Annie said as she slid up behind him and placed her hands on his sides. "I'm sorry. Oh my gosh. It's okay. I've got you." She held him tightly.

As long as Annie's hands were on his waist, Finn found he didn't so much mind accepting her help. He would swallow his male pride down if it meant being near her.

"It's okay, Mommy," Tammy said with a smile. "I've got him." She looked up at Finn with eyes as blue as her mother's. "Hold on with both hands. *Both* hands."

Finn nodded and exchanged a quick grin with Annie.

"Let's get Mr. Church over to the gate," Annie suggested.

"He's okay now, Mommy. Do you want to go around the rink?"

The little girl's innocent question sent a wave of panic through Finn. Did he want to risk falling on the ice and looking like a moron in front of a crowd of children and mothers? Of course not. But then Annie moved closer behind him and tightened her grip on his waist... and there was no way he was saying no.

He nodded.

Tammy grinned. "Okay. Just listen to me and you'll be fine."

Tommy skated up and grabbed the edge of the rink to stop. "You can go on ice?" he said. His mouth flopped open. "But you've got a fake leg." His mouth snapped shut and his eyes grew huge. "Do you have attachments for it with treads for ice, like a tank?"

"Tommy!" Annie clenched her fist in front of her throat, a sign to Tommy to stop talking.

"It's fine." Finn looked over his shoulder at her, but had to quickly look forward again or lose his balance.

Annie shifted so she was side by side with him, one arm wrapped around his waist.

"I don't have any attachments for it," Finn said. The boy's grin faded. "But I'm thinking about adding a hidden rocket launcher."

"No way!" The little boy almost fell over, and Tammy giggled. "Really? Can I see your leg?"

"Not now." Annie waved him on.

"Later?" Tommy pressed.

"Sure," said Finn.

Annie leaned in close. Her breath was warm against his neck, and his skin tingled. "Are you sure you don't mind?"

Finn looked down into her sparkling blue eyes and nodded. He didn't mind. Not one bit.

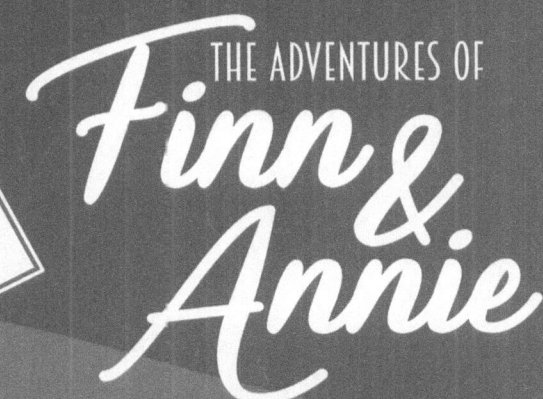

THE ADVENTURES OF
Finn &
Annie

THE CASE OF THE
WAYWARD
RIDE

CHRISTOPHER GREYSON

A MiniMystery Series

THE ADVENTURES OF

Finn & Annie

THE CASE OF THE WAYWARD RIDE

WALL STREET JOURNAL BESTSELLING AUTHOR
CHRISTOPHER GREYSON

GREYSON MEDIA

CHAPTER 1

F innian Church stood at the side of the road, looking across a field of the prettiest wildflowers he'd ever seen. He raised his chin to the sun and drank in the intoxicating fragrance of daisies, poppies, and lupines.

Then the wind shifted, and the floral scent was mixed with gas and oil from the car that had slid off the road, down a gravel slope, and into an enormous oak tree. Finn wasn't here to enjoy nature. He'd been summoned to the scene to investigate a fatal accident.

His smile faded when he recognized another odor, barely discernible beneath the others.

Death.

The body of Nate Taylor had been removed from the wreckage hours ago, but the smell remained. There's something about death that lingers long after the body's removed. And it isn't only the smell; death itself has a presence.

The hairs on the back of Finn's neck prickled as he listened to the quiet of the country road and the beating of his heart. He headed back to his car to retrieve his tablet and measuring wheel.

A rumble sounded from down the road—like a dump truck on its last legs—and Annie Summers's old sedan appeared around a bend. Her dented car was the color of a bruised banana a week past its prime, but that was the least of its troubles—sparks were shooting out as the muffler dragged against the uneven pavement.

Seemingly oblivious to the thunderous noise and fireworks display from the underside of her battered car, Annie parked on the side of the road and hopped out.

"Morning!" She gave Finn a huge wave before ducking back into her car to grab her camera equipment.

Finn ran one hand down his face, wrestling with himself not to shout. *It's not her fault. She probably doesn't even realize her muffler is shooting sparks at her gas tank.*

He walked over to her, loosening his tie, and took a deep breath. He was working on stress-reduction techniques. His therapist had encouraged him to perform little micro-rhythms: loosen tie, take a deep breath, long exhale, let the stress float away. It never worked, but he was still trying.

Annie shut the car door. "Is everything all right?" She looked at him quizzically.

He made sure he spoke slowly and looked directly at her so she could read his lips. "Your muffler fell off and is dragging underneath your car. Sparks were flying everywhere. It's incredibly loud and probably dangerous."

Annie grimaced and stomped over to the rear of her car. She got down on her knees and peered underneath. Finn expected tears or swears, but instead Annie just shrugged.

She rose to her feet, and her smile returned to light up his morning. "I've got a coat hanger in the trunk. I'll tie it up again after we finish."

"Again? Did it fall off before?"

"I was hoping it would make it until the end of the week. It was a toss-up between fixing the hot water heater or the muffler, and Tammy won't take a cold bath, so the heater won."

Annie had two kids to take care of, but still, she shouldn't be driving around with her car like that.

Finn took out his phone. "My brother-in-law's a mechanic. I can have him take a look at it."

Annie shook her head, and her blond hair danced across her shoulders. "I just don't have the funds for it right now."

Finn thought he saw the shadow of a rare sadness on Annie's lips, but it was gone in a second as she took in the scenery. "What do we got here? Oh!" Her mouth fell open as her gaze traveled down the slope to the wildflowers. "That field is so beautiful." She raised the camera and started snapping away. She kept panning until she reached the mangled car, then lowered the camera, concern shining in her eyes. "Was the driver badly hurt?"

Finn had known Annie only a short time, but it hadn't taken him long to realize that not only did she have the eyes of an artist, she had the sensitive heart of one, too.

He nodded. "Driver was killed. Died on scene. Nate Taylor, forty-nine. His passenger, Wendy Hall, is being treated at Mercy Hospital. They're keeping her for observation for a head injury, but I'm hoping she can make a statement this afternoon."

"It's a miracle she survived." Annie pointed at the short tire tracks in the field. "It looks like he didn't have time to hit his brakes." She started taking pictures of the accident scene.

Finn studied the gravel slope, wondering again how he would make the trek down the uneven surface with his prosthetic leg. "Let's start up here," he said.

He and Annie walked down the road and stopped at a set of skid marks.

Annie's shoulders sagged. "Poor guy. If the car had traveled just another ten feet, he would have hit the guardrail."

Finn set his measuring wheel down at the end of the

guardrail and let it roll until it reached the skid marks. "More like seven-point-four feet."

"Can you tell how fast he was going?"

Finn shook his head. "The car went airborne—see where the skid marks leave the pavement?"

Annie nodded.

"That's going to make it difficult for the police to calculate the rate of speed."

"Did the passenger say anything?" Annie asked.

"She told the officers that Nate was going too fast. But her story is . . . a little complicated. That's why I'm hoping we can interview her and get some answers."

Finn had already gone over the police report, and he'd completed background checks on both Nate and Wendy. The two were polar opposites; Nate's background was as clean as Wendy's was dirty.

"Complicated?" Annie's blue eyes searched Finn's, and he felt the heat rising up his neck.

Finn pointed down the road. "Are you familiar with Abernathy Park?"

"Yes, it's wonderful. I take the kids there all the time."

Finn cringed. "Well, after dark it isn't so nice. It's actually got a pretty well-known reputation for prostitution."

Annie's lip curled. "Where do they . . . do it?"

Finn felt his cheeks warm. He wanted to look away, but then Annie wouldn't be able to read his lips. "I guess the parking lot. But the only reason I'm bringing it up is Wendy. She's been arrested there twice for prostitution."

"Oh, so she and Nate . . ."

"I don't know yet. It's one of the questions I'm not looking forward to asking her. Or Nate Taylor's widow." Finn looked at the ground, then forced his face back toward Annie's. "Taylor was a minister."

Annie winced. "I'm glad it's you asking the questions and

not me." Annie fiddled with her camera lens. "Do you even have to . . . you know, go there?"

"Unfortunately, I do. It's our job to find out the where, when, and why."

Finn peered down the road, and something caught his attention. He waved for Annie to join him as he walked over to get a closer look.

There was another, lighter set of tire marks at the beginning of the curve. Finn awkwardly squatted down to examine them. But with his prosthetic, which started just below his knee, even this simple act made him feel like he was on a balance beam.

"It looks like he tapped the brakes and cut the wheel here," he said.

Annie started clicking away as Finn took measurements.

"Are you certain these tire marks are his?" Annie asked.

"No, but the police will be able to tell us." Finn pulled out his tablet and flipped through his notes. "There's no mention of a second set of marks in the police report. These are really faint, so the police may not have seen them."

"How anyone can tell anything from brake marks is beyond me."

"I don't think these are actually brake marks at all." Finn stood up. "I'm not an expert by any stretch, but it's not the rubber from the tire that leaves marks; they're caused by friction from the tire heating the oil in the tar. And these are so faint, it looks like Nate may have just cut the wheel here. I'll have to call this in."

"You sure sound like an expert to me." Annie smiled as she took close-ups of the marks.

Finn tried to picture the car rounding the curve. Judging by these new tire tracks, the car would have traveled into the other lane as it came to the bend. "If the car swerved here, he'd try to straighten back out." Finn walked back over to the point where the car left the road. "He could have overcorrected, and by the time he hit the brakes, the car was in the air."

Finn turned his head at the sound of an approaching vehicle. Annie was squatting down taking pictures of the tire marks, completely oblivious to the sound of a car racing up behind her.

A surge of panic shot through Finn. "Annie!" He shouted the warning, but without her looking at him, it didn't matter how loudly he yelled. He could have set a bomb off without her knowing.

The car was almost at the curve.

Finn ran awkwardly toward her, but he could tell he wouldn't get to her in time. In desperation, he threw the measuring wheel at her feet. The handle snapped off, and the pieces bounced past Annie's legs. Startled, she jumped back just as the car rounded the bend.

Finn frantically waved his arms, gesturing for her to get out of the road. The gray minivan screeched to a stop just a few feet away from where Annie was standing. Finn reached her side, but she wouldn't look at him. Her eyes glistened with tears, and her hands were shaking.

The minivan pulled over to the side of the road, the driver's door opened, and a middle-aged woman got out. She was flushed and wiping tears away as she hurried over. "I'm so sorry. I didn't see you."

"It's my fault." Annie's voice was louder than normal. "I was lost in concentration." Her hand balled into a fist. "I'm supposed to keep my head on a swivel whenever I'm on a road, but I just..."

She gritted her teeth, and Finn found himself doing the same. He knew all too well the frustration and anger she was feeling about dealing with a disability.

"It's my fault," said the older woman. She placed a comforting hand on Annie's arm, but Annie shook it off.

"No. It is all mine." Annie turned her head away to hide her embarrassment.

"Honey, I was the one lost in concentration. I didn't see you because I wasn't focusing on the road. Please accept my apology."

Annie stood in silence, staring down at her feet. The silence grew awkward, and the woman looked to Finn.

Annie caught the silent exchange. "I'm deaf."

"You're—oh!" The woman choked back a sob and turned her head. For the first time, she seemed to notice the wrecked car by the side of the road. She took one look and burst into tears.

Annie immediately switched into sympathy mode. She wrapped an arm around the woman's shoulders and led her back to her minivan.

Finn was unsure what to do or where to go. From the woman's reaction upon seeing the wrecked car, he was certain that she had known Nate. Could she be his widow?

After a few minutes, Annie waved him over. The woman was seated in the driver's seat, and Annie stood beside her with a hand on her shoulder.

"Finn," said Annie, "this is Karen Taylor. Nate's wife."

"My condolences, ma'am."

"You're investigating the accident?" Mrs. Taylor asked, still sniffling.

Finn nodded.

"I don't care what the police are saying. My husband wasn't giving that woman a ride." The widow's eyes met Finn's, and he was taken aback by the hard resolve he saw there.

"As insurance investigators—" he began.

"I don't care about the insurance or the money. My husband was a *good man*, and I won't see his reputation destroyed."

"Ma'am, I'm not passing judgment."

"You're not, but the community, when the story reaches the

paper . . . It will be hard enough for his congregation to get through losing their pastor, but it will be unbearable if there is *another* scandal." She dabbed her eyes and blew her nose. "I won't see all of Nate's hard work die with him."

"Mrs. Taylor—"

"Please. Call me Karen."

"Karen. I haven't spoken with the passenger yet—"

"I'm telling you, my husband would not be in the car with a woman without telling me. This has nothing to do with her being a prostitute. My husband wouldn't give *any* strange woman a ride."

"Karen," Finn said carefully, "do you think it's possible that if someone needed help, he may have acted as a good Samaritan?"

Karen shook her head. "I know it sounds puritanical, but if my husband were to give a single woman a ride, he would have texted me. And the woman would sit in the back. My husband even went so far as to keep his office door open whenever he was meeting with someone. It's an accountability system he established. He was above reproach."

"Because of the other scandal you mentioned?"

Karen twisted the tissues into a knot between her fingers. She nodded.

"Again, I'm not judging your husband, but isn't it possible for a man to . . . stumble again?"

Karen closed her eyes. She slowly shook her head, and when she looked up, her tears had stopped. "Not my Nate. And he didn't stumble the first time. *I* did. Nate started that whole accountability thing to help *me*."

CHAPTER 2

After Karen left, Finn and Annie spent the rest of the morning taking pictures and measurements of the scene. As lunchtime neared, Finn's phone buzzed.

"Wheels up," he announced after reading the text. "We need to head over to Mercy General. Wendy is ready to give a statement."

Annie frowned. "It's going to take me a few minutes to get my muffler tied up."

"We'll have to do that afterward. You can ride with me and I'll bring you back."

Annie bit her lip and wrinkled her nose. "You don't think it'll get towed if I leave it on the side of the road?"

Finn typed a text to his brother-in-law and hit send. "I can assure you, it'll be fine."

Annie followed Finn to his car, but she cast a worried look back at her car as they pulled out onto the street.

They rode in silence for a few minutes, Finn driving and Annie looking at her phone, then Finn's stomach grumbled loudly. "Excuse me," he said reflexively before remembering that she wouldn't have heard the sound.

"Are you hungry?" Annie asked. She reached for the bag at her feet.

"Starving." Finn's eyebrow ticked up. "How did you know my stomach rumbled?"

"The way you looked at it." She imitated looking down at her own stomach and made her eyes widen in shock. "When I lost my hearing, I became a little more observant of body language." She went back to staring at her phone.

Finn loosened his tie a bit, wondering if his body language had revealed anything he wanted to remain hidden. "That's quite remarkable," he said. He had to make an effort to angle his face toward her as he spoke while driving.

She shrugged. "It's not really a conscious thing, it just sort of happened."

Finn felt an overwhelming urge to ask Annie about her hearing loss, but he couldn't figure out a way to phrase the question without overstepping. Besides, if anyone could relate to not wanting to be asked about an injury, he could. At one point in his recovery he'd considered writing down the story of how the IED blew his leg off, so he could just hand it out whenever anyone asked. Of course, he wasn't serious about following through, but he *was* tempted.

"What are you thinking about?" Annie asked. She leaned forward so she could look at his face more full-on. "You're scowling." She wrinkled her brow.

Her expression bothered him. Not that he felt she was mocking him, but because her angry face was such a contrast to her sunny disposition.

"Do I really look like that?" His question tumbled out unfiltered.

Annie glanced down at her phone and nodded. "Sullen is not your best look."

Finn slowed for a red light. "I was thinking about my leg."

"Oh . . . is it okay?"

Finn shifted uncomfortably in his seat. *Is it okay?* The question took him aback, and he was about to fire off the familiar sarcastic quip: *No, it's gone.* But he held his tongue.

"I mean . . ." Annie struggled for the right words.

"I'm fine. I just sometimes find myself wondering 'what if,' you know?"

Annie shook her head. "What if what?"

"You know, what if the accident hadn't happened. Do you ever wonder that?"

Annie's eyes scanned the phone screen and her smile returned. "I have enough to worry about today without worrying about something I can't change. I don't think about it really. I try to figure out ways to improve myself right now."

"Improve how?"

She held up her phone. "Well, like you and me talking like this. Normally I feel too self-conscious to try to talk to someone while they're driving. Besides, it's dangerous for you to have to look at me. So I'm trying this new speech-to-text app. It's translating your voice very well."

The car behind them beeped, and Finn noticed the light had changed. He gave an apologetic wave and started forward.

"I was wondering how you were doing that," he said.

Annie chuckled. "Doughnut that."

"Excuse me?" Finn felt his face flush.

"The app." Annie wiggled her phone. "It's not perfect. It translated what you said as *I was wandering how you were doughnut that.*"

Finn laughed too. "Speech-to-text technology has come a long way."

"It's a blessing. Really." Annie closed her eyes for a moment. "I'm very blessed."

Blessed? You lost your hearing. How is that blessed? Finn swallowed down the sarcastic response, but he couldn't derail the train of thought. His stomach growled even louder, and this time he not only glanced down but self-consciously placed a hand over his gut like it would suppress the noise.

"I forgot. You're hungry." Annie set her phone on the seat beside her and picked up her bag.

"There's a little place ahead that makes a killer gyro. I figured we could stop there."

Annie checked her phone. As she read what he'd said, her lips pressed together. "Um, I actually brought lunch. PB&J." She reached into her bag and pulled out two bagged sandwiches. "Today was pizza day at Tommy's school. It's his favorite, so I have a spare sandwich." She looked at Finn hopefully.

Finn looked down at the slightly squished sandwich and tried to recall the last time he'd eaten a PB&J. It had to be elementary school. He was about to extol the taste of the steak-and-cheese gyro when he remembered that Annie didn't have enough money to get her car fixed. He opened his mouth, about to offer to pay for lunch, but then he saw Annie's smile slowly fading. Taking away that smile would be right up there with kicking a puppy.

"I'd love a PB&J." He plastered a smile on his face and forced himself to look straight ahead as they zipped past the restaurant.

"Really?"

"Yeah. I was just thinking I can't remember the last time I had one. Do you want me to pull over or . . . ?"

"No, keep driving; we can eat on the go. That way I can get back to my car sooner. I know you think it will be fine parked on the side of the road, but the last thing I want is for it to get ticketed or towed."

Finn's phone beeped with a text message. It was from his brother-in-law. GOT THE CAR AND BRINGING IT BACK TO GARAGE NOW. GIVE ME AN HOUR.

Finn smiled. "I promise, your car will be fine. Trust me, okay?"

Annie nodded and unwrapped her sandwich.

Finn took a bite of his and had a difficult time opening his mouth through a mouthful of the stickiest peanut butter he'd ever wrestled with.

"Oh, sorry." Annie started rifling through her bag again. "I forgot that Tommy and jelly had a falling-out and I made the sandwiches with just peanut butter."

Finn nodded and did his best to swallow.

"Here." She triumphantly held up a green-and-yellow kids' drink box, inserted the plastic straw, and handed it to him.

Finn took two eager gulps before the sour explosion made his eyes cross. He swallowed down some of the mixture of goopy peanut butter and candy-flavored drink, then gasped for breath.

Annie took a sip herself, stuck her tongue out, and immediately began apologizing. "I'm so sorry. I didn't read the box. It's super sour!"

Finn nodded, trying to resist the urge to power down his window and spit it all out. When Annie did just that, he burst out laughing.

"Sorry." She hid her face with her hand and spat again. "Oh, that's *so* gross."

Finn lowered his window and spat, too, putting some force behind it to launch the ball of peanut butter clear of the car.

Annie rummaged around in her bag again and produced a water bottle. "Here. I only took a couple of sips." She undid the cap and handed it to him.

Finn took the bottle and tried not to hesitate. He'd been a germaphobe even before he lost his leg, and he was worse now. Just the thought of infection filled him with dread, but one look at Annie's blue eyes—combined with the sour tang still burning his tongue—convinced him to take a sip.

He took another bite and said through a full mouth, "How does that app work with peanut-butter mouth?"

Annie read the screen and her feet drummed off the floorboards as she giggled. She held it up for him to read.

HI FAT APPLE WIMPY BATH

Laughing and joking, they shared the water between them and managed to force down the sandwiches. All too soon for Finn, they pulled into the hospital parking lot. His sides were sore and it took him a moment to realize it was because he'd been laughing so hard.

He turned in his seat to face Annie. "Thank you," he signed.

Annie's eyes rounded. "Thank you for learning sign."

"Just starting." Finn's fingers moved awkwardly as he tried to remember the movements. "I didn't realize how difficult it was to read lips."

Annie shrugged. "I'm really good at it, but most people have it very hard. Communication is very important . . ." She suddenly looked away and held up a hand.

For Finn, it was like a cloud had blotted out the sky. He hadn't intended to get her upset, and this conversation was clearly painful for her. And now, with Annie facing away from him, he was in a bind and didn't know how to respond. It felt too personal to touch her, but how else would he get her attention?

"We should get going." Annie grabbed her bag and opened her door.

Finn reached out for her arm but stopped before he touched her. She glanced back toward him.

"Thanks for lunch," he said.

Her smile returned but it wasn't as bright. She nodded and got out of the car.

CHAPTER 3

They found Wendy Hall propped up in her hospital bed, her phone in one hand, a chicken salad sandwich in the other.

"We appreciate you agreeing to speak with us, Ms. Hall."

"I'm not feelin' very well, so I'd like to just get this over with, if you don't mind."

It was clear from Wendy's expression that Finn and Annie were the last people she wanted to talk to. She pulled the blanket higher up her chest. She texted one-handed on her phone as she spoke.

"I already told the police everythin'," she said. "There isn't really much else to tell."

"Can you start with how you got into the car?"

"A friend of mine dropped me off at the park. I was meetin' another friend but they didn't show up, so I started walkin'. I wasn't hitchhikin'." She pointed her half-eaten sandwich at Finn for emphasis, sending crumbs raining down on her tray and blanket. "This guy just pulls over and asks me if I need a ride."

"And you got in the front seat?"

Wendy rolled her eyes. "Yeah. It's not like it was a limo or nothing."

"Where did he pick you up?"

"On the road."

Wendy continued to text, and Finn tried not to let his irritation show. *Deep breath in. Deep breath out.* "How far away from the park were you when you got in the car?"

Wendy shrugged. "I don't know. I was only in the car a minute or two before we crashed."

"Did the man who gave you a ride say anything?"

"He said, 'Need a ride?' I said yeah. He said, 'Get in.' We drove a little and then he drove right off the road and boom! We hit the trees."

"He was just driving and then he went off the road? Did he swerve, or was there something in the road?"

"That's, like, five questions. How am I supposed to know?" Wendy made a face, and her phone pinged with an incoming message. She read it and scowled. "Look, that's all I know." Another ping, and her eyes narrowed. She typed something back. "I knew the guy for less than a minute. But he's at fault, right?"

Wendy's ringtone sounded, and her lips mashed together. "I gotta get this. Can you gimme a second?"

"Certainly." Finn looked at Annie and gestured toward the door. She followed him out into the hallway.

Finn rolled his eyes. "Are you getting the feeling that Wendy doesn't seem to be the most forthcoming witness?"

Annie didn't answer him. She was looking back into the room, watching Wendy, who was whispering into the phone. The longer Annie stared, the tighter her eyebrows pinched together, until she looked furious. She raised her camera, pressed a button, and surreptitiously pointed it at Wendy.

"You okay?" Finn asked.

"That woman is absolutely despicable."

"She's not winning any congeniality contests, but maybe you should cut her some slack. She just survived a serious car accident."

"No, she didn't." Annie's free hand had balled into a fist.

Finn looked back and forth between Wendy and Annie. His eyes widened as he realized what Annie was doing: reading Wendy's lips.

He yanked out his phone and fumbled for the video app.

"I'm already recording with my camera," Annie said.

"You're a genius!" Finn resisted the urge to kiss her cheek. "What is she saying?"

Annie held up a hand. "I can't read both your lips at the same time."

She paused, then relayed Wendy's words: "I'm tellin' you, they don't believe me. They're gonna figure it out." Another pause. "I'm *not* freakin'. But they're gonna figure out I lied. Someone could have seen me get into the car after it hit the tree . . . Okay. . . I will. Bye."

Finn tried to look casual, but Wendy's confession was pure gold. He stepped in front of Annie, his back to Wendy, blocking Annie's scowling face. "Don't let on that you heard," he said. "We need to check with the police and make certain that the video is admissible."

"Hello?" Wendy called out, snapping her fingers. "I'm not feelin' well. I have a back injury. Can you get your stuff out of here and bounce? I wanna take a nap."

They both ignored her.

"What do you mean?" Annie asked Finn.

"This is a 'one-party consent' state, which means that for a recording to be legal, you need the permission of one party in the conversation."

"But I didn't record the audio," Annie said. "They can read her lips from the video."

"I'm not sure what the law is on that. But that's why I have to check with the police." Finn grabbed Annie's shoulders. "Trust me. I've got a feeling that if we give the detectives what you just figured out, they'll get Wendy to tell them the truth."

CHAPTER 4

F inn and Annie practically skipped out of the hospital to the parking lot. They had spoken to Detective David Montrose, who had actually performed a little jig in the hospital's lobby when he heard Annie's analysis. He'd then re-interviewed Wendy, and she confessed to the whole scheme.

"I still can't believe someone would do that. How could she not help?" Annie shook her head. "She admitted she was hitchhiking and stepped into the road so Nate had to swerve to avoid her. She caused the accident. But instead of calling 911, she ran and got into the passenger seat and pretended to be hurt. She took advantage of a dying man. It's sad and disgusting. I sure hope there aren't many people like Wendy in this world."

Finn pulled out of the parking lot. He didn't have the heart to tell Annie that the world was filled with people like Wendy. He was thinking about a case the insurance investigator who trained him had told him about. A garbage truck hit a bus. When they pulled surveillance video from a liquor store across the street, they found a dozen people rushed to get on the bus *after* the accident. All of them filed claims against the garbage collection company, looking for insurance payouts.

Annie crossed her arms. "At least Karen Taylor will know without a doubt that her husband was a good man."

Finn smiled at her. The world might be filled with Wendys, but there were still good people in it. Like Annie Summers.

"Do you mind giving me a ride back to my car?" Annie asked.

"We're on our way to it now," Finn replied, turning right.

Annie's eyebrow arched and she pointed to the left. "But it's that way."

Finn slowed down as they approached the auto shop. Half a dozen cars were parked outside, including Annie's. Her eyes darted back and forth between her old yellow car and the bright yellow sign above Dave's Towing and Repair Shop.

"Oh, you've got to be kidding me." Annie smacked her thigh. "I just knew my car would get towed." She closed her eyes and sighed. "I don't want to know how much this is going to cost. We'll be eating peanut butter sandwiches for a month." Her eyes snapped open. "Wait a second. How did you know my car got towed here?"

Finn smiled. "Do you remember my mentioning that my brother-in-law's a mechanic?"

Annie looked embarrassed. "But I don't have the money to pay a car repair bill right now."

"My brother-in-law owed me a favor, and I was happy to pass that favor on to you. Besides, you just solved our case in a day. I hope you don't mind. I'm just paying it forward."

Annie suddenly threw her arms around him, hugging him tightly. Her hair was soft against his cheek, and the warmth of her body awakened a deep hunger within him. He moved his lips to speak, but no sound came out.

"Thank you, Finnian," Annie whispered in his ear.

THE ADVENTURES OF

Finn &
Annie

THE CASE OF THE PHANTOM PET

WALL STREET JOURNAL BESTSELLING AUTHOR

CHRISTOPHER GREYSON

A MiniMystery Series

THE ADVENTURES OF Finn & Annie

THE CASE OF THE PHANTOM PET

WALL STREET JOURNAL BESTSELLING AUTHOR
CHRISTOPHER GREYSON

GREYSON MEDIA

CHAPTER 1

F innian Church parked his car outside Annie Summers's house. The little ranch home was in need of some TLC. The paint was peeling, the gutters needed cleaning, and the grass was eight inches high. He glanced up and down the street at the other homes on the tidy cul-de-sac—all of them immaculately kept—and his thoughts turned once more to his assistant Annie's personal life.

He knew that she had two children and that she had lost her hearing later in life, but other than that, he didn't know a lot about her—not nearly as much as he'd like to know. He was grateful to get the insurance investigation call this morning, because that meant he had an excuse to see Annie. He'd never considered himself shy, but for some reason, whenever he was around Annie and her sunny personality, his tongue felt as clumsy and unfamiliar as his prosthetic leg.

He straightened his tie and checked his appearance in the rearview mirror, then got out of the car and headed up the walkway. His footsteps slowed when he saw a red violation notice affixed to the door. It appeared that his estimation of the height of the grass was correct — eight inches—and the town inspector had deemed it over the limit.

Finnian felt sweat bead up on his brow. He never wanted to be the bearer of bad news, especially with Annie, but there was no hiding the full-page red notice stuck on the door. He rang the doorbell and waited.

The door shuddered, vibrating from top to bottom. Someone on the other side grunted, and the door moved a half an inch and stopped. It was catching on the threshold—probably swollen from the humidity—and whoever was trying to open it was really struggling.

Accompanied by more grunts and groans, the door flew open and Tammy, Annie's five-year-old daughter, stood triumphantly in the doorway. "Hi, Finnigan."

"Finnian." He instinctively corrected the little girl but quickly added, "If you want, you can call me Finn."

"Okey-dokey." She gave him a sweet smile.

Footsteps thundered down the hallway and Tommy, with six-year-old energy, skidded to a stop, grabbing the doorframe before he slid all the way out the front door. "Hey, Finn." He glanced up and saw the sticker. "Oh, crap."

Tammy's eyes went wide. "Bad word! Bad word!" She turned around and bolted down the hallway with her brother chasing after her.

"Don't tell Mom I said it!" he pleaded.

Finn found himself standing alone by the open front door.

A minute later, Annie appeared, tugging on her jacket, both kids at her heels. Finn waved, but her focus was on the red paper stuck to the door.

"Tommy said a bad word!" Tammy said. She crossed her hands in front of herself like a referee calling a penalty.

"Hi, Finn." Annie's cheeks were pink with embarrassment as she pulled off the sticker—taking a good amount of peeling paint with it. She gritted her teeth and signed something that made both of the kids' mouths drop open.

"*Super* bad word, Mommy!"

Annie squatted down and pulled both Tammy and Tommy into her arms. "Mommy's super, super sorry. She's just having a bad day."

"But you said don't let the day make you, you should make the day," Tommy reminded her.

Annie nodded. "You're right. And that's what I'm going to do! Mommy has to go to work now. Kisses, then go over to Jonny's."

The kids gave her a quick kiss, waved to Finn, and dashed to the house next door.

Annie watched them until they were safely inside the house and then turned to Finn. "Sorry about that—" She said something more, but he completely missed it. He was too distracted by the flecks of gold that sparkled in her blue eyes when she smiled.

Finn knew she needed to face him directly when they talked—it was essential for reading lips—but whenever his eyes locked with hers, his brain just shut down.

He closed his eyes and shook his head. "Could you please repeat that last part? I spaced out for a second." Finnian felt his cheeks flush.

"I'm ready to go whenever you are."

"Don't you need your gear?"

Annie's nose crinkled up. "I'm a dope!" She darted into the house and came back hauling her duffel bag heavy with equipment. "Now I'm ready."

As they walked to Finn's car, he filled her in on the case. "The insured's name is Jerry Durham. He was rear-ended two weeks ago, but he just filed an addendum to his claim, and they want us to check it out."

"More damages?" Annie asked.

"Over ten thousand dollars more. They're going to digitize the paperwork and send it over to me, but I don't have it yet. The office network is down."

They got into Finn's car and he pulled away from the curb. They were still working out the best way to communicate while he was driving. They'd worked out a system where he would raise his hand before speaking, and Annie would use the speech-to-text app on her phone.

"Sorry you saw that stupid violation notice," Annie said. "My lawnmower died. I'm hoping it's just the fuel filter, but I'm starting to think it's the motor."

"Do you need a hand fixing it?" Finn asked before thinking it through. He didn't know the first thing about motors.

She shook her head. "Thank you for the offer. I'm looking it up online."

"If you change your mind, just let me know." Finn handed Annie the folder. "Here's what we have on the accident so far."

Annie read as they drove. When they arrived at Mr. Durham's house, Finn checked his phone, but there was nothing new from the office.

Finn and Annie walked up the brick walkway and Finn rang the front doorbell. After a full minute, he rang it again, and knocked for good measure. Finn was about ready to leave when he heard movement inside. He held up his index finger and tapped his ear twice. He hoped that he was signing correctly.

Annie's eyes grew larger. She smiled and signed something he didn't understand.

He shook his head.

She signed as she spoke. "I still can't believe you're learning to sign."

Finn felt heat rising up his neck. "Just a little. There's a lot of videos on the internet." He moved his hands forward and back, with the tips of the middle fingers brushing together as they passed. That was the sign for the internet—he just hoped he was doing it correctly.

"The internet?" She smiled when he nodded.

The front door opened to reveal Jerry Durham, a big man dressed in a flannel bathrobe and wearing a thick neck brace. He grimaced as though just standing there was painful. "Can I help you?"

"I'm Finnian Church, and this is Annie Summers. We're from A. G. Maxwell Insurance."

"Are you here about the addendum I filed?"

"Yes, sir. We'd like to discuss that and your original claim. Do you have a few minutes?"

"Certainly. Please come in."

Durham stepped back, letting Finn and Annie enter. He shut the door behind them and led them into a cluttered living room. He motioned to the sofa while he moved to a motorized recliner that assisted people who had trouble standing up and sitting down. It was brand-new—it still had the manufacturing tags on it. He leaned into the chair, pushed a button on the remote, and the chair slowly lowered him into a sitting position.

"Did you bring the settlement check?" he asked.

"No. That would be sent out by the office," Finn said. "We're just here to gather information regarding the addendum. Unfortunately, the office network went down, so I haven't received all your paperwork yet, but—"

"Oh, great," Durham muttered. "So, I have to go over it all again?"

"If you don't mind." Finn forced a polite smile and loosened his tie. *Don't let this guy get to you. Just let the stress go.* His new stress-reduction techniques were becoming habitual.

"I do mind, but I will. I apologize, but this is very upsetting. It's traumatic to relive it. You see, the claim is for my dog." Durham grimaced as he pointed to a framed picture on the coffee table—a photo of a bulldog stretched out on a red cushion on a window seat.

Annie picked up the picture and studied it closely. "This is a great photo. The natural light is just perfect."

"Thank you." Durham smiled without showing any teeth. "I took it right over there." He pointed toward the window seat below a large bay window in the front of the house.

"The addendum is for your dog?" Finn asked, puzzled. "I thought you were injured in a car accident."

"I was. Bun was with me, and she was killed."

"I'm sorry for your loss," Finn said, unsure how to continue. "But I'm a little confused. Your initial claim didn't mention a dog."

Durham winced and lowered the motorized recliner a few more degrees. "As my paperwork states—if you had it—I didn't even realize the extent of my own grievous injuries until I returned home. And I was unaware until later that Bun suffered what turned out to be a fatal injury."

Finn took out his tablet. "Would you mind starting just before the accident? The initial report said you were driving north on Main Street and stopped at the traffic light at the intersection of Maple Street?"

"Exactly. I came to a full stop and then a second later, *blam*, he hit me going full speed."

"This photograph is really, really good." Annie tapped the framed photo of Bun.

"Thank you," Durham said.

"But in your report," Finn said, "you wrote that you heard a car skidding."

"That's right. It may have been another car braking that I heard. I don't think the car that hit me could have been slowing down, not with how hard it struck me."

Finn nodded. "After the initial impact, you pulled into the

Franklin Shopping Center parking lot and exchanged papers with the other driver?"

"Yes. I just knew I should have contacted the police then, but the other driver was insistent otherwise. He was very intimidating."

"Martin Berry? The other driver?"

"Yes, that was his name."

"Did he threaten you in any way?"

"Nothing explicit. It was more a physical thing. Leaning in on me. Puffing his chest out."

Finn wrote down some notes. He'd already interviewed Martin Berry, who was five foot four, slender, and had just turned seventy. Jerry Durham was thirty-nine years old, an even six foot, and two hundred pounds. Finn had a hard time believing that Berry, a retired postman and volunteer librarian, could have physically intimidated Durham—or had the temperament to do so.

"You're now claiming that you had a dog in the car with you when you were in the accident?" Finn asked.

"I *did* have my dog in the car with me. Bun was a French bulldog. A very expensive French bulldog. By the time I got home I couldn't even turn my neck because my whiplash was setting in. I took Bun to the vet, even though the whiplash was so bad, because I was concerned about his condition. After all, if I was hurt so badly, Bun must have been injured, too. The vet noticed there was a problem right away." Durham's lips pressed together. "He did what he could. There were x-rays and tests, but it was too late. He had to put Bun down."

The shutter of Annie's camera clicked as she snapped photographs of the framed picture of the dog.

"What are you doing?" Durham asked. "I included the picture in my report."

"I'm sorry." Annie smiled. "It's just that this picture is stunning." She got up, walked to the bay window, and took another photo.

"Miss? *Miss*?" Durham raised his voice.

"She's deaf," Finn explained, waving his hand to get Annie's attention.

"Well, I'm not comfortable having you both walking all over my house," Durham said. "As a matter of fact, I apologize, but I'm just not comfortable at all. I need to lie down." The motor on his recliner whined as he powered the chair to a standing position.

Annie was so focused on her camera, she didn't notice Finn waving at her, and when she did finally turn around, she was oblivious to Durham's irritation. "What lens did you use to shoot that photo?" she asked as she walked back over to the table, picked up the picture, and angled the photo so Durham could see it. "The depth of field is so soft that your focus goes right to Bun and he just pops."

"I used my phone," Durham said curtly.

"You took the photo with just the built-in camera on your phone?" Annie was clearly surprised.

Durham glanced at the camera dangling around Annie's neck and smirked. "If you have natural talent, you don't need any of that fancy equipment."

"Annie's a fabulous photographer," Finn said, placing a restraining hand on Annie's forearm. Her whole body was vibrating with indignation.

"I'm sure she is. Now, if you'll excuse me, I really have to lie down. The pain, you see."

Annie gave a terse nod and marched toward the door.

Durham's comment must have really gotten under her skin.

"Of course. Thank you for your time." Finn said as he handed Durham his card. "We'll see ourselves out."

CHAPTER 2

Annie stormed to the car her focus straight ahead. Because she wouldn't look at him, Finn felt helpless to get her attention. She'd told him that he should gently touch her arm or shoulder, but right now he didn't think that was the best idea.

They both got into the car, and Annie slammed her door.

"Can you believe that man?" Her hands were a blur as she made a number of signs. Even if Finn hadn't been trying to learn sign language, he could guess what some of them meant.

Finn raised his hand to get her attention. "I don't believe Durham about your photography skills, the accident, *or* his injuries. Did you notice how easily he stretched his arm out when he took my card? He was so focused on you, he dropped his guard. I think he's full of it."

Annie exhaled, and her eyes dropped down to her lap. She gave a slight shake of her head. "I'm sorry. I didn't notice." She took her phone out and turned on her speech-to-text app.

Finn gave her a reassuring smile. "No worries. He was a jerk." He started the car and headed back to Annie's. "I think this is one of those cases where it's going to be the doctors who make the call. I have my suspicions, but I can't prove them yet."

Annie opened the initial report and flipped through a few pages. "But there were skid marks at the scene of the accident." She turned to the next page. It showed a green, mid-sized SUV with a small dent on the bumper. "And Mr. Durham's car only had a scratch."

Finn nodded. "We'll write up all the details and recommend a follow-up."

Annie crossed her arms over her chest and closed her eyes.

Finn frowned. He knew she was upset, but the simple act of closing her eyes shut her off from him, and the feeling really bothered him. He always considered himself a laid-back guy, but ever since he lost his leg, he struggled when he felt helpless. He knew Annie's anger was only temporary, but the fact that he couldn't even try to comfort her weighed heavily on him.

When he reached the right turn that led toward Annie's house, he went left instead.

After a few more minutes, Annie opened her eyes and glanced around, confused. "Where are we going?"

"I need to make a quick stop before I drop you off. I hope you don't mind."

"No, that's fine." Annie gently put her hand on his forearm, causing goose bumps to race up his arm. "I'm sorry I got so upset. But when I saw that great photo, and Mr. Durham said he took it with just his phone . . . it's just . . . I'm trying to start a new career, and I don't know if I'm good enough to do it."

"Are you kidding me?" Finn rolled his eyes. "Your photographs are fantastic."

Annie reached into her pocket and held out a business card.

Finn glanced at it as he drove. The top line read: *SUMMERS PHOTOGRAPHY*.

"You're starting a business?"

She nodded timidly. "I just put the money from our last job into a light diffuser and these business cards. Then my stupid lawnmower broke. Maybe I'm just foolish trying to be a businesswoman."

Finn waved his hand dismissively. "No, you're not foolish at all. And I have an idea about your lawn." He turned down another road and then into his own driveway.

"Is this your house?" Annie grinned as she eyed the immaculate little cottage. "It's adorable."

Finn started to frown but couldn't keep it going. No guy wants his house described as adorable—but when Annie said it, he didn't mind so much. "I'll be right back." He got out of the car and forced himself to walk at an even pace to the detached garage. Another challenge of his prosthetic leg was changing his walking speed. He had "normal" down pat, and he was getting better at "slow," but when it came to walking fast, he ended up limping like a dog with its leash wrapped around its legs.

He unlocked the garage and pulled out the old-fashioned push mower, a paintbrush, and a half gallon of red paint. With no motor, the mower was lightweight, and he had no trouble putting it in the trunk.

When he got back into the car, Annie was shaking her head. "I can't borrow your lawnmower."

"I'm not letting you borrow it."

She shot him a puzzled look. "But I thought . . ." She trailed off. "I'm sorry, I assumed that's what you were doing."

"Nope." Finn backed out of the driveway and headed back to Annie's, trying to hide the impish grin that fought to spread across his face.

"Why did you put your lawnmower into the trunk then?"

"You'll see."

When they reached Annie's, they both got out of the car, and Finn headed for the trunk with Annie following after him.

"I thought you weren't going to let me borrow your lawn-mower," Annie said.

"I'm not. I'm going to cut your grass and take my mower home with me when I'm done." He grinned.

Annie reached for the handle. "No. I'll do it."

Finn didn't budge. "Really, you'll actually be helping me out."

Annie laughed. "That's a good one. Letting you mow my lawn is helping you?"

"Exactly." Finn pushed the lawnmower over to the corner of the property. "My physical therapist is a little . . . eccentric. Think *Karate Kid*, Mr. Miyagi, paint-the-fence kind of crazy. He thinks the push mower is great rehab, and I'm starting to agree with him. It's helping with my walking over uneven surfaces because I get to hold on to something while I'm doing it. It's a lot less boring than a treadmill, too."

He watched Annie's thoughts play out on her expressive face. He was surprised when she shook her head. "I can't just *watch you* mow my yard. I have to help."

"Why don't you help with the case then? You don't believe Mr. Durham's telling the truth either. Maybe you can find something that proves that." Finn held up his phone. "The office emailed me Durham's addendum. I just forwarded it to your email. Why don't you compare that to his original story and see what you can find out?"

Annie thought about it for a minute.

Finn watched her blond eyebrows start to knit together, and he suspected she was going to say no again. He didn't give her the chance. "Great! It's a deal!" he announced and started mowing the grass before she could argue.

"But I didn't agree to that!" she called after him.

Finn just gave a wave and a thumbs-up as he pushed the lawnmower in the opposite direction. He kept his eyes focused on the grass until Annie begrudgingly headed for the house.

CHAPTER 3

A half hour later, Finn had moved on to the backyard. Annie came toward him with a glass of water in one hand and waving with the other. "Finn! You're not gonna believe it!" She rushed over to him, handed him the drink, and took him by the other hand. "I have to show you this."

When Annie tugged on his arm, he stumbled forward and spilled most of the water.

Annie's hand shot over her mouth. "I'm so sorry. I forgot. I just got excited."

She wrapped an arm around his waist. He didn't need her to steady him, but he couldn't tell her that, because having her close felt too good. If anything, he hammed it up and wobbled a bit.

Annie pulled him closer and looked up at him. "I got you."

"Thanks." Finn cleared his throat and took a sip of water. "What did you find out?"

Annie beamed. "I *am* a good photographer!"

Finn chuckled. "You didn't need to figure that out. I could have told you that."

Her blond hair danced as she shook her head. "Mr.

Durham doesn't have a clue about what a good photographer is, because he *isn't* one! And there's more, but it'll be easier to show you." Annie motioned inside.

She kept her arm around Finn's waist as they headed for the house. He was perfectly capable of walking now that he had his balance, but he told himself that the lawn *was* a little uneven.

When they reached the front door, Annie took him by the hand and led him through her house. The décor was eclectic, to say the least. Finn was used to military drab and symmetry, whereas everything here had bright colors and didn't match. The sofa was an overstuffed giant with three different seat cushions and an assortment of throw pillows. The fluffy recliner was being held up by a large book where one of the legs used to be, and Finn suspected the entertainment center was a repurposed bookcase. It was the opposite of his place, and a part of him loved it.

Annie led him to a corner of the living room that had been transformed into a computer area with a couple of mismatched monitors sitting on stacks of books, and two photos pulled up on the screen to the right. One was clearly the picture Annie had taken of the framed photograph in Mr. Durham's living room. The other was a picture of the same dog and looked identical...

Finn stared at the monitor. Maybe his eyes were playing tricks on him? He looked back and forth between the two until finally he was sure that the pictures of Bun were the same. But one appeared to be a photograph of Bun from a magazine.

"I'm so confused." Finn gestured to the monitors. "Bun was in a magazine?"

"Yes, but Bun isn't Mr. Durham's dog!" Annie did a little happy dance. "I *knew* there was no way he got the depth of field in that photograph using just a phone. It's impossible. But I thought maybe there was something I was missing. So I posted the photo of Bun on this photography forum, and everyone backed me up. They said there was no way to achieve that effect using just a phone camera." She took both of Finn's hands and swung them back and forth like she'd hit the lottery.

Her happiness was infectious. In the reflection of the monitor, Finn noticed the big grin on his face—and he didn't even care how goofy it looked. He hadn't been this happy in a long time.

"And that got me thinking," Annie continued. "So I did a reverse image lookup and . . ." She held her hands out to the monitor like she was Vanna White revealing a puzzle. "Bun is really an English bulldog named Henry the Eighth. He's won five dog shows in England."

"So Durham stole the picture off the internet?"

Annie nodded emphatically. "Check out the difference in the windows." She pulled up the photo she'd taken of Mr. Durham's window seat, and placed it beside the other photos.

Finn studied them. "You're right. The molding along the top of Durham's window is different. His window has a rounded edge and the one in the dog pictures doesn't."

"Busted!" Annie gave Finn a high five.

"Way to go!" Finn tapped his temple. "Durham faked the picture, but how did he fake the supporting documentation? Can I sit down?"

"Sure." Annie pulled out the chair.

Finn carefully maneuvered himself into the tight spot and managed to sit without putting too much weight on the rickety desk. He expected Annie to pull up a chair beside him, but when she stepped behind him, placed her hands on his shoulders, and lowered her face so it was right beside his, he almost forgot why he'd sat down.

"Uh . . . I wanted to . . ." His mind went blank as Annie's curls brushed his neck.

He suddenly realized the monitor on the left had a display

of everything they'd said since he entered the room, ending with his awkward *Uh, I wanted to . . .*

"Are you using speech-to-text in here, too?" he asked.

Annie gave his shoulders a little squeeze. "I have to while I'm working on the computer. The kids call out to me all the time."

"That's smart." Finn sat there, staring at the addendum. "And this is fraud."

"Do you think there were more people involved in the scam?" Annie asked.

"Yes." Finn snapped his fingers. "From the look of this file, it's way more complicated than Durham stealing a picture off the internet and claiming that he had a dog."

Annie leaned forward as she started absentmindedly rubbing Finn's shoulders. His breathing hitched, and he tried to focus.

"What are you looking for now?" Annie asked. Her face was so close to his that her breath warmed his chin.

"The dog . . . the place where Mr. Durham bought the dog." His fingers hovered over the keyboard, but he couldn't think of the word. The only word that was coming into his mind right now was *Annie.*

"A kennel?" she said.

"Kennel! That's the word. Your lips—" Finn coughed, and his eyes went wide. "I mean, I . . ."

Annie's eyes narrowed as she read the speech-to-text on the screen. "Sorry. My app is having a hard time understanding you."

Finn cleared his throat again and tried to focus. "I'll try to speak slower."

"Let me get you a refill." Annie picked up his empty glass. "I'll be right back.". Annie shot from the room like a dart and returned fifteen minutes later with water and a plate of cut up veggies and dip.

"Thank you." Finn took a long sip. "This whole story is bogus." He leaned back in the chair and said, "Annie, you're a genius." He pointed at the monitor with a carrot stick. "The kennel where Durham supposedly bought Bun is part of the veterinary clinic where he said she was treated after the accident. They're both owned by the same veterinarian whose name is on the bill of sale for the dog, the medical bills, and the cremation paperwork. So I did a little digging on the vet. You won't believe who the vet is married to. The former Lisa Durham! Lisa is Jerry Durham's sister."

"No way! Are you serious?" Annie patted his back. "The vet is Mr. Durham's brother-in-law? They were in on it together!"

Annie jumped up and held her hands out to Finn. Puzzled, he took her hands and stood. Annie started to do her happy dance, but Finn's joy turned to shock when he realized she wanted him to dance along.

What is she thinking? I have a hard enough time walking, let alone dancing.

"I can't," he said, shaking his head.

"It's easy." She smiled. "Just sway or move your hands. We did it again!"

Finn awkwardly moved back and forth. The front door banged open, and Tammy and Tommy raced into the room. Finn tried to pull his hands away, but Annie held on tight.

"We solved another case!" Annie cheered.

"Yeah!" Tammy ran over. "Are you doing your happy dance? Can I dance, too?" She grabbed Finn's hand and Annie's, then laughed and danced in place.

"Hey," Tommy jerked his thumb toward the door. "Someone's mowed half the lawn. They used one of those super old lawn mowers with no engine."

"Finn is doing it." Annie said, her eyes sparkling. "Isn't that nice?"

Tammy let go of their hands and gave Finn a big hug. "Thanks, Finn!"

Tommy's face lit up. "Can I help?"

Finn looked questioningly at Annie. Her nose wrinkled up. "If you wear your boots, I might—"

"Sure, Mom!" Tommy dashed off, disappearing down the hall.

Tammy started to run after him, but Annie placed a restraining hand on her shoulder. Tammy stuck out her bottom lip. "But I want to help, too, Mommy."

Finn smiled down at the little girl. "There *is* another job that needs to get done," he said. "The problem is, I need someone who is a *really* good artist."

Tammy's hand shot in the air. "Me! *I'm* an artist!"

"Oh, that's right," Finn said. "Well, the front door needs a coat of paint and—"

"I'll go get my smock!" She zipped out of the room.

Annie bit her bottom lip and looked up at Finn, her eyes glistening with tears of gratitude. "I don't know how to thank you, Finnian." Her words caught in her throat.

He shrugged. "If we're keeping score, I think I owe you. You're the one who solved the case."

Annie's face suddenly brightened. "You're staying for dinner."

"No, no, I can't. I mean, you don't have to do that."

"I do. Please?" Annie stood close to him, and once again, Finnian looked into those blue eyes and lost the ability to speak. He held his fist up at shoulder height and bobbed it back and forth to make the sign for *yes*.

Annie moved even closer to him. "Do you mind if I help?" Without waiting for an answer, she placed her hand over his and gently turned his hand so the palm was facing out.

Finn drank in her sweet scent as she taught him to sign *yes, yes, yes.*

"Mom, what are you making Finn say yes to?" Tommy asked smiling from the hallway.

Annie and Finn burst out laughing in unison, their hands still entwined.

"That I'll be staying for dinner." In fact, at that moment, he didn't want to be anywhere else.

A MiniMystery Series

THE ADVENTURES OF

Finn &
Annie

THE CASE OF
THE DISAPPEARING DIAMOND

CHRISTOPHER GREYSON

A MiniMystery Series

THE ADVENTURES OF
Finn & Annie

THE CASE OF
THE DISAPPEARING DIAMOND

WALL STREET JOURNAL BESTSELLING AUTHOR
CHRISTOPHER GREYSON

GREYSON MEDIA

CHAPTER 1

Annie Summers's eyes fluttered open, and a smile quickly spread across her face, making her look like a kid on Christmas morning. The gift she was looking forward to was a chance to spend time with Finn. He'd texted her last night about a job this morning, and over the last few months working as a photographer and videographer with Finnian Church on his insurance investigations had been exciting, fun, and—something else as well.

Just thinking about someone in a romantic way was so foreign that it was actually scary. She hadn't even entertained the idea of dating since her divorce from Camden, but her rush of excitement last night when she heard from Finn, and her happy anticipation when she woke up left little room for doubt —she had a crush on her boss.

The former soldier was the exact opposite of her ex-husband. Maybe that was part of Finn's appeal. Where Finn was patient, Camden's reactions to the same events were random, unexpected, and often fueled by anger. Finn was as kind and thoughtful as Camden was cruel and arrogant. Finn was self-sufficient; Camden was spoiled and wanted to be waited on hand and foot.

It hadn't always been that way. There was a time when Camden was . . .

Who was she kidding? Camden had always been a jerk. The truth was, she'd put up with his flaws and mistreatment because she felt he was all she deserved. After she lost her hearing, when she was fourteen, her mother had planted two ideas in Annie's head: she was broken—damaged goods—and if any boy gave her a second look, never let him go.

So that's exactly what happened. Annie turned Camden's head and then she clung to him like a drowning swimmer to a life ring, grateful that he had rescued her from a lonely life. Her mother frequently reminded Annie of her debt to Camden and her need to keep him happy at all costs, since there was *no way* she would ever get so lucky again. For years Annie overlooked Camden's abhorrent behavior, cruelty, and contempt. And she would have probably still been with him if the legal system hadn't stepped in; Camden, blaming her somehow for his downfall, divorced her while he was incarcerated.

She looked around the bedroom. It needed a fresh coat of paint, but she loved the windows. The kids each had their own room and said they loved the house. She was only renting, but she had a new job and a new life, and she wouldn't let Camden steal any of her happiness. Not today. Not anymore.

The light above her bedroom door flashed. A second later, Tammy rushed across the floor and leapt up onto the bed. Annie's four-year-old little angel was wearing her princess footsie pajamas with an addition all her own, a bright pink tutu.

Tammy signed, "Shark is here."

Annie's smile grew. "I thought you were a dolphin," Annie signed back.

Tammy giggled and shook her head. "Not me." She then signed each letter: F-I-N-N.

Annie sat bolt upright and looked at the clock. 8:00. He wasn't supposed to be here until . . .

She grabbed her phone off the nightstand and reread Finn's text.

Hi Annie,

We're scheduled to meet the client at 9:00 so why don't I pick you up an hour earlier?

Finn

"Oh no!"

Pulling an oversized, comfy shirt over her head, she dashed to the door and yanked it open. She'd made it two steps into the hallway when Tommy walked into view, followed by Finn. The little boy was giving him a tour of the house.

Wearing only the shirt, Annie darted into the hall closet. In the darkness, she felt the flush on her cheeks as she pictured Finn standing at the end of the hall, slack-jawed and wide-eyed.

He must think I'm crazy.

The door behind her opened and Tammy peered in. She was giggling.

"What are you doing, Mommy?"

"Is the coast clear?"

Tammy nodded. "Tommy's showing Finn his fish tank."

Annie peeked into the empty hallway and bolted into the bathroom. Her embarrassment grew as she saw her reflection in the mirror. Her blond curls stuck out at all angles like she'd been electrocuted, and the shirt barely covered the tops of her legs.

There wasn't enough time for a shower. She pulled her hair into a ponytail, slapped on deodorant and mascara, and took a swig of mouthwash from the bottle in record time, but now she had to make it back to her room to get dressed. Once again she sped down the hall, back to her bedroom, to yank a pair of slacks on, pull a blouse over her head without unbuttoning it, and shove her bare feet into the shoes nearest the door. She emerged from the bedroom out of breath.

Tucking in her blouse all the way while trying not to hyperventilate, she hurried down the hallway to the living room. It was empty. Pushing aside the frustration of not being able to determine where her children were without seeing them, she walked to the front window. Finn's car was still parked outside. Glancing over her shoulder, she noticed shadows moving in the kitchen.

The three of them were sitting at the kitchen table eating cereal. Finn held up his princess bowl and smiled sheepishly. "Tammy made me breakfast."

"But it's my cereal!" Tommy said proudly.

"And it's delicious." Finn set his bowl down. "Thank you both."

"Watch this, Mom!" Tommy held up his spoon with a marshmallow perched on the end. With a flick of his finger, he knocked it into the bowl. "Home run!"

Annie's eyes widened and she used the universal sign language of mothers to get him to stop—the mom look.

Tommy set his spoon down and Tammy giggled.

"Sorry I'm late," Annie said. "I just need to grab my bag."

Finn glanced at his watch. "We still have time. I added some padding to the schedule."

Annie blushed. *Probably because of my habit of running late.*

"They need to get to the bus stop." Annie signed *Hurry up* to the children as she spoke.

Her embarrassment came roaring back as Tommy and Tammy lifted their bowls to their mouths to slurp the sugary milk at the bottom. But when Finn followed suit, she laughed along with the kids.

"Don't forget my baseball game tonight!" Tommy said as he grabbed his school bag.

Annie gave him a thumbs-up and breathed another sigh of relief. Spending time with Finn wasn't the only reason she was grateful for the job today; she needed the money to pay for Tommy's T-ball uniform.

After kissing the kids and watching them run to join the group waiting at the bus stop, Annie got into Finn's car. "Tommy must really like you. He shared his Frosted Rings with you. Normally he saves them for Saturday morning."

"I'm flattered."

He smiled at her, and she had to force herself to look away from his eyes, sparkling with humor and kindness. "Again, I'm sorry I'm late." Annie turned on her speech-to-text app. "I misread your text."

Finn gave a dismissive wave that changed to a full-blown parade wave as he noticed the kids jumping up and down at the bus stop. He followed it up by tapping the horn three times. Annie waved and blew kisses, causing Tommy to roll his eyes and Tammy to start blowing kisses back.

"They're great kids," Finn said, his words coming up on Annie's phone screen. "Tommy's very excited about starting T-ball."

"He's also very nervous," Annie said. "He has a problem with playing."

"What's he having a problem with? I used to play."

"Just the hitting, catching, and throwing parts." Annie's nose crinkled up. "I've tried to help him but the truth is, I'm worse at those than he is."

Finn cocked his head to the side. "Those skills are a big part of the game. Ah, do you think Tommy really wants to play?"

"More than anything," Annie said. "All of his friends are on the team."

"I could help him, but I don't want to step on any toes . . . What about his father?"

Annie swallowed. Finn had never asked about the children's

father, and he was the last thing she wanted to discuss. "He's out of the picture. Where are we heading today?" she asked, eager to change the subject.

Finn opened and closed his mouth. He looked like he still wanted to discuss Tommy and baseball, but he pressed his lips together and gave a little nod. "We're looking into a claim regarding a stolen diamond ring. The ring is valued at fifty thousand dollars, and the home owner took a special rider out on her jewelry." Finn reached down and handed Annie a manila folder. "Mrs. Esther Larson is also pursuing charges against her maid, Ms. Sonia Gonzalez. We're going to interview her first."

Annie sat up, her excitement rising. When she took this job, she'd just expected to take pictures and be told what to do. But Finn included her in everything and valued her opinion. To him, she mattered—and she loved this strange, new feeling.

CHAPTER 2

Sonia Gonzalez buzzed them up to her little apartment on the third floor. There was no elevator and poor Finn had to climb the steep stairs. With his prosthetic leg, Annie didn't know how he managed it. Not wanting to embarrass him, Annie stopped on the first landing to retie her left shoe, and the right one on the second landing. She was certain that he at least suspected she was stalling for him, but he didn't mention it. If anything, he appeared grateful.

The door to the apartment was open and Ms. Gonzalez was waiting for them. She was a petite woman with medium-length dark hair. Her large, brown eyes were red-rimmed. She stood ramrod straight as she greeted them. "Good morning. You are from the insurance company?"

"Good morning, Ms. Gonzalez. Yes, we're from A. G. Maxwell Insurance. I'm Finnian Church and this is Annie Summers."

"Please come in." She stepped to the side and Finn and Annie entered directly into the living room.

Ms. Gonzalez's modest apartment was immaculate.

Although tiny, its open floor plan made it feel a little larger than it actually was.

"Please sit down," Annie read on her speech-to-text app.

Finn and Annie sat on the couch and Ms. Gonzalez stood nervously beside a high-back chair.

"Wouldn't you like to sit down, Ms. Gonzalez?" Finn asked her.

Ms. Gonzalez nodded and sat in the chair. She was rubbing the back of her right hand with the left. Annie was well acquainted with this self-comforting gesture. Her therapist had pointed out that Annie did the same thing to calm herself.

"Please call me Sonia." Ms. Gonzalez sat down. "I am . . . nervous." Her lip trembled.

Finn took out his phone. "Would it be okay with you if I recorded this conversation?"

The frightened maid frowned. "My English is not so good."

Finn said something that read on the text app as gibberish. Annie cast him a puzzled glance.

"I asked if Sonia would be more comfortable speaking in Spanish," he explained. "She said she would." He turned to Sonia, spoke to her, and then translated. "I told Sonia that you are deaf. She said you must understand how challenging communicating can be at times."

Annie smiled and nodded. Communicating was a frustration that she was all too familiar with, but working with someone who understood this went a long way toward closing the gap.

Finn pressed record and started interviewing Sonia. He translated both his questions and Sonia's answers into English for Annie.

"We're here to ask you about Mrs. Larson's ring."

"The police already talked to me. I didn't take it. I swear." Sonia placed her hand over her heart.

"How long have you been working for Mrs. Larson?"

"Only a week. But I work very hard. I tried to make sure that everything was done correctly, but . . ."

Finn folded his hands and waited for her to continue. Annie admired his patience. He didn't press her or goad her.

"Mrs. Larson was unhappy with talking to me."

"Why?"

"My English is not very good and Mrs. Larson does not like repeating herself. I understand it better than I speak it, but I'm trying to improve. I'm taking English."

Finn nodded. "I'm sure you're getting better. It takes time. Mrs. Larson also reported that a pair of pearl earrings is missing. She said they disappeared two days before the ring."

"I didn't steal anything. I saw the earrings on the table, but I didn't take them."

"Mrs. Larson said no one else was in the house."

Sonia nodded. "That is true. It was just me and her in the house. I can't explain the disappearance of the jewelry, but I'm not a thief. I would never steal."

"Did you see the diamond ring?"

"Yes. On the table in her bedroom. I did move it. I had to."

"Why was that?" Finn placed his hands on his knees and leaned forward.

"To dust properly. Mrs. Larson is allergic, so I wanted to be extra thorough. I took everything off the table, polished it, and I put it right back."

Finn nodded. Annie was surprised he wasn't taking notes. Maybe it was because he was recording the conversation. Or perhaps he was already pushed to his multitasking limit, translating the bilingual conversation.

"Would you be willing to take a polygraph test?"

Sonia said something that Finn didn't translate.

"It's a lie detector test," he clarified.

Sonia's hands went into overdrive as she wrung them together. "The police asked me that, too. It's just that I'm so nervous. My neighbor, she watches all those NCIS shows. She said sometimes if you're nervous, you fail."

"That is true but—"

Sonia's lips trembled. "I didn't steal anything. I promise. But I don't know about taking that test. Could I pay for the ring?"

Finn sat up straighter and so did Annie. Then he asked what Annie was thinking: "Why would you offer to pay for something that you didn't take?"

"I'm trying to become a citizen. If I'm convicted of a crime, they will not let me."

"The ring is fifty thousand dollars."

Sonia burst into tears and buried her face in her hands.

Finn had cautioned Annie about being objective on cases, but Annie couldn't help herself— her heart ached for this woman. She moved to one side of Sonia's chair and placed a comforting hand on her shoulder.

Finn picked up a tissue box and offered her a tissue. Sonia wept uncontrollably for a few minutes.

Finn caught Annie's gaze and signed to her, "Let's go talk to Mrs. Larson." The look on Finn's handsome face said it all. He believed Sonia, too.

CHAPTER 3

Mrs. Larson's house—a grand white colonial set high on a hill—was palatial in comparison to Sonia's tiny abode, and it dwarfed even the other expensive homes around it.

Mrs. Larson opened the heavy front door and her expression soured. "Are you from the maid service?"

"No, ma'am." Finn held out his card. "I'm Finnian Church and this is Annie Summers. We're from A. G. Maxwell Insurance. We made an appointment to ask you some questions about your claim."

Mrs. Larson glanced at her watch. "You're five minutes early."

It wasn't at all difficult for Annie to read her lips. The woman's brusque demeanor made her bristle, but Finn seemed unruffled.

"We can come back if you'd prefer." Finn smiled.

Mrs. Larson looked at her watch again like she was actually considering his offer. She stepped to the side, holding open the door.

Annie expected Mrs. Larson to lead them into a living room or study, but the woman stopped in the foyer and crossed her arms. The fresh flowers on the marble table drooped as if the toxic environment was sucking the life right out of them. "I've already spoken with the police. So far, they've neglected their duty and haven't arrested that woman. Have you read their report?"

"I have," Finn responded.

"Then why are you *here*?"

Finn pressed his lips together and Annie noticed the slightest tightening around his eyes. But his voice remained calm when he responded, "We need to ask you some additional questions and take some photographs."

Annie smiled at his emotional discipline. Her ex-husband would have blown up on the front steps.

Finn took out his phone. "Do you mind if I record this conversation?"

"I do." Mrs. Larson's face puckered in disgust.

Finn nodded, tucking away his phone. "I will need to take notes then. As I mentioned, I have read your report. Can you please show us the bedroom where the diamond ring was located?"

"It's upstairs." Mrs. Larson turned on her heel and briskly crossed the foyer to the grand staircase.

Finn hurried after her and Annie watched him with concern. Finn had been a soldier and he radiated a deep strength, but Annie found herself fiercely protective of him. She couldn't understand it. It went beyond his prosthetic leg. He never showed it, but for some reason she had a sense that he was injured in another way that still hadn't healed.

Annie placed a gentle hand on his arm in an attempt to slow him down. "Do you want pictures downstairs?" She pointed back to the foyer.

"No, thank you," Finn signed.

Finn turned his head and looked up. Mrs. Larson must have

said something, but of course Annie hadn't heard it, and the app hadn't picked it up either. Annie smiled and held onto his arm.

"I'm signing. Annie is deaf."

Mrs. Larson tapped her foot impatiently. "This way."

Finn and Annie followed Mrs. Larson up the stairs and into a bedroom almost the size of Annie's whole downstairs. The tight-weave carpet was silver with golden flecks—very chic, but it felt hard, not plush. The furniture looked to Annie like antiques, good ones, though not particularly comfortable. A grand canopy bed sat in the center. The room was very neat and immaculately clean.

"Who else has access to this room?" Finn asked.

"Myself, my husband, who's been in Morocco for the last three weeks, and the thief." Mrs. Larson's nostrils flared as she glared at Annie. "What is she doing?" She thrust a finger toward Annie as she marched to glower at Finn. "I specifically informed you that I was not to be recorded. That is a violation of the law."

Finn squared his shoulders. "Annie is not recording your conversation. She is using a speech-to-text app so she can understand—"

"I am not comfortable with that. Have her shut it off."

Finn inhaled slowly. One look at him and Annie knew that Mrs. Larson's rudeness had just crossed some line. The muscles in his jaw flexed.

"That's fine," Annie said, holding up her phone so he could see her text—I CAN READ HER LIPS.

She put her phone in her pocket, and Mrs. Larson smiled smugly. Finn loosened his tie. Annie noticed that it was a habit of his that he did at times of stress. She resisted the urge to reach out to him.

"Where was the diamond ring the last time you saw it?"

Mrs. Larson walked over to an antique table and pointed down. "Right here."

Annie started taking photographs. The table was very ornately carved with legs that tapered down to pencil-thin feet. A vase of roses sat on the table. Like the flowers downstairs, it looked as if the life was being sucked from them. Petals littered the table top.

"Two days prior," Mrs. Larson continued, "that woman stole a pair of pearl earrings."

Finn's brows knit together. "The earrings aren't listed in your claim."

"They were inexpensive, roughly a thousand dollars, so they were beneath my policy. Still, they show a pattern of theft, do they not?"

A thousand dollars is inexpensive? Thoroughly disgusted, and glad she wasn't the one who had to talk to the woman, Annie concentrated on taking photos in between reading lips.

"Have you hired another maid?" Finn asked.

"Not yet." Mrs. Larson glanced down at her watch. "And it looks like I won't be hiring one today. They are late. Why do you ask?"

Finn pointed to the table. "The flower petals on the floor have been cleaned up."

Annie's mouth opened slightly. She hadn't noticed it before, but the floor was clear of petals, while the table was covered with them.

"They were vacuumed up."

"By you?" Finn asked.

"Of course not."

Finn raised an eyebrow. "If only you and the maid were in the room, how is that possible?"

Mrs. Larson walked over to the nightstand and pressed a button on a console. From out of the closet appeared a robot vacuum. "Normally it is on a set schedule."

Annie watched as the vacuum crossed the room, bumped into the wall, turned slightly, and continued on its way.

Finn eyed the machine. "How often do you empty the bag?"

"Never." Mrs. Larson's look of irritation with Finn's questions seemed to be rising. "It's automated. Are we almost done here?"

Finn gave a little push to the table where the diamond had been. It wobbled slightly and a petal floated off the table and onto the rug. Without saying a word, he turned and walked into the closet.

"Excuse me!" Mrs. Larson crossed her arms. "Where do you think you are going?"

With his back to her and without her app, Annie couldn't tell what his response was.

A moment later, Finn reappeared holding a little vacuum bag. "Your vacuum returns to its station to get recharged and the dustbin is emptied into this bag. I'd ask if you've checked it, but I'm guessing the answer is no."

"Excuse me?" Mrs. Larson's nostrils flared.

Finn walked over to the trash can and held the vacuum bag up next to his head and gave it a shake. He awkwardly bent over, and Annie caught her breath as he wobbled slightly. He carefully opened the bag and felt inside. He pulled out a pearl earring, followed shortly by another one and, in a moment, the diamond ring.

Setting them on the table, he turned to face Mrs. Larson. "I will inform the agency that you are canceling your claim. You will need to contact the police station and let them know that you were mistaken about the theft."

Instead of being relieved that the jewelry was recovered, Mrs. Larson seemed even more perturbed. "How do we know that woman didn't plan to have the jewelry vacuumed up and was going to retrieve the vacuum bag from the trash later?"

Annie stepped forward, ready to let Mrs. Larson know

exactly what she thought about her, but Finn placed a restraining hand on her shoulder. She nodded to let him know she understood, then photographed the dust-covered jewelry and vacuum bag for the file.

"How do we know that wasn't your plan all along and you filed a false insurance claim?"

"How dare you!" Mrs. Larson stamped her foot.

"Let me be clear." Finn spoke calmly but the tightness around his eyes made his handsome features appear very stern. Annie didn't know what his rank had been in the army, but she could easily picture him giving orders to troops. "If you do not cancel your police report, the insurance company will pursue a fraud case against you."

"You can't do that."

"I can and I will. As a policy owner, you have a responsibility to perform a minimum of due diligence before filing a report. Checking the wastebasket is far below the threshold. And you are aware that ongoing investigations are public knowledge."

"I will be canceling my policy," Mrs. Larson said crisply.

"That is your prerogative, but it will have no effect on whether we decide to pursue an investigation or not."

Mrs. Larson's eyes narrowed. "I suppose the important thing is that I have my ring back. That also means there is no reason for you to be here. Thank you." She held her arm out toward the door.

Finn didn't say a word as he marched out of the room and toward the stairs. Annie hurried around him so she could descend the stairs first. In spite of Mrs. Larson huffing impatiently behind them, Annie made sure to take her time so Finn didn't rush.

She felt like she'd emerged from a crypt as they exited the house and a warm breeze caressed her face. The door flew shut behind them. Annie's chuckle turned into a light laugh as she looked at Finn's face, which was twisted in confusion and anger.

"How can you laugh about that beastly woman?" Finn asked.

Annie checked her speech-to-text app and shrugged. "I'll forget Mrs. Larson, she doesn't bother me. But I can't wait to tell Sonia. Do you have any idea how happy she'll be?"

"She'll still be out of a job."

"I think I'd rather be unemployed than work for that woman." Annie smiled.

Finn stopped at the driver's side of the car and smiled back. "You have a way of always finding the bright side of things."

Annie felt the color rising in her cheeks. "Well, you have a way of figuring things out. I think that was the fastest I've ever seen you solve a case."

Finn's smile grew. "Do we have time to stop by Sonia's and tell her the good news in person? I'd like to make sure that she has all the facts, just in case Mrs. Larson goes back on her word."

Annie peered at the clock on her phone and made a face. "Tommy has his first T-ball game tonight and I promised that I'd try to help him practice a little. I don't know how much help I'm going to be, though, since I only know what end of the bat to hold."

Finn chuckled. "If it's okay with you, I love baseball. I played in college. I'd be happy to help. We can call Sonia on the way to the game."

"Are you sure? I don't want to put you out."

"I'd love to. I told Tommy I'd go to his game."

Annie swallowed. It wasn't that she didn't want Finn to go. But Camden was coming to the game, too.

CHAPTER 4

Annie sat on the metal bleachers with Tammy beside her. The little girl was so excited about her brother's game that she could hardly contain herself. Her feet were tapping, and Annie could feel the constant vibration through her body.

And Annie's heart was pounding in her chest, too, thumping like a poorly packed washing machine because of the three men in her life. It was whirling with excitement at seeing Finn. Then, when she thought about how nervous Tommy was, it started beating heavily, and when she thought of Camden showing up, it clunked like a load of washing shifting.

She didn't understand why Camden was coming at all.

When Finn said that he'd played in college, she knew Finn wasn't bragging, but Tommy's father had played in the major leagues—though only for one season. Camden tore his rotator cuff in a car accident, was arrested for DUI, and released from the team. His career was over before it really started. The other driver sued and they lost everything. Annie stayed beside Camden through it all. Everyone had told her to divorce him, but Camden was the one who'd left, and had taken a job in another city. They didn't see him often, and she wanted to curse the bad timing of this visit.

Tammy pulled on her shoulder and pointed at the dugout. Tommy was waving at them. He was smiling, but Annie could see how nervous he was. She gave him a wave and a big thumbs-up.

Tammy's feet danced happily on the bleachers and she pointed in a different direction. "Finn's here!"

Annie stood up. Both of her children were signing Finn's name by holding a hand palm up and slowly rotating it as they pushed their arm forward—like a shark swimming. Finn was walking along the fence, searching the crowd for her. When he saw her, his face lit up. The look alone made Annie smile, but the feeling behind it made her feel like she was flying. He was happy to see her. He wanted to be here.

Just as important for her, he'd said he would come and he did. Camden had broken his promises so many times that the kids no longer trusted him at all. That thought made her calm down a little, and the load in the washing machine settled a little. Maybe Camden would stay true to form and not show.

Annie looked back at Finn. His smile had faded. He wasn't looking at her; his attention was on the bleachers. *I'm an idiot!* Annie wanted to smack herself. Tammy loved sitting in the top row, so that's where they headed, without considering how Finn would have to climb up to them.

"We need to move to the bottom," Annie said, gathering up their things.

"But I like sitting here, Mommy," Tammy whined.

"Finn can't climb up here," Annie signed.

Tammy nodded rapidly, sending her blond curls bobbing about her shoulders as she scrambled like a soldier over an obstacle course to get down to greet him.

"You didn't have to move on my account," Finn said, still

staring up at the bleachers like it was a mountain he wanted to scale.

"We didn't." Annie tried not to lie. "We were sitting up there... so we could spot you coming. Now we can sit up close."

Tammy clapped her hands. "You can sit next to me." She took Finn by the hand and pulled him down to the space beside her on the bleachers.

The game started and the three of them clapped for all the other players and cheered them on. Every time a player got up to hit, Tammy asked when Tommy would bat. Annie knew that every player got a chance, but as the game wore on, even she started to worry.

Tammy sat down and stopped clapping, clinging to Annie's side like she was scared. Annie didn't need to see him to know that Camden had arrived. A small crowd greeted him as he arrived. He was a mini-celebrity at the ballpark, mostly because he never missed an opportunity to let everyone know that he'd played professionally. Annie caught his gaze and she sat down, too. He sneered in her direction and swaggered over to the chain-link backstop. There was nothing she could do about his being there—even though Camden was still on probation, the restraining order had ended.

The boy at bat hit a single and Tommy came running out of the dugout. Finn and Tammy started clapping and cheering, but Annie couldn't take her eyes off her son. He froze when he noticed his father, then gave a stiff wave.

One of the coaches moved Tommy up to the T-ball. Tommy choked up on the bat and swung as hard as he could. He missed it by a foot. Camden dramatically threw his hands in the air and shook his head. Finn yelled something and clapped.

Annie's speech-to-text app was just about useless in this situation, and even focusing on one person to read lips was difficult—but she could see Tommy wasn't doing well. Her stomach lurched when he swung again and bashed the plastic pole holding the ball. The ball fell off and landed at his feet.

As the umpire put the ball back on the T, Tommy glanced back at his mom. Annie could tell that he was close to tears. She hurried over to the fence and gave him a big thumbs-up. Camden, a few feet away, cupped his hand to his mouth and shouted something to Tommy, who took another swing and missed.

Camden turned to Annie, shaking his head. "He must get his baseball skills from your side of the family. How do you strike out in T-ball?"

"You can't," Annie shot back. "He gets another turn. Please try to be encouraging."

Camden's face twisted in disgust. "Are you kidding me? I bet he gets a participation trophy too?"

"He's six," Annie said.

"Tell him I'll come when he's playing a real game." Camden spun on his heel and started for the parking lot.

Annie's hands balled into fists. She turned back to look for Tommy. He was standing next to the dugout, and Finn was looking into his eyes, speaking earnestly, with one hand on the boy's shoulder. Tommy nodded several times as he wiped his eyes with the back of his hand. Annie was worried he might have a full meltdown, so she was taken aback when the little guy laughed.

Tommy and Finn exchanged a knuckle bump and Tommy walked back to try batting again. He took his stance as Finn moved over and stood by Annie's side.

"What did you tell him?" Annie asked.

"He's missing the ball because he keeps closing his eyes. I told him to picture the ball as a giant marshmallow."

"Like the cereal this morning!" Annie clapped.

"Exactly." Finn grinned.

Tommy swung and hit the ball and watched in amazement,

along with everyone else, as the ball skittered far into right field, then he ran. In his excitement, he carried the bat all the way to first base.

The crowd leapt to their feet and erupted in applause. Tammy and Finn did a little celebration dance. Without thinking, Annie grabbed Finn and kissed his cheek. Both of them flushed red and Tammy clamped her hands over her mouth.

"You kissed Finn!"

Annie shook her head. "It wasn't a kiss-kiss. I was just so happy." Annie scooped Tammy up and gave her two quick kisses on both sides of her cheeks. Tammy giggled and kissed her back. The three of them waved at Tommy, standing proudly on first base.

"Are you happy, Mommy?" Tammy signed.

Annie nodded and held her a little tighter. The truth was, she was happier than she'd been in a very long time.

A MiniMystery Series

THE ADVENTURES OF

Finn & Annie

THE CASE
OF RAINING
NAILS

WALL STREET JOURNAL BESTSELLING AUTHOR
CHRISTOPHER GREYSON

THE ADVENTURES OF

Finn & Annie

THE CASE OF RAINING NAILS

WALL STREET JOURNAL BESTSELLING AUTHOR

Christopher Greyson

GREYSON MEDIA

CHAPTER 1

Annie Summers opened her newly painted front door, looked out across her freshly cut front lawn, and pictured Finnian Church smiling as he pushed the old-fashioned lawn mower last week. Finn couldn't have come into her life at a better time. He'd given her a job, the break she needed to make it as a photographer in an unfamiliar arena—the insurance industry. And now, like a knight on a white horse, he'd not only fixed her car but cut her grass and painted the front door as well.

She made a mental note to do something special for him. With very limited funds, buying something was out of the question, but she could always make a thank-you present. The biggest question was—what to make? Finn was a former soldier. Would he really want something she made with the arts-and-crafts supplies she kept on hand for projects with the kids?

A determined smile crossed her face as she squared her shoulders and marched out to the car. She'd come up with something. *Today is going to be a good day and nothing is going to stop me.*

At least that was what she kept telling herself—one of the affirmations she found in some self-help book after Camden divorced her. She could still remember her panic when she first read the divorce papers. Sole custody. It was what she'd asked for, but the realization that she would be raising their two young children on her own made her head spin. Camden's lawyer argued that there was no way a young, unemployed, deaf woman could possibly provide the care that these kids needed on a full-time basis, that his client—the one who had never changed a diaper in his life— was best suited for parenting. Thankfully, the judge recognized that Camden's filing for full custody stemmed from him trying to dodge paying child support, not a desire to actually raise his kids.

But Annie was making it on her own. They might be only scraping by, but she was moving forward. Each day she tried to improve herself and their situation, and step by step she was succeeding. Her confidence grew as she backed her old, rusted car out of the driveway.

Powering down her window, she let the warm air blow her blond hair back and sweep her worries away with it. As she crossed town, she stopped frequently, letting other drivers pull out with a smile and a wave. The other motorists waved and smiled back, creating a positive feedback loop in her brain that encouraged her to keep at it. But when she glanced down at the clock, her eyes widened. She only had five minutes to get to Finn's house. She'd been late twice before, and although he hadn't said anything, she knew tardiness bothered the buttoned-down former military man.

Annie stepped on the gas and zipped down the side streets. She was careful not to go too fast, but she still managed to pull into the driveway just as the clock changed to nine on the nose.

Beaming, she hopped out of the car and jogged up the manicured walkway. Though she'd never been a neat freak, she had to admit that there was something charming and comforting about Finn's organizational prowess. Even the flower boxes were orderly, each with three petunias and two geraniums.

Annie rang the bell and waited.

After a minute she rang the bell again, and her phone buzzed in her pocket with a text from Finn.

RUNNING LATE. COME IN. HELP YOURSELF TO ANYTHING IN KITCHEN. NEED A MINUTE.

Annie opened the front door and stepped inside. "Good morning!" she called out, staring down at her phone, hoping he'd text back that he'd heard her. "Take your time!"

One of the hardest things she had to deal with about being deaf was the feeling of isolation. Right now, that horrible prickly sensation of panic trickled down her back. There could be a crowd of people in another room, but she wouldn't have any idea. She was in her own bubble of silence.

Her phoned buzzed.

TY! COFFEE IN KITCHEN.

Annie smiled as she followed the aroma past the living room and into the bright kitchen. It was immaculate and suited the house beautifully, with its white Shaker cabinets and Carrera marble countertops. She wasn't a big coffee drinker, but the rumbling in her stomach made her realize that she'd skipped breakfast again. She opened the cabinet above the coffeemaker and felt like Mother Hubbard—the cupboard was bare. The next one contained only a set of four cups and matching saucers on the bottom shelf. But they looked too fancy for a morning cup of coffee.

In search of mugs, she kept opening cabinets until she had circled the kitchen. Everything was meticulously placed, but the lack of kitchenware puzzled her.

Is he a minimalist?

Without another option, she took down one of the four

cups and saucers she'd found earlier and poured her coffee. She set the cup down and took out her phone.

WOULD YOU LIKE A CUP? she texted.

NO TY.

Annie closed the cabinet and opened the refrigerator, hoping to find cream, but the refrigerator, too, was nearly empty, except for a couple of neatly closed Chinese take-out containers, condiments, and a bottle of water.

Vibrations from someone coming down the hallway made her close the refrigerator and turn around. Finn smiled when he saw her, but his expression turned serious as he limped into the kitchen, leaning on the crutch under his left arm. She didn't often see him use the crutch—she suspected he resorted to it only when he was in great pain.

He looked at the floor but kept his face angled toward her so she was able to read his lips. "I, ah ... overdid it a little with ... therapy. Are you ready to go?"

From the set of his jaw, it was clear that he didn't want to elaborate, but Annie was torn. Part of her wanted to ask him if he would rather reschedule the appointment. He'd lost his left leg just below the knee, and if it was bothering him ...

Before she could think of a response, Finn turned and headed for the front door. Now unable to hear him, Annie poured her coffee down the sink and followed after. He held the front door open for her, and she took out her phone and turned on her speech-to-text app.

"Would you mind driving today?" Finn asked. "I'll pay for gas."

"No problem," Annie said as they headed for her car.

"I apologize for being late," Finn said. He got in and awkwardly placed the crutch beside his leg and his briefcase on his lap.

"No need to apologize. I'm the one who's usually late."

Annie hitched her thumb toward the backseat. "You can put the crutch back there if you'd be more comfortable."

"I'm fine. Thank you."

Annie hurried around to the driver's side, started the car, and waited.

Finn stared out the window. After a moment, he said, "I don't really want to discuss it."

Annie blanched. "That's okay, but I don't know where we're going."

Finn chuckled and shook his head. "My apologies again. I thought you were waiting for me to explain what happened. Our appointment is north of town, 327 Westmorland."

Annie punched the address into her GPS and pulled out of the driveway. "And we're off!"

Finn stared down at his leg. Every time he shifted in his seat he winced slightly. "We received a claim regarding a damaged windshield." He opened his briefcase, took out a tablet, and closed it again. "Mr. Silas Bennet."

"That sounds pretty straightforward."

"It may not be." Finn read from the report on the tablet. "Mr. Bennet claims the windshield was damaged when it started to rain nails."

CHAPTER 2

Annie moved several throw pillows and sat next to Finn on Mr. Bennet's fancy white couch. Mr. Bennet, a small, older man with a very animated way of speaking, was standing in the center of the ornate carpet and acting out the incident as if he were onstage.

"I was driving along Route 40 and I needed to get off at exit III." He pantomimed steering a car, complete with pulling down the rearview mirror as he checked for traffic. "And just as I went under the overpass it began to rain snails!"

Annie raised an eyebrow and held her phone out to Finn. As she'd hoped, he got a chuckle out of the mistake.

"Annie is deaf," Finn explained to Mr. Bennet. "Her speech-to-text app thought you said it rained *snails*."

Mr. Bennet's face twisted in disbelief. "Nails. I clearly enunciated the word. I was a professor of communication before I retired." He then turned and strutted over to the mantel. Like a prosecutor producing the murder weapon, he seized a shiny nail off the marble and triumphantly set it down on the coffee table. "Exhibit number two!"

From the way the corners of Finn's mouth turned up, Annie

suspected he was trying not to laugh. "And what would be exhibit number one?"

"Why, the video, of course." Mr. Bennet thrust out his chest and grinned proudly. "I have a dash cam. It recorded the entire incident—including the damage."

"Would it be possible for us to view this video?" Finn asked.

Mr. Bennet nodded excitedly. "I planned for that. Can I offer you some refreshments? Tea?"

Finn politely declined, but Annie's stomach grumbled in annoyance at being neglected. "I'd love a cup," she said.

Mr. Bennet hurried into the kitchen and quickly returned carrying a tray loaded with a teapot, three cups, and an assortment of cookies, mini-muffins, and scones. His grouchiness gone, he was brimming with excitement about his preparations for his guests.

"Wow," Finn said as Mr. Bennett set the tray down on the coffee table in front of them. "This is quite an assortment."

Annie smiled happily. "It looks delicious, thank you."

While Mr. Bennet set out the cream and sugar, napkins, and small plates, Annie glanced at the pictures around the large living room. All of the photographs were dated, and all featured Mr. Bennet and a woman. Annie scanned until she located a wedding picture from the '60s, the vibrant, curvaceous Mrs. Bennet smiling at her new husband with sparkling eyes.

Mr. Bennet must have noticed Annie staring. He nodded toward the photos and said, "My wife Mary and I. She's been gone almost seven years now. She would have set out home-made desserts. Please forgive these, they're store-bought."

Annie and Finn both rushed to thank him and reassure him that everything was wonderful, and Finn fixed a cup of tea in spite of his earlier refusal. Annie was truly grateful for the sustenance and felt her brain working better as soon as she took her first bite of a delicious blueberry muffin.

Seemingly satisfied that his guests were taken care of, Mr.

Bennet powered on the TV and DVD player. He shut off the lights and stood beside the television like a professor giving a lecture. After five minutes of watching traffic on the I-40 through the windshield, Mr. Bennet said, "Here I'm coming up to the exit and I drive under the overpass. Watch what happens next!"

Annie and Finn put down their teacups and leaned forward.

Just as the car drove clear of the overpass, sparkly objects bounced off the windshield and the hood. Mr. Bennet mumbled something that Annie's speech-to-text app didn't pick up. Then the windshield wipers moved back and forth a few times.

Mr. Bennet paused the video again and pointed at the screen, grinning as if what he was indicating was self-evident. "Did you see that?"

"I'd need to see it again," Finn said cautiously.

"You can't see the scratches on the windshield very well on the video, but didn't you hear that?" Mr. Bennet gasped, his eyes widening. "I'm so sorry, my mistake."

Annie shook her head and smiled. "No problem. What was I supposed to hear?"

Now it was Mr. Bennet's turn to look confused as he seemed to be struggling with what to say. "There was a sound like . . ." He thought for a minute.

Finn turned to Annie. "Do you remember what fingernails on a chalkboard sounded like?"

Annie cringed at the memory, even though she'd give her right arm to hear the sound again. "I do. Did something get stuck under the wipers?"

Mr. Bennet plucked the nail from the coffee table and lifted it up. "Exhibit number two!"

"Can you please rewind the video until we can see the overpass?" Finn asked.

"Certainly, but it doesn't show the person or persons throwing the nails," Mr. Bennet said. "I think it was most likely some juveniles."

Mr. Bennet found the spot and played the video again. Because of the cement barriers, Finn couldn't see the far side of the overpass, but he reached for his tablet and jotted down some notes.

"You can't see anyone, but there is a car driving by," Finn pointed out.

Mr. Bennet rewound the video and watched it again. "That's very true! I missed it before, but you can see the headlights illuminating the sign."

Without thinking, Annie patted Finn's leg and the poor man winced in pain.

"I'm so sorry." Annie grimaced.

"It's okay," Finn said through gritted teeth. He turned back to Mr. Bennet. "Can we see your windshield? Annie will need to take pictures." Finn placed his hand over his pant leg as he rose and picked up his crutch. "First, could I please use your bathroom?"

"Certainly. Second door on the right." Mr. Bennet walked to the front door. "Take your time. The car is right out in the driveway."

As Annie watched Finn limp to the bathroom, she had to resist the urge to rush over to him. She felt horrible that her light touch had caused him such pain. *He must really be hurting.*

Mr. Bennet held the door open and Annie followed him out, getting her camera ready. In the sunlight, the deep scratches to the glass were clearly visible. After she'd taken shots from several different angles, she felt the vibrations from the front door closing and looked up to see Finn awkwardly coming down the steps with his crutch. As he approached, she noticed a small smear that looked like a bloodstain on his pants near his knee.

Finn held his right hand out. "Thank you for your time, Mr. Bennet."

"Would you like to come back inside and watch the video again?" Mr. Bennet asked, shaking Finn's hand.

"We're good. But is it possible for you to send me a copy by email?" Finn handed him a business card with his contact information.

"Certainly. If you need any other information, just let me know."

As Finn and Annie headed back to the car, Finn's face was hard.

"Are you okay?" Annie asked. She was on his right side and couldn't see the bloodstain on the other side, but the exact shape of the small dark patch was burned into her mind's eye.

"I'm good, thanks, but I received a text message from the office. Another claim's been filed, and the accident was at the same exit where Mr. Bennet's windshield was damaged. This driver wasn't as fortunate. Their tire blew out, and the car struck the guardrail and then rolled over. They're in the ICU. We need to head over to Mike's Autobody and take pictures of the wreck. But first"—a shadow crossed his face—"we need to stop at my house for a moment."

CHAPTER 3

Annie backed out to the left and headed to Finn's house. He was looking out his window and not at her, which meant he was not talking—or not in the mood for talking. He sat with his hand covering the spot on his knee.

"Is everything okay?" she asked again, wanting so much to help him and feeling completely helpless.

Finn's smile was tight. "Fine. The office is sending me the new report. I've asked them to CC you on those from now on."

"Thank you." Annie smiled, suddenly uplifted. Once again Finn had made her feel included and encouraged. *'From now on'* *... this really is working out.* She was thrilled to feel like part of a team—especially with Finn. "Are we going to the police station, too? We'll need their report, and if kids were throwing things off the overpass, there may be more information."

Finn's eyes were closed and the muscles in his jaw flexed and stuck out like miniature boulders of granite. Annie pulled over. Finn looked up, confused.

"Why are you stopping?"

"You're hurt. Can I help?" Annie couldn't stop her glance

darting down to where his left hand was covering the spot. "Is it your leg?"

"My leg is fine." Finn's expression hardened and he glared out the windshield. "I have a headache. Can we please continue?"

Annie recoiled a little at his clipped words. She nodded, checked her mirrors, and pulled out. They rode the rest of the way without speaking.

As Annie pulled into Finn's driveway, he turned to her and said, "I apologize if I was short with you." He signed *Sorry*. "I should only be a few minutes, if you don't mind waiting in the car. I . . . It's . . ." He looked away from her and got out of the car, then shut the door and hobbled up to the house on his crutch.

Annie sat staring at the door. She knew Finn was hurting, but his curt manner had dredged up horrific memories. Camden had had a hot temper and a short fuse. Her hand instinctively went to the side of her face and she cringed. Although she was deaf, Camden's cruel words still echoed in her head. He was long gone, but his physical and psychological abuse had left scars.

She closed her eyes and took a deep breath in order to repeat her self-help mantra from this morning—*Today is going to be a good day and nothing is going to stop me*—even though she didn't believe it.

A few minutes later, Finn reappeared, dressed in new suit pants and using both crutches now. He swung himself down to the car, opened the back door, and put the crutches in before sitting down.

Holding up his hand slightly to get her attention, he met Annie's gaze. His eyes were rounded and soft. He signed *Sorry*, making circles around his heart with a closed fist. "Please let me apologize for my earlier behavior," he began. "I let my . . . emotions get the better of me and I was rude. Thank you for asking about me, and again, I'm sorry for my outburst."

Annie beamed at him. In all her years with Camden the words *I'm sorry* had never escaped his lips—not even after he hit her or called her some horrible name. And here Finn was apologizing for being a little rude, when he was obviously in pain.

"Thank you. Finn, I . . . I just want to help. You've really helped me." Annie signed *Thank you.*

Finn looked like he was about to say something more, but then he shook his head. "Your driving is a big help. And I called the police station while I was in the house and they're sending me incident reports on that part of the highway. That was a great idea."

"Okey-dokey." Annie smiled as she put the car into reverse. "Next stop, Mike's Autobody."

CHAPTER 4

Mike's Autobody was like some three-headed monster—used car lot, garage, and junkyard all squished together. From the inflatable waving tube men and gaudy signs promising the best deals anywhere, down to the towering piles of rusted cars stacked on top of each other, Mike's Autobody took up one entire block of a commercial zone.

No sooner had Annie parked than two different salesmen, both in cheap suits, appeared to be racing each other toward her car.

The taller salesman opened her door and stuck out his hand. "I can see what brought you in today. Let me take that clunker off your hands."

"Please excuse my charming coworker," the shorter one said, shooting a sharp glance at the other salesman as he opened Finn's door. "I bet you're here to find something for the little lady that she's not embarrassed to drive."

Finn held out his card. "Finnian Church, A. G. Maxwell Insurance. We're insurance investigators."

The taller salesman turned on his heel and left his coworker to fend for himself.

"You'll want to speak with Mike, then. He's in the office." The salesman handed Finn his card back.

Finn rolled his eyes as he took out his crutches. Annie hurried around the car to shut the door for him, but he used his hip to push it closed.

They made their way slowly toward the entrance. The gravel shifted beneath Finn's crutches, no matter how hard he jabbed down into the rocks for leverage. By the time they got inside, Finn was sweating and his face was tight.

They made their way through the crowded showroom, filled with cars, magazines, and desk spaces, over to the counter at the back of the room. Behind it sat a young woman with blond hair teased high and a blue blouse pulled low. She introduced herself as Candi.

Finn introduced Annie and himself, then said, "We're here about an insurance claim regarding the SUV that rolled over last night near exit III."

"Oh." Candi's nose wrinkled. "We sell cars, fix 'em, or junk 'em. We don't sell insurance."

Annie tried not to smile as she read the text translation of what the woman had said and saw Finn's confused expression.

"We're not here to buy insurance, Candi. We're insurance investigators. Did an SUV get towed here last night?"

Candi's shoulders rose up to the base of her dangly earrings. "Maybe. Is that what you're investigatin'? Was there a problem with the tow? Or do you wanna pay for it at billin'?"

Finn cleared his throat. "Would it be possible to speak with Mike, please?"

Candi frowned. "One minute. I'll get him."

As she flitted away on her sky-high heels, Finn turned to look at Annie. "I hope this Mike is easier to deal with. That was pretty frustrating. She just wasn't getting what I said."

A moment later, the office door was whipped open and a large man in a cowboy hat strutted out, pulling up his belt. The buckle was the size of a license plate. "What's this about you having a problem with a tow? That car was totaled before we even put it on the wrecker."

"I'm not here about that—" Finn started to say, but Mike cut him off.

"It's a seventy-five-dollar hookup fee and five dollars a mile. Simple."

"Actually—"

Mike turned and shouted, "Hey, Judy! Pull the mileage report for Truck B and give it to this guy." He turned back to Finn. "All of our trucks have GPS in 'em." He leveled a finger in Finn's face. "I don't pad mileage and *no one* comes into my place and accuses me of doing that."

Annie noticed the sinews in Finn's neck were standing out, but otherwise he seemed calm. "I'm not accusing you of anything." Finn held his card up like a badge. "My name is Finnian Church and I'm with A. G. Maxwell Insurance. We're here to take photographs of the wreck for the insurance claim."

Mike took his hat off and ran his fingers through his hair. He stared back and forth between Finn and Annie like he was debating whether Finn was telling him the truth, before looking over his shoulder and glaring at Candi, who was walking over to the soda machine in the corner. She shrugged.

"Sorry about the mix-up!" Mike's angry scowl vanished and was replaced with a charming grin. "Being in the towing business, you get people in all the time complaining and accusing you of all sorts of stuff—missing radios, sunglasses. None of it's true, of course!" He laughed. "Tell you what, I was in the middle of a sales call, so I'll have Judy show you where the wreck is. Nice meeting you."

He turned around and as he marched back to his office he hollered, "Hey, Judy! Show these two out to the rolled SUV we brought in last night. It's still on the truck." He shut his door and opened it a second later. "Don't take them into the yard!" he shouted and shut the door again.

As Finn and Annie waited for Judy, everyone else in the dealership avoided even looking in their direction. Annie's phone beeped with a text from Finn.

DO I SMELL OR SOMETHING?

He tilted his head and pretended to sniff his armpit.

Annie had to fight back a case of the giggles. She even tried holding her breath, but she burst out laughing. Like ground-hogs, heads popped up from the cubicles and then darted away.

"Sorry for the wait." A flustered-looking woman hurried across the showroom. "I'm Judy. Here's the GPS report for Truck B for the last week. You can see that the truck came straight back here from the accident scene."

"Thank you," Finn said, handing the paperwork to Annie. "We're not disputing mileage, however. We need to photograph the vehicle for our records."

"Oh." Judy looked as if she was calculating something in her head. "I'll take you out there. It's on a wrecker in the back lot."

"Would it be okay if we drove?" Annie asked.

Finn shook his head, but Judy lifted up a key and smiled. "I saw the crutches and I've got a bad hip myself. We're taking the golf cart. It's right outside."

Annie exhaled. Finn was grimacing so much, and the last thing she wanted was him walking further than he had to.

"I just need to grab my camera gear out of the car," Annie told him.

Outside, as she popped the trunk on her bruised banana of an automobile, a different salesman came hurrying over.

"It's a good thing I caught you." The man grinned and adjusted his tacky tie. "No one in their right mind would give you a nickel for that trade-in except me."

"Insurance investigator." Annie flashed one of Finn's business cards like it was a badge, just as she'd seen Finn do earlier.

The gold seal of A. G. Maxwell acted like a cross to a vampire. "Ah . . . I have someone on the phone I need to talk to. Excuse me." The man swiftly headed in the opposite direction.

Smiling, Annie got her camera bag out and joined Finn in the golf cart. She was going to tell Finn about her cool handling of the salesman, but her joy was short-lived. With every bump and pothole the cart hit as it drove past the towering piles of cars, Finn winced and grimaced. By the time they reached the wrecker, his knuckles were white from grabbing the handle.

"Why don't you wait here?" Annie said. "I'll take the pictures and you can check if we need any others."

Finn nodded and flashed her an appreciative smile. "I've got a couple of questions for Judy."

While Finn spoke with Judy, Annie hurriedly photographed the SUV. The vehicle looked like it had rolled over at least once, causing extensive damage to the front, back, sides, and roof. When she started snapping pictures of the driver's side and noticed blood, she said a silent prayer for the driver.

As she made her way around the car, she stopped at the passenger-side tire. Three long silver nails were sticking out of the tread, and they looked to Annie very much like the nails Mr. Bennet had shown them. She took closeups and then looked for more, and found two in the rear passenger-side tire. She finished up and walked back to the golf cart.

Finn's color was better but he still looked pale. "We're all done here. Did you get some good pictures?"

"I did. Would you like to see them?" Annie held out her camera.

Finn shook his head. "Actually, I'm not feeling so well. I think we should get going."

Annie quickly stuffed her bag into the golf cart. "I'm going to run back and get the car. The shock absorbers will give you a more comfortable ride."

"I can drive you," Judy offered.

"That's okay." Annie took off running. She couldn't accept Judy's offer, because then Finn would be left standing there until she got back.

She made it to the car in no time and gunned it back to Finn. She was in such a rush that when she hit the brakes she skidded to a stop, kicking up a dust cloud that enveloped the golf cart and its occupants.

"Sorry about that!" Annie said as she grabbed her bag and tossed it in the trunk, then opened Finn's door.

Finn coughed as he limped to the car. "Thank you for all your help," he said to Judy.

"Call me if you need any more information," Judy said, waving her hand.

Annie wasn't sure if she was chasing the dust away or waving goodbye, so she waved back just in case. "Thank you!" she called out over her shoulder as she opened the rear door for Finn.

Finn sat and swung his legs in slowly. As he put his crutches beside him, Annie noticed the rivulets of sweat running down from his hairline and sideburns. She closed the door, and Finn let his head sag over and rest against the window.

Annie's heart went out to him. It was obvious that he was in a lot of pain, but what could she do?

CHAPTER 5

Back at Finn's house, he practically collapsed into the chair in the living room.

"Thank you. I'm sorry I was a dead weight today. An anchor, for goodness' sake." Finn grimaced.

"You have nothing to apologize for, but I'm really worried about you." Annie glanced down at the fresh bloodstain on his new pair of trousers. "Do you need to see a doctor?"

"No." Finn shook his head. "I just pushed myself a little too far."

"You're bleeding. It's more than just overdoing it." Annie took a deep breath. Even she had to admit that backbone had never been her strongest feature, but her growing concern for Finn overrode her lack of fortitude. "You have three choices: I give you a ride to the doctor's, I call an ambulance, or you let me look at it."

Finn shook his head. "I'm fine. I just need to rest."

Annie switched off the speech-to-text app on her phone, pressed 91, and let her finger hover over the 1.

"You wouldn't." Finn raised a disbelieving eyebrow.

Annie started to dramatically lower her finger.

"Wait!" Finn held up a hand. "Compromise? Let me rest and I'll go to the doctor's tomorrow."

Annie shook her head. "I don't think it can wait until tomorrow."

"It can." Finn smiled, but he was pale.

"Then let me be the judge of that. I took a semester of nursing."

"Really?" Finn asked.

"After Tammy was born. I'm familiar with bandages. Let me check yours. Please?"

Finn's eyes searched hers. The longer they did, the more Annie saw. *He's afraid.* He looked down at the floor.

He's more than afraid . . . he's embarrassed.

Annie reached out and took his hand. "Please?"

Finn shook his head. Annie lifted her phone.

"Okay." Finn exhaled. "But . . ." He gestured down at his leg. "How?"

"Let me get you a towel. And where do you keep your bandages?"

"In the bathroom."

Finn pressed his lips together and Annie got a glimpse of the stoic soldier within; in pain, yet in control. This was a wounded vet, a proud man who felt vulnerable, and the last thing she wanted to do was make him feel needy or weak.

"I'll be right back," Annie said, trying to sound as professional as possible. She hurried down to the spic-and-span bathroom and picked out two large towels. She gathered an assortment of bandages and antiseptic from the cabinets and brought them out to the living room. In her own messy house, she thought with regret, it would have taken her forty-five minutes to find everything.

Without saying a word, she draped the largest towel over Finn's waist and bent down to untie his shoes. Finn unbuckled his pants, and while he held the towel in place, she tugged at the hems of each pant leg, removing his trousers.

"Let's place another towel under your leg," Annie said. "Let me know if it hurts."

Finn grimaced as he lifted his injured leg. Annie slipped the towel beneath him and blinked rapidly at the bloody bandage and Finn's prosthetic, wishing the sight before her looked better than it did. There was no way she could treat the wound with the prosthetic attached.

Finn's chest rose and fell rapidly. "I don't know if I'm comfortable with you seeing me like this."

"I'm not comfortable seeing you in pain. Please?" Annie stared back into his eyes.

Finn's fingers shook slightly as he unhooked the prosthetic and eased it off the blood-soaked bandage. Annie gently laid it on the floor.

The skin all around Finn's wound was inflamed and in two places it had been rubbed raw by the plastic and was bleeding.

"Should you even be wearing that with your leg in this condition?" The words tumbled from Annie's mouth. "I'm sorry. I'm probably overstepping in a big way, but . . ."

Finn's eyes opened and he looked like he was breathing easier just from having the prosthetic off. "Actually, you're right. I shouldn't be wearing it."

"Why are you? Why not just use the crutches and give yourself time to heal?"

"I didn't want you to see me as less than a whole man." Finn gave her a look that tore at her heart. There was a desperation in his eyes that she longed to fix, but there was no bandage for that pain.

Annie shook her head. "As if. I could never think less of you, Finnian." She swallowed and quickly looked down. She'd spoken without thinking, and generally she'd found that was a bad thing.

Finn cleared his throat. "Why did you stop going to school for nursing?"

Annie felt the color continue to rise in her cheeks. "I typically faint at the sight of blood."

Finn chuckled. "You're something else, Annie Summers. Thank you."

Ten minutes later, she had cleaned the wound and sprayed it with antiseptic. The swelling and redness were already starting to recede ard Finn was beginning to look more like his regular self.

She returned the first-aid supplies, and when she came back into the living room, he had drifted off to sleep in the chair. She let herself out after a last look at his handsome face. With the trust he had shown her, she was beginning to think that her distrust of all men needed an update.

CHAPTER 6

F inn slowly emerged from his dream, but kept his eyes closed. He'd woken up sometime after Annie left and changed into a comfortable shirt and pair of shorts. For some reason he'd gone back out to the living room. Perhaps it was the fact that when he slept in the recliner he didn't toss and turn, or maybe it was the fact that sitting there, he remembered Annie touching his leg and the relief it brought. It hadn't taken him long to fall back asleep.

But now, a faint breeze was blowing across his face in little puffs. He thought he'd left a window open until he smelled cotton candy.

"Don't wake him up," Annie said softly from the kitchen.

"What about the lasagna?" That sounded like Annie's son, Tommy, from the right side of the recliner.

"He looks hungry," whispered Tammy on Finn's left side, wafting cotton candy toward his nose. He had to fight not to burst out laughing.

Annie's voice came closer. "He needs to rest. We'll leave it for him to eat when he wakes up."

Finn opened his eyes. Both kids gasped and jumped,

causing Annie to jump even higher and give out a little scream. Then the children broke out in giggles.

"Why hello!" Finn said, sitting up and rubbing his eyes. "I didn't know I had guests coming."

"Hi, Finn!" both kids shouted in unison.

"I'm so sorry," Annie said, hurrying over. "I told them not to wake you up."

"We didn't, Mommy." Tammy shook her head. "He woke up all by himself."

Finn chuckled and looked up at Annie. Her cheeks were flushed.

"I, ah, brought something by to say thank you for everything." She smiled at him, her blue eyes twinkling.

Finn shook his head. "But I didn't do anything."

"My job, my car, mowing my lawn, painting the front door? It's a long list."

"Don't forget helping me with my baseball! I would have been toast without you Finn!" Tommy interjected.

"I was happy to help. It's nothing."

"So is this. And it's almost ready. Are you hungry?"

"Starving, actually." He had gotten a whiff of cheese and garlic and sauce from the kitchen.

"Where do you want to eat?"

Finn thought quickly. He'd changed into a pair of comfortable shorts and was not wearing his prosthetic leg. He didn't want to take a chance of frightening the kids and was grateful that his secret was hidden by the blanket covering his lower body. "How about we eat out here?"

Annie seemed to pick up on his situation and nodded understandingly. It was another trait that endeared her to him —she was so empathetic. "We'll have a little picnic out here. Tommy, can you give me a hand?"

Both children clapped, and Tommy rushed to help his

mother in the kitchen. Tammy grabbed the arm of the chair and climbed over and onto Finn's lap.

"Whoah!" She tottered back and forth as she sat on his right leg. "I forgot Mommy said you took your leg off."

Finn's eyes went wide. The only person besides his doctors and Annie who had seen him without his prosthetic was his ex-fiancée. She had been so revolted by the sight that she asked him to put it back on. But this little girl was very different. She didn't seem bothered by it in the least. Just like her mother.

"Where is it?" Tammy asked as she regained her balance.

"Where's what?" Finn asked, though he knew what she meant.

"Your leg."

"It's right here." Finn patted his right leg. A smirk formed on his face as Tammy grinned infectiously at him.

"No. Your . . ." She wrinkled her nose as she thought about which leg was missing. "Your left leg."

Finn gasped jokingly. "What?! It's gone!" He clamped both hands to the sides of his face like Kevin in *Home Alone*.

Tammy laughed and wobbled. She glanced around and saw his prosthetic. "There it is." She scrambled down and picked it up. "It's not that heavy."

"Because you're so strong."

"I'm stronger than her!" Tommy called from the kitchen.

"I'm strong too!" Tammy said, lifting the leg up over her head. "Look how strong I am."

Both Tommy and Annie walked out of the kitchen and Annie nearly fell over when she saw what Tammy was doing.

"No, no, no." Annie rushed over and took the prosthetic, then stood, unsure what to do with it.

Tammy looked like she was about to cry.

"It's okay." Finn chuckled. "Tammy was just pulling my leg. Get it? Pulling my leg?"

Annie and Tommy stared at Finn with their mouths hanging open.

Tammy sniffled, wiped her nose with the back of her hand, and then laughed like she'd just heard the funniest joke in the world. "Pulling your leg! I get it. Like a joke!"

All four of them laughed. Finn was certain they were laughing more at Tammy's cute giggles than his joke, but he didn't care. The important thing was, none of them were bothered by the fact that he was missing a leg.

CHAPTER 7

Annie finished washing the dishes and came out into the living room. Both children were asleep on the couch. Finn was in his recliner, reading something on his tablet. His brow was knit together and he was squinting at the screen.

She walked over and held out her phone. As more time passed since her hearing loss, it was becoming harder for her to know the volume of her own voice, and with the kids sleeping, she didn't want to wake them up.

Finn read the text on her phone and raised a puzzled eyebrow.

"Everything's fine," he typed back. "Why are we texting?"

She pointed at the kids and he nodded.

She texted, "Can I check your bandage? I should change it before I go."

Finn took a deep breath. She could see him debating it. She'd hoped when she changed his bandage before that he'd gotten over his embarrassment, but he looked worried now. She didn't wait for a reply and headed to the bathroom to get the supplies.

She quietly walked back into the room and set the supplies on the table next to Finn. He shook his head, but she ignored his protests and gently grabbed the blanket covering his leg. Finn kept his hand on the blanket, but when her sparkling blue eyes met his, he yielded and let go.

The wound looked much less inflamed. Most of the redness had dissipated, but she still gently washed the area, sprayed it with antiseptic, and wrapped it up again.

"Should you go back to the doctor's?" she typed.

"No. It happens. I just won't be able to go out for a few days."

"Why?"

Finn's fingers hesitated over the phone. "I shouldn't put my prosthetic on."

"Then go out without it."

Finn paled and shook his head. "People would stare."

"They stare at you anyway," Annie typed. Finn went even paler, so she quickly added, "Not because of your leg. U R so handsome." She hit return and froze, then closed her eyes, wishing the earth would swallow her up. She knew she must be blushing from ear to ear.

Opening her eyes and staring at the phone screen, she tried to change the subject. "Do we have another case?"

He nodded and typed, "But we need to finish the paperwork on this one first. Something is still bothering me."

"What?"

"The lady doth protest too much, methinks," Finn typed. "That was *Hamlet*, but in this case, I'm talking about Big Mike. Do you remember how mad he got about the mileage records?"

Annie nodded. "He flipped out. He sure seemed worried. Paranoid even."

"That's because he was fined in the past for doing just that —padding his mileage." Finn switched his screen over to a report from the Better Business Bureau. "But as far as I can tell, he's not hiding anything about mileage now. They're not—" He stopped typing and his finger hovered over the screen. He looked up at her excitedly and his hands quickly signed something, but she couldn't understand what. He handed her his tablet, picked his crutches off the floor, and pointed toward the kitchen. Annie stepped away from the chair.

Finn yanked the blanket off his lap, but then froze. He stared up at Annie with fear in his eyes. She made sure she held his gaze. She placed a comforting hand on his shoulder and smiled, never once breaking eye contact.

Finn nodded and powered up the recliner. He set his crutches under his arms, stood up, and moved rapidly into the kitchen, with Annie following. She was surprised when he went all the way to the back door and awkwardly opened it. She held the door open until he went outside, onto the porch, and then she closed it behind them.

"You're not going to believe this!" he said, his face aglow. "Pull up that video that Mr. Bennet sent us, please."

Annie switched to the mail program and found exhibit number one, as Mr. Bennet called it. Finn moved closer to Annie so he could see the screen.

Annie's hand shook slightly as their shoulders pressed together. Finn was so excited by whatever he had discovered that for him personal space had gone out the window. His face was side by side with hers. The scent of his aftershave was cedarwood, and she drank it in. The muscles in his strong forearms flexed as he gripped his crutches. Her eyes wandered down to his leg. The muscles in his thigh were tight and defined. She was wondering if he was that toned all over when Finn suddenly stopped the video and shouted, "There! There! Do you see it?"

Annie reddened. She hadn't been paying any attention to

the video, just Finn. She looked at the screen. Mr. Bennet's car had just gone under the overpass and she could see a glint of something metal against the windshield.

"The nails?" Annie blurted out.

"Yes, but look at the time!" Finn pointed at the bottom of the screen and the text—5:17 PM.

Annie shrugged.

Finn switched apps to the GPS report Judy had given them and he scanned in. "Look here: 5:17 PM. Look where Tow Truck B is."

Annie gasped. "It's on the overpass! Do you think the driver threw the nails?"

Finn nodded. "That's exactly what I think happened. And look at this." He scrolled down the report to the following day at 6:02 AM. "Truck B was on the same overpass two minutes before that accident. Big Mike's drivers are creating towing business by throwing nails out onto the road to pop people's tires!"

"That's horrible."

"It's criminal. We'll have to bring this to the police."

Annie felt her smile growing. "You did it again, Finn. You're brilliant." She moved in to hug him.

As she wrapped her arms around his waist, Finn leaned forward and his right crutch fell from his hand. His breathing sped up and she held him tighter.

Finn looked down at her and she gazed up at him. The stars had already come out and the moon was large, almost full. His lips moved, but she didn't think he was saying anything. Part of her wanted to take out her speech-to-text app just in case, but then she'd have to let him go, and that wasn't an option.

Finn gazed down at her for a long time. The lights from the porch sparkled like stars in his damp eyes. He lifted his right hand and signed *Thank you*.

Annie signed *You're welcome*, but that wasn't what she wanted to say at all. She wanted to thank Finn. Thank him for all he'd done for her, but more importantly, for trusting her and making her feel...wanted.

Finn held on to her and she squeezed him a little tighter. Together, they stood there watching the stars.

A MiniMystery Series

THE ADVENTURES OF

Finn & Annie

THE CASE
OF A MOUSE IN MY SOUP

WALL STREET JOURNAL BESTSELLING AUTHOR
CHRISTOPHER GREYSON

A MiniMystery Series

THE ADVENTURES OF
Finn &
Annie

THE CASE OF A MOUSE
IN MY SOUP

WALL STREET JOURNAL BESTSELLING AUTHOR
CHRISTOPHER GREYSON

GREYSON MEDIA

CHAPTER 1

Finnian Church ran his hand across his freshly shaved jaw and stared into the bathroom mirror, speaking to his dad's reflection—because he couldn't stand the look of self-doubt in his own eyes. "I don't know, Dad. Maybe I should cancel."

"Don't be ridiculous." Howard Church leaned his tall frame against the door of the small bathroom and smiled. "You'll have a great time. It's not a big deal. You're just going to lunch."

"You're the one who always told me to never date someone I work with."

"So it's officially a *date*?"

"No." Finn splashed a little cologne on his neck. "But it might be a step in that direction." Finn reread Annie's text asking him if he'd meet her at the Imperial Garden for lunch.

THERE'S SOMETHING I NEED TO ASK YOU.

He couldn't tell much from the text; he needed to see her expressive face to read her emotions. After working together with Annie for the last six months, he'd learned that she was both proud and shy, fierce and soft, and a lot of information was conveyed in her smile and her eyes, her quick gestures . . .

"Her text doesn't sound like a date invitation," Finn said, and heard the disappointment in his own voice.

Howard nodded again. "It could be. It could also just be lunch. No pressure. Try to relax and go with the flow. Annie sounds super."

"She is." Finn smiled. "But I don't want to mess things up for her. She has two kids. I know it's a baby step, but what if it leads to something? What if we start dating and it doesn't work out? She might not want to work for me anymore or I might not be able..."

Howard held up his hand with all the authority of a retired policeman. "Hold on there. Don't worry about tomorrow. Today's trouble is enough for today."

"*Today's* what I'm talking about, Dad." Finn walked past his father and into the living room.

Howard made a low grumbling sound like an old dog letting you know you were starting to aggravate him. "You're fighting a battle in your head that hasn't taken place yet. A nice woman asked you to lunch, not to meet her at the altar."

Finn grabbed the handle of his briefcase and stared at his father. "I'm glad you stopped by, but I wish you'd called before driving all the way across town for such a brief visit. I have to go now or I'm going to be late to pick up Annie."

The muscles in Howard's jaw flexed, which wasn't a good sign.

Finn's heartbeat ticked up. "You didn't drive over here to just say hi." His grip tightened on the briefcase.

"No, I didn't." Howard removed an envelope from his back pocket. "Someone dropped this off at the house."

Finn took the envelope, turned it over, and froze. His name was written in a delicate script across the front, but that wasn't what made his mouth go dry. He recognized the hand writing —Karen, his ex-fiancée. He stuffed the letter in the pocket of his jacket. "I'm not doing this now."

"You don't have to do it at all. I thought we should just throw it away, but your mother feels it should be your choice. But I think you should pull an Elvis." Howard curled his lip and ran his hand over his balding head. "Return to sender! Address unknown—"

Finn rolled his eyes. Since he was a little kid his father would do Elvis impersonations, but for some reason they seemed to get worse as time went by.

"I'll think about it." Finn held open the front door. Could he just throw the letter away? Did he have the strength to pitch it without opening it?

Howard stopped on the front step and blocked Finn's exit. "You don't need Karen back in your life or in your head." His eyes were rounded in concern and he suddenly looked much older than when he first came in. "After everything she did to you, you don't owe her anything."

Just like his father, Finn's aggravation showed in the tension in his jaw and the rumble in his chest. "I'm not talking about this anymore. I need to go."

Howard moved out of the way and Finn angrily limped to his car. It wasn't sympathy and advice Finn needed; what he needed and wanted more than anything was just to forget. But his scars were a constant reminder. Not only had Karen accidentally posted on social media for all the world to see that she was leaving Finn because she needed *a whole man,* but she'd been unfaithful to him and everybody had known it except for him. And that still wasn't the deepest cut.

It was whom she had been with that nearly killed him.

CHAPTER 2

Annie stood in her tiny bathroom fussing with her blond curls. She badly needed a conditioning treatment and a trim, but it seemed like every day brought an unexpected expense and the first thing cut in the budget was always one of her own needs. She opted for a ponytail today; she just couldn't bear to see the split ends. Anyway, with her hair back from her face, her blue eyes blazed brighter.

Working with Finn had not only helped her financially; he also gave her morale a boost, and his courage and strength in adversity were inspiring to her. He was so different from Camden, her ex-husband, who was almost a year behind on child support and didn't even seem interested in seeing his children.

She knew she could take Cam to court, but his not paying support was a mixed blessing. If he was current with support, he could see the kids, and the thought sent a chill straight through her. Tammy was too young to remember the horrors of living with her father, but Tommy hadn't forgotten. The poor little guy still had nightmares and he'd never sleep over at a friend's house because he was afraid he'd wake up screaming or wet the bed.

Annie wiped away a tear. Losing her hearing was hard enough personally, but the impact it had on her children was torture for her. Tommy's nightmares had gone on for weeks before he finally told her. He'd been waking up screaming in the middle of the night, but of course she couldn't hear him. Then he'd lie in bed crying, too afraid to leave his bedroom and go get her.

She'd tried every app she could find, but nothing worked. She finally settled on a simple solution—a shake alarm. If Tommy woke up, he could press a remote that would make a device under her pillow vibrate. It wasn't perfect, but it worked.

The overhead light blinked on and off, signaling Annie. She opened the bathroom door.

Tommy was standing in the hallway shifting his weight from one foot to the other. "I gotta go. You've been in there, like, half an hour."

"Sorry!" Annie stepped into the hallway as Tommy darted past her. "Where's Tammy?"

Tommy signed *Kitchen* and then slammed the bathroom door shut.

Annie went to the kitchen to see what Tammy was up to, and her daughter looked up from her coloring book. "Wow!" she gushed. "You're so pretty, Mommy!"

Annie blushed as she ran her hands down the front of her dress. She loved the way the full skirt moved. It could use a quick iron, but Finn had never seen this one. She could never quite catch him looking at her—he was too well-mannered for that—but lately she thought she saw a twinkle in his eye when she wore a nice outfit.

"Are you going to marry Finn, Mommy?" Tammy smiled.

Annie exaggeratedly signed her surprise at the question. *What? No. Finn and Mommy just work together.*

Tammy looked confused. "But you're all dressed up like you're going on a date."

It's not a date, Annie signed emphatically. *Can I see what you're coloring?*

Tammy didn't take the bait of her mother's attempt to distract her. "But you said you're going to a restaurant."

Annie switched to speaking. "We are, pumpkin."

"It's lunch with just you two?"

"Yes, but—"

"And it's not work."

"But—"

Tommy rushed into the hallway. "Then it is a date!"

"You are getting married! Yeah!" Tammy did a little dance.

"No." Annie tried not to smile, but when Tommy joined Tammy's dance a wide grin spread across her lips.

The lights in the living room flashed.

"Someone's here!" Tammy said.

"I got it!" Tommy charged for the door with Tammy at his heels.

Tommy opened the door and Tammy shot past him.

Finn's eyes went wide as the little girl leapt up at him with her arms open. Catching her around the waist with his left hand, he grabbed the railing with his right and somehow managed not to fall down the steps.

Her heart in her throat, Annie rushed forward, ready to scold her daughter, but Finn held up his hand and mouthed, *It's okay.*

Annie knew that both children were excitedly speaking with Finn, but with their backs to her, she had no idea what they were saying. Tammy's curls bounced on her shoulders as Finn held her on his hip and Tommy tugged on his jacket, vying for his attention.

Annie took Tammy in her arms while Tommy grabbed Finn by the hand and pulled him inside, no doubt eager to show him his latest project—a diorama of the log cabin where President Lincoln was born.

Annie mouthed *Sorry* and Finn rolled his eyes. He signed, *All good.*

She wanted to kiss him then and there. She didn't know if it was the fact that he was learning sign language to communicate better with her, how patient he was with her children, his good-natured smile, or a combination of all three, but her whole body tingled and glowed when she gazed at him.

"I'm ready." She picked up her purse.

"Mommy's super-excited about your date." Tommy clamped his hand over his sister's mouth, but the words had already escaped.

Finn's mouth froze. His smile remained, but Annie picked up on each emotion flashing across his face—puzzlement, awkwardness, and one more that she couldn't figure out. In some ways, Annie's deafness had made her other senses hypersensitive. While she'd lost the ability to pick up emotions in the sound of people's voices, her ability to read their facial expressions bordered on a superpower. But right now, her power was short-circuiting and she couldn't tell how Finn felt about what Tammy had said.

Tammy yanked Tommy's hand down. "Sorry. Mommy said I shouldn't call it that."

Finn's expression changed again, but this time Annie read his emotion clearly—hurt. "We're just going to lunch," he said with a smile and disappointed eyes.

What could she say to make it better? She'd love it if it was a date, but was she ready for that? And what if Finn didn't feel the same way about her? And is dating your boss ever really a good idea? She was fine with it, but was he? And she needed this job—

Someone tugging on her arm made her realize that she'd shut her eyes tight, which was like stepping into her own privacy chamber, though she knew it didn't actually make her invisible. She opened her eyes and Tommy squeezed her hand. He must have picked up on her embarrassment as he launched into his role as his mother's protector.

"What my little sister was trying to say is that Mom isn't calling it a date because then Tammy thinks you're getting married."

Now Annie wanted to crawl under the sofa. She could actually see the red flush creeping up Finn's neck. His ears were as bright as Rudolph's nose.

Tammy's eyes went wide and she clapped her hands. "I like weddings."

Finn looked at Annie like he wanted to hide under the sofa with her. His mouth opened and closed several times but he failed to form any words.

"Let's go!" Annie marched to the door and pulled it open. Sunshine slapped her in the face and warm spring air swirled her skirt. She took a deep breath and kept moving as the kids rushed around her legs. She kissed the tops of their heads and pointed to the neighbor's house. "Tell Mrs. MacEntire I'll be back by two thirty. And don't play too roughly with BonBon."

BonBon was Mrs. MacEntire's chocolate Lab who had to be close to twelve years old but acted like a puppy around the kids.

"Bye, Mommy." Both kids kissed her, waved at Finn, and started to take off. But Tammy suddenly turned around. She rushed back over to Finn and motioned for him to bend down. "I *really* like weddings," she said and kissed his cheek, then ran to catch up with her brother.

Annie swallowed and smiled awkwardly at Finn. "Sorry about that."

Finn touched his fingers to the spot where Tammy had kissed his cheek, and from his expression Annie could tell that the little girl's gesture really meant something to him. But all he said was, "Just kids being kids," before walking over to the car and opening the door for Annie.

"I'm sorry . . . I, ah, just went into autopilot and opened your door." Finn's cheeks were as red as his tie.

"Don't be sorry. Your autopilot is very thoughtful," Annie said, flattered by his attentiveness. Sometimes Camden had the engine on and was in drive before she was even sitting down.

Finn waited until she got settled in and was facing him before he spoke again. It was another thoughtful gesture that made her melt.

"Is there a reason you picked the Imperial Garden?" he asked.

"Yes," Annie said. "I need your help."

CHAPTER 3

At their table in a corner of the bustling, cheerful Chinese restaurant, Finn played with a sugar packet in order to avoid getting lost in the deep blue sea of Annie's eyes. It was a losing battle. The more she spoke, the longer he looked and the deeper he fell.

Annie suddenly stopped talking and took a deep breath. Finn's arm froze, the water glass halfway to his lips. He had no idea what she was going to ask him or what kind of help she needed. Truth was, he'd spent half the night wondering, and the other half dreaming about it. Some of the dreams were wonderful—others, full-blown nightmares where Annie would start laughing at him and Karen would suddenly appear and join in.

But Finn was a soldier. He set his water glass down on the table and smiled like he was the calmest man without a care in the world. Privately, he regretted not taking an antacid before he left the house.

"The reason I asked you to come here—" Annie was cut off when a short man rushed over.

"Annie!" He grinned broadly but his brow was creased. "Thank you so much for coming. You must be Finn."

Finn stood to greet him.

"So nice to meet you." The man bowed and shook Finn's hand. "I appreciate this so much." He pushed and pulled Finn's arm up and down like an old-fashioned water pump. "Really. We're so grateful."

Finn cast a puzzled glance toward Annie.

"Finn, this is Jacob Manning. His wife, Yu, and I are old friends. She and Jacob own the restaurant."

Jacob finally let go of Finn's hand. "Yu is at the supermarket. I'm pulling double duty in the kitchen. One of our chefs moved, so we're short-staffed. Have you asked him yet?"

Annie shook her head. "I was about to—"

"You want to eat first. Of course." Jacob motioned the waiter over. "We're making a special lunch. It's the least we can do. Just a simple dish."

Annie laughed and patted Jacob's shoulder. "Jacob's very modest," she said to Finn. "He spent four years in culinary school in China."

"That's impressive," Finn said. "Is that where you met your wife?"

Jacob chuckled. "I met her here. She fell in love with my cooking before she ever noticed me."

A waiter brought over a tray with two bowls of soup on it.

"I'd better get back in the kitchen," Jacob said. "Thank you again." He looked at Annie and raised crossed fingers before hurrying away. The waiter set down the soup and scurried after him.

Annie asked, "Do you mind if I say grace?"

"Not at all." Finn started to close his eyes but stopped. "What?"

"Nothing." He shook his head, clearly embarrassed.

"Please tell me what you were just thinking," Annie leaned forward.

Finn hesitated for only a moment before those blue eyes sucked him in once more. "It's a little silly," he admitted, "but I was wondering how it would work if I said grace. With your eyes closed, you couldn't read my lips."

Annie blushed. "I pray with my eyes open. It kinda weirds people out, but I figure God doesn't mind."

"I doubt it would bother Him." Finn chuckled.

Annie reached across the table and took his hand. Finn felt a flush of guilt wash over him when he made a mental note to pray more if it meant holding hands with Annie.

Annie looked directly at him while she prayed. It was actually difficult for Finn not to close his eyes. "Dear Lord, thank you for this time together today and for this food. Help us to help Jacob and Yu through this situation and let us know what to do. In Jesus's name, Amen."

Finn was starting to piece together why Annie had asked him to this restaurant. He was certain that the favor she was going to ask had something to do with her friends. The fact that it didn't seem to be a personal matter regarding Annie was both a relief and a disappointment.

Annie folded her hands on the table. "I have a big favor to ask."

"Anything." Finn smiled and picked up his spoon. The soup was a kind of miso and it was fabulous.

"I've been friends with Yu since we were little. She and Jacob put everything they had into opening this restaurant and it's just starting to take off."

Finn took another sip and glanced around the dining room, which was quickly filling up. "I can taste why. This soup is amazing. What could be the problem?"

Annie sighed. "A customer came in the other day. Her name

is Inez Pope and I think she's trying to extort money from them."

"That's a pretty serious allegation. If you believe that, we should go to the police."

Annie shook her head. "Yu doesn't want to and neither does Jacob. Inez said she doesn't want to ruin their reputation, but if they don't settle with her out of court, she'll have no choice but to go to the police."

"What's her complaint?" Finn asked as he scooped up a tender shumai dumpling.

"She claims there was a mouse in her soup."

Finn's spoon landed in his bowl with a splash.

CHAPTER 4

F inn swallowed and stared down at his soup. Now he *really* regretted not taking an antacid before he left his house.

"She's lying, of course," Annie quickly added. "The kitchen is immaculate and they've never had an issue with rodents." She gestured around the room. "And you can see how clean they keep the dining room as well."

Finn set his spoon down. "It's not just a matter of cleanliness." He chose his words carefully, but it was killing him as Annie's smile started to fade. "One hungry little mouse could sneak in anywhere. And more quickly follow."

"I understand that, but please hear me out." She reached across the table and once again took his hand. Finn had always been a big advocate of personal space. He didn't like shaking hands and the only people he hugged were his parents. But with Annie, those rules went out the window.

"It's not just the fact that Inez found a —" Annie flicked her finger back and forth over the tip of her nose, which he guessed was sign language for mouse. "It's all the other things she's done."

"Like what?"

"Yu said Inez didn't freak out when she found the mouse. She calmly called the waiter over and demanded he get the manager."

"Some people react to situations differently."

"Not to sound like a traitor to womankind, but I don't know any woman who doesn't get freaked out by a"—she flicked the end of her nose—"let alone one who ate half a bowl of soup before finding a dead one in it."

"True."

"Inez took a bunch of pictures of the mouse and left. But she showed up this morning saying she had to go to the emergency room and get a rabies shot. Then she demanded twelve hundred dollars or she was going to go to the police."

"Why so little? Cases like that settle for a lot more."

"That's what I was thinking. Why would she only want twelve hundred?"

"Maybe she's asking for an easily attainable amount. Something they could get from an ATM or likely have on hand." Finn leaned forward and looked into her blue eyes. "She's probably lying about going to the doctor, but I don't know how anyone could prevent her from going to the police."

Annie squeezed his hand. "You think she's lying about seeking medical care?"

"I can't know for certain that she's lying until we speak to her, but if a doctor suspects you've been exposed to rabies, you don't just get one shot. It's a treatment regimen of multiple shots administered over the course of days to weeks. And there is another reason that I don't believe she went to the doctor."

"What is that?"

"No one came back for the . . ." He imitated her sign for "mouse" and flicked his nose.

Annie shook her head no.

"Any doctor worth their salt would want to run tests on the . . . carcass."

"Annie?" A young Chinese woman nearly bowled a waiter over as she darted across the dining room. She had tears in her dark eyes as she embraced Annie. "Thank you for coming."

Finn awkwardly slid out of the booth. He'd made the mistake of sitting with his prosthetic leg on the outside, which made it difficult to get out.

Annie turned to Finn. "Yu, this is Finn. He's already poked some holes in that woman's story and he suspects she's lying. And he'll prove it. He's absolutely brilliant." Annie beamed with pride.

Yu broke out in a huge smile, and then she suddenly shot forward and embraced Finn. He was caught off-guard; his prosthetic hit the edge of the booth and he pitched backward.

His arms flailed out as he reached for anything to break his fall. For one brief second he thought his hand was grabbing a tall chair, before he saw he'd just brought his arm down on a tray of food carried by their waiter. Cups, bowls, and plates were overturned and catapulted a salvo of food into the air. Finn landed flat on his back, gritting his teeth as the steaming food smacked against his chest and burned his face.

As Annie and Yu stared down at him in horrified disbelief, Finn struggled to stand up, but in his embarrassed haste, he initially rolled the wrong way and onto his prosthetic.

A young man started to clap, while the woman sitting with him tried to hide her giggles. Shame washed over Finn, followed quickly by white-hot rage.

An older, heavy-set man with a thick beard jumped up from his table, grabbed the young guy by the scruff of his neck and his belt, and bum-rushed him out the front door. The girlfriend started to protest, but the old man glared at her as he jerked his thumb toward the door. "Get moving or you're going the same way your boyfriend went."

"I'm so sorry. Are you all right?" Yu said as she grabbed a towel from the apologetic waiter.

After helping Finn up to a chair, Annie, Yu, and two waiters tried in vain to clean him up by wiping, dabbing, and using soda water, while Finn stared at the old man who had rescued him from the indignity of someone clapping at his misfortune.

The old man nodded. "You a soldier, son?"

Finn nodded, unsure if his voice would cooperate if he tried to answer.

"Me too." The man pulled up his pant leg to show a metal prosthetic above his boot. "Nam."

"Thank you," Finn managed to say.

"No need," the man said, turning back to his table. "I did it for myself as much as you."

"Let's get you cleaned up in back," Annie suggested.

Finn nodded and followed after her. Just before he reached the double doors of the kitchen, he glanced back at the man. He was sitting alone. His head was turned in Finn's direction, but judging by look on his face, he was thousands of miles and decades away.

Finn understood the look all too well. There was not a day that went by that Finn didn't close his eyes and return to that fateful road in Iraq. It was hot as hell and just as dangerous, but back then he'd had two legs. He'd give anything to go back.

CHAPTER 5

Annie paced outside the men's room door close to tears. She had asked Finn for a favor and now he was in the bathroom changing into a T-shirt Jacob had lent him. Yu had sent the jacket across the street to the dry cleaner's, but Annie doubted the assortment of stains would ever come out.

But her worries about Finn's suit being ruined paled when she remembered the look on his face. Annie whipped away a tear as she pictured it. He was so embarrassed, even though the accident was no fault of his own. When that creep started to laugh and clap, it was all Annie could do not to break a chair over his head. How could anyone be so cruel as to find someone else's misery funny?

"Is he okay?" Yu asked, walking back into the kitchen with Jacob at her side.

"I'm sure he's fine." Annie felt a pang of guilt because she wasn't sure about that at all. Who would be okay falling in the middle of a crowded restaurant and getting covered in hot food?

The door to the bathroom opened quickly. "Ta-da!" Finn raised his hands, now dressed in his suit pants and the plain white undershirt Jacob had given him. "For my next trick, I will attempt to eat my lunch without getting it all over me!" He laughed.

Annie forced herself to laugh, too. She could see the brave act that Finn was putting on and she had his back.

"I'm so sorry," Yu said again.

"Not your fault." Finn graciously smiled and held his arms out. "Besides, I think I look good in white. What do you think?"

"You look hot in white," Yu said and gave Annie a wink. "I can see why she's on you like—"

Annie stamped on Yu's foot.

"Any chance you're still hungry?" Jacob asked sheepishly.

"I'm starved," Finn said. "Why don't we try that again while we discuss the case?"

"You'll still help us?" Yu lit up.

"Of course," Finn said, holding his arm out toward the dining room.

"Maybe we should eat in here?" Annie suggested.

No sooner were the words out of her mouth than she felt like she'd stabbed Finn. He looked pained and beyond hurt.

"That way we can discuss the mouse without having to do this . . ." Annie flicked her nose.

Finn's smile returned. "Okay. Great. That makes sense."

"We can eat in the break room," Jacob offered.

The four of them sat down to a wonderful meal while Yu explained what had happened. It was the same story that Annie had relayed, but Yu provided more details, including Inez Pope's phone number and address. She told them that the woman had only given them until tomorrow to make their decision or she was going to the police, then to the TV station and posting the pictures on the internet.

"Bad reviews are hard enough to deal with." Jacob rubbed his eyes. "But this would kill us."

Finn set down his chopsticks. "This food is delicious. Who could possibly give you a bad review?"

"We only have fourteen reviews, but two are bad!" Jacob wrung his hands. "Someone gave us one star but wrote that they loved the food. I think they just got confused about the reviewing system, but still . . ."

"And the other one said his dessert was soggy," Yu fumed. "He just doesn't mention that he ordered fried green-tea ice cream and had it delivered. I told him we don't offer it for delivery because it gets soggy in transit, but he begged us, saying that his wife was pregnant, so I made an exception."

"And now this!" Jacob was turning a sickly white color. "Our inspections from the Department of Health have always been excellent. That is very unusual for a new restaurant. I clean the kitchen every night. I clean as I go, too. Look!"

Annie glanced out the open door of the break room to the immaculate kitchen. "It's spotless."

"I don't think I've ever seen a better-looking commercial kitchen," Finn agreed.

"But people won't believe that," Yu said. "We can post pictures and deny it, but people will read that review and . . ."

"Excuse me." Jacob's lips trembled. "Please forgive me for my outburst."

"Nothing to forgive," Finn said.

Annie wanted to hug the poor man. "We can tell how hard you've worked on creating such a fine establishment."

Finn drummed his fingers on the table and chewed his bottom lip. He appeared to be trying to figure out how to ask something. "Where is the mouse now?"

"I'll go get it." Jacob walked out of the room.

Yu leaned closer to Finn and Annie. "Jacob has killed himself doing everything to build this restaurant, but you have to understand how much more it is to him. He taught himself Mandarin. He worked and scrimped to go to China so he could learn how to cook authentic Chinese cuisine using traditional cooking methods. And it was so hard there for him. He was the only non-Chinese student. He only says nice things about it, but one of his friends from there told me it was brutal. But Jacob did it. This is so unfair."

Annie squeezed her hand. "Finn will help." She smiled at him, hoping she wasn't putting too much pressure on him to solve this. But if anyone could help her friends out, it was Finnian Church.

"Here it is." Jacob came back in carrying a little lunch cooler. "I packed it in ice and kept it in my office."

"Why?" Annie blurted out.

Jacob's shoulders sagged. "I don't know. I thought you may want to examine it or something."

Yu stepped to her husband's side. "They do that with humans but not animals. It was a good try. I think Finn is going to start by interviewing the woman or something."

Finn shook his head. "Actually, Jacob's idea is as brilliant as his food."

CHAPTER 6

With Annie beside him in the passenger seat and both their windows down all the way, Finn knew he would quickly forget the scene in the restaurant but would always remember the way the wind blew back Annie's blond hair and occasionally wafted her perfume his way. She smelled like spring and smiled like summer, and the way she gazed at him made him feel like he could leap tall buildings in a single bound.

But the realization that it might be next to impossible for him to prove that the mouse was planted in her friends' restaurant brought him back down to earth. "Are there any cameras in the dining room? I didn't think of it at the time."

Annie shook her head as she read her speech-to-text app. "Yu never thought they'd need them. They're going to buy them after you solve this."

Finn swallowed. *If I solve this.*

"Where are we going?" Annie asked as Finn pulled into the parking lot of the County Coroner's Office.

"To see my sister Olivia."

"Does she work here?" Annie asked.

Finn smiled proudly. "She's chief coroner. One of the youngest in the country."

"That's amazing. Let me see if I remember all three brothers and three sisters."

Finn felt his back stiffen as soon as she began talking about his family.

Annie closed one eye and counted them off on her hand. "The sisters are Emma, Olivia, and Amelia. Liam and George . . . but I'm missing one brother." She turned to look at Finn.

Finn stared straight ahead. They hadn't spoken in almost a year. Right now, he had a hard time even saying the name.

"Arthur."

Finn didn't know how, but Annie must have picked up on the fact that he didn't want to discuss his brother.

Not now.

Not ever.

He zoomed into the closest parking space and had to stop a little too quickly. Annie shot forward, her blue eyes widening as she grabbed the roof handle.

"I'm sorry," Finn said.

"It's okay. I'm fine," she said, but her ever-present smile had left her face.

It pained him to realize that he'd frightened her, even just a little bit. "No, it's not." Finn shut the car off. "I don't like talking about my brother, but that's no reason for me to drive aggressively. I'm really sorry, Annie."

Annie grinned like he'd given her a present. Her reaction puzzled him. He expected her to frown on either his losing his temper or his constant apologizing—he was ashamed of those behaviors himself—but instead she appeared to appreciate his openness.

"It's totally fine." Annie nodded. "If you don't want to talk about him, we won't."

Finn's jaw flexed. Part of him *did* want to talk about his

brother. He wanted to talk about Arthur's betrayal and how deeply it had cut him. But how could Annie help with this? He'd already spent too much time screaming at the sky and was no closer to understanding why than on the night it happened.

"Thank you for understanding," he said simply and got out of the car.

Annie followed him inside. The Coroner's Office looked and felt like a cross between a college and a hospital: stately brick and marble tastefully mingled with white tile and stainless steel, with a perfume of antiseptic in the air.

As he made his way downstairs to his sister's office, Finn was wondering why she had chosen a windowless cell in the basement when she could have had a corner office with a beautiful view of the park. A little smile crept across his face when he remembered his sister growing up. She was a total nerd but also loved the outdoors. Olivia reasoned that the temptation to escape work was too strong if you were staring nature in the face, so she shut herself away until quitting time. Finn figured that with the kind of grisly things she had to see in her line of work, a chance to look out the window at something pretty would be a healthier choice, but the formula worked for her: she got her work done and was outdoors with her family every chance she got.

Finn knocked three times, paused; two times, paused again; then once more. It was their signal since they were kids. Olivia was the eldest and still as protective as a mother to her baby brothers, especially Finn, the youngest.

The door was whipped open. Olivia's smile flickered momentarily when she noticed Annie beside Finn. "Good afternoon, Finn." She looked him up and down and raised an eyebrow. "That's an interesting look for you."

Standing there in a white undershirt and suit pants, Finn felt his cheeks redden. "Olivia, this is Annie Summers. Annie, Olivia."

"Annie!" Olivia's arm shot forward and she shook Annie's hand with gusto. Finn was momentarily surprised by his sister's greeting Annie with such affection, until Olivia said, "My mother has told me so much about you."

Finn kept the smile on his face as he made a mental note to speak to his mother. He wasn't upset, it was his mother who had recommended Annie for the job after all, but he had to find some way to get her to stop talking about his personal business to the entire family.

Olivia's psychic connection with him seemed to kick in and she said, "Mom just likes to talk about her little baby boy." She reached out and pinched Finn's cheek.

Annie smiled.

Finn's eyes hardened and Olivia let go of his face.

"What brings you by?"

Finn held up the Igloo cooler. "Can we talk in your office?"

Five minutes later, Olivia sat behind her large desk rubbing her temples. "You want me to do an autopsy on a *mouse?*"

"Exactly." Finn smirked.

Olivia turned to Annie. "Is he serious? This is a prank, right?"

Annie shook her head. "Nope."

Olivia eyed them both suspiciously.

"If you don't think you're able to do it—"

"Ha-ha." Olivia scowled at Finn. "Do you really think you can goad me into doing it?"

Finn shrugged, feigning innocence. Since they were children, the words *I dare you* had been Olivia's kryptonite. "I'm sure it will be difficult, considering the small size and its being outside your usual practice. Would you be able to recommend another coroner, perhaps one with more experience—"

Olivia cut him off by throwing her pen at him. "Shut up, I'll do it. I'll call you with the results."

Finn grinned, handed the cooler to his sister, and winked at

Annie. Olivia helping him out was never in doubt. His sister had always been there for him.

"I can't thank you enough." Annie reached out to shake her hand.

"Sure you can." Olivia stood up and grabbed Annie's hand. From the way the muscles in her forearm rippled, Finn was certain she was putting some pressure on Annie. "Be good to my baby brother. I watch out for him."

Annie swallowed and nodded, while Finn rolled his eyes and frowned at his sister.

Olivia met his gaze unflinchingly. He understood the subtext in her stare: *I didn't say anything about your last relationship, little brother, and it nearly killed you. I'm not going to stay quiet this time.*

CHAPTER 7

The following day Finn had to force himself to slow down as he drove over to Annie's. Olivia had emailed him the results of the mouse-topsy, as she called it, but he hadn't read them yet. Annie had asked him to wait and he'd foolishly agreed. The suspense was killing him, but the fear that his sister had found nothing was even worse.

Maybe I can peek?

He picked up his phone and quickly set it down. There was no way he could lie to Annie—ever. He'd have to wait to find out the results.

Annie must have been just as excited, because she was sitting on her front steps waiting for him. The sight of her hair reflecting the sunshine like ripe wheat, and the hem of her white dress blowing gently in the breeze, made his breath catch in his throat.

Finn almost crashed into the mailbox because he couldn't take his eyes off her. Somehow, he managed to park in her driveway, though it was a lopsided attempt.

She got up and ran to the car, climbed into the passenger

seat, and squeezed him in a hug. She smelled like fresh-cut flowers and her hair was soft against his neck.

"Finn?" Annie asked, pulling away. "Is everything okay?"

Finn cleared his throat and opened his eyes. "I'm f— Fine." His voice rose higher than normal.

Does she notice that?

Annie couldn't hear the change in pitch, so maybe she wouldn't pick up on his awkwardness?

She blushed and he wanted to kick himself. Of course she would notice him stuttering like a teenage boy.

I'm a moron.

"Well, ready for the big reveal?" He held up his phone.

Annie leaned shoulder to shoulder with him and spoke directly into his ear. "You haven't read it, have you?"

Her warm breath tickled his neck. He turned to tell her he hadn't, but she was so close to him their lips were only inches apart. He quickly shook his head and looked down at the phone in his shaking hands.

Annie cupped his hands in hers. "I'm nervous, too."

Finn nodded as his hands trembled more. It wasn't the results of the mouse-topsy that were short-circuiting his brain as much as her proximity.

He opened the email.

Hey, little brother!

I've written out a formal report below, but I'll give you the summary here. It was actually a great exercise for my staff. I utilized it as a "teaching moment," so if you ever need me again, don't hesitate. We all got a lot out of it without the grimness of a human corpse.

Anyway . . . here goes.

We treated the mouse-topsy like we would a human case. The first thing we tried to determine was cause of death. We try to make no assumptions, but it's not a big leap to think the victim either drowned or was boiled alive.

Annie made a face and Finn had a difficult time not chuckling. He forced a sympathetic expression on his face and waited for her to open her eyes before he continued to read.

We determined that the victim was not cooked at all. In human terms, the victim received first-degree burns, indicating that the body was only in the soup for a limited time. One of my techs actually ran a test and his data indicates that the mouse would have been exposed to moderate temperatures (approximately 115–125 degrees Fahrenheit) for only a brief period. Long story short, the mouse was either never in the cooking pot or was in there for a matter of seconds.

The next test determined that there was no soup in the mouse's lungs. None. That means not only did it not drown, but it wasn't alive when it went into the pot.

As the "moustery" (sorry, Finn, I couldn't resist) deepened, we all decided to carry on as we would with a human victim in determining the cause of death. After bringing the mouse to X-ray, we discovered that three vertebrae in its neck were broken. So, in my official—off the record, of course!—opinion, the mouse was killed by a mousetrap and added to the soup postmortem.

Who was the chef behind the mouse-drop soup? I can't say, but one thing is clear: the mouse was dead before it went into the soup du jour.

Annie hugged Finn, but his joy at her touch was short-lived.

"We're not out of the woods yet. Like Olivia said, this doesn't prove how the mouse got into the soup."

Annie flopped back in her seat and stared up at the ceiling. "So there's no way to prove Inez did it then?"

"Not necessarily." Finn grabbed the steering wheel. "We just need to get her to confess."

CHAPTER 8

Finn and Annie parked outside Inez Pope's apartment complex, which was only a few blocks from the Imperial Garden. Finn shut the car off and exhaled. "Are you sure you want to go in?" he asked.

"Of course!" Annie sat up straighter. "Is there a problem with my going? I can use the speech-to-text app. I've done all right on the other interviews." Her blue eyes searched his. "Haven't I?"

"It's nothing to do with . . ." Finn struggled for the words and decided to level with her. "We're positive that Inez is trying to extort money from Jacob and Yu. People willing to commit that crime could be willing to commit others. It could be dangerous and I don't want anything to happen to you."

Annie beamed. "I thought it was something to do with my performance. I'm not worried, I'll be fine."

Finn looked at the well-maintained apartment complex and reluctantly nodded. "We have a mountain of evidence of the crime. Because of medical confidentiality, the hospital couldn't tell me if Inez had been treated there, but we can ask to see the bills. Then I'll bring up the results of the mouse-topsy. I'm going to threaten to go to the police, but she might not back down."

"She'd be crazy to go through with it if she could be charged with a crime."

Finn grimaced. "I think she's crazy for doing it in the first place. Sometimes when people get on the crazy train, they can't get off."

Annie squeezed his hand. "I'm sure you can do it."

"I wish I believed in myself a quarter as much as you do," Finn blurted out.

Annie's eyebrow rose and she checked her phone. "What do you mean?"

Finn wanted to crawl into the backseat and hide. He checked her screen and her app had recorded what he said correctly. How could he expand on that without sounding defeatist?

"I know Inez might not confess," Annie said. "But either way, I'm just so grateful that you're willing to try. If she doesn't confess, I'm sure we'll figure something out."

The curtain in the window of Inez's apartment was pulled back and quickly shut again.

Finn grabbed the door handle. "Let's do this."

He expected the front door to open before they reached the bottom step, but whoever had peeked out the window was now nowhere in sight. He rang the doorbell and waited. After a minute, he rang it again and knocked.

"I'm so glad you're here," Annie said. "Sometimes I've left people's homes thinking no one was there, having no idea that they were inside calling out for me to come in."

Finn found himself once again in awe of Annie's fortitude. She had a real smile on her face. She'd been knocked down countless times, and again and again she simply dusted herself off and stood up. *Resilient, courageous, kind . . . and beautiful.*

The door opened a crack. A woman with red-rimmed eyes peered out. "Yes?"

"We're looking for Inez Pope," Finn said.

She nodded and opened the door. "You're the police?"

"No." Finn shook his head, waiting to enter until he explained who they were. "I'm Finnian Church and this is Annie Summers. We're investigating your accusation that you found a mouse in your soup at the Imperial Garden."

A baby began crying inside and a cloud of heavy sadness and weariness passed across the woman's face. Inez Pope did not strike Finn as crazy or evil.

"Please, come in." She pointed to a little kitchen table. "We can talk there. I'll be right back."

Finn and Annie sat down, and Inez came back a minute later cradling an infant in her arms. She sat opposite Finn and held up her hand when he started to speak. "Stop. I need to explain something," she said. She bit her lip and rocked the child in her arms. "I withdraw my claim. I'm not going to pursue it."

"Why?" Annie asked loudly. She was scowling.

Inez covered her face with her hand. "I just . . . Please, just forget about it."

Annie cast a puzzled look at Finn and he realized that with Inez covering her face, Annie was unable to read her lips.

"She wants us to forget about it," Finn said to Annie. When Inez looked up, he explained, "Annie's deaf."

Inez's shoulders started to shake as she began to cry. "I'm sorry."

"You made the whole story up," Annie said, her voice rising. "The couple who own that restaurant have worked so hard—"

"I'm sorry!" Inez wailed, holding the child against her breast. "Can we please just forget the whole thing?"

"Forget it?" Annie said. "Do you have any idea what you've put them through? You've committed a serious crime!"

Inez broke into ragged sobs, as the infant continued to cry.

Finn put his hand on Annie's shoulder, but she didn't back down, demanding, "Why would you do such a thing?"

"I . . . needed money. My husband has been laid off. He looks for work every day, but still no job. Our car died, so now he takes the bus into the city, but if he doesn't get something soon, we're going to be evicted."

"That's why you asked for twelve hundred dollars," Finn said. "Is that your rent?"

Inez nodded. "This building has a mouse problem. The other day, when I was pulling another dead one from the trap, this crazy scheme of planting the mouse in a restaurant came to me. It was wrong. I was desperate but . . . I can't go through with it. I'm so sorry I caused them such grief."

Annie leaned back in her chair and glanced at Finn. "Have you done anything else like this?"

"No. Never." Inez took a few gulps of air. "I'm so ashamed. Please don't tell my husband."

"He doesn't know?" Finn asked.

Inez shook her head. "My husband is a good man. He'd be so hurt. He's really trying." She sobbed again.

Annie stood up, grabbed a tissue, and then surprised Finn by draping an arm around Inez's shoulders. The poor woman cried louder. Annie motioned for Finn to take the baby.

She might as well have asked him to fall on a grenade. He had zero experience with kids, but when Annie mouthed *Baby*, he moved. Inez shifted the baby to his outstretched arms and buried her face in her hands. Finn stood there gently rocking the child. The infant looked up, as mystified as he was, and then smiled at him.

"What did your husband do for work?" Annie asked.

Inez shook her head. "You're not going to believe this. It makes what I did so much worse. He's a chef."

CHAPTER 9

As the kids finished their feast, Annie and Finn smiled at each other across the table.

"That was awesome!" Tommy gushed.

"I'm stuffed." Tammy stuck her tummy out and patted it.

Annie and Finn were chuckling as Yu and Jacob approached the table accompanied by a young man.

"My compliments to the chef." Finn raised his water glass. "That meal was scrumptious."

The children imitated him and Annie joined in.

"*Chefs,*" Yu said, smiling. "I'd like to introduce our new assistant chef, Marcus Pope."

The young man gave a bashful wave.

Everyone clapped. They all knew who he was, of course. The only one not in on the cover-up was Marcus. After Annie explained the reasons Inez did what she did, Yu asked for an apology face-to-face. Once Yu met with Inez, she too ended up in tears. The decision was made to interview her husband for the job and that no one would mention Inez or her actions.

"Thank you very much." Marcus beamed. "I'm just so grateful to Jacob and Yu. Thank you, both of you."

While the rest of the table started chatting with the chefs, Yu motioned Annie over. "I have something for you."

Annie followed Yu back to the office. Yu picked up an envelope from the desk and lifted a dry-cleaning bag off the chair and brought it to Annie.

"Finn's suit!" Annie winced. "Did the stains come out?"

"Every last one. How can I ever thank you?"

"Not me—Finn. I told you, he's unbelievable."

Yu grinned impishly and wiggled her eyebrows. "He is. When are you going to try to move out of the friend zone?"

Annie blushed. "Well—"

"Yu!" a waitress called out as she came into the kitchen. "The credit card machine is doing that thing again!"

"Hold that thought," Yu said to Annie. "I want to hear *all* about it." She winked, then hurried after the waitress.

Annie lifted up the plastic and breathed a sigh of relief when she saw the jacket looked as good as new. She turned the envelope Yu had given her over. It was blank. Annie assumed it was a note for her. She opened it up. Inside was another envelope, the ink of the front had smudged to the point it was illegible. Annie opened the second envelope and removed the letter inside. She began to read the handwritten, delicate script:

I hope this letter finds you well. I can't begin to tell you how sorry I am. I know I can never undo the hurt and pain my actions caused you, but know this—my feelings for you have only grown.

Can you find it in your heart to forgive me?

Annie's hand shook as she tried to make herself stop reading, but it was like looking at a car accident on the side of the road—she couldn't tear her eyes away.

Please remember all of the good times and not my mistake from one drunken night. That was the biggest mistake of my life. Was I scared of getting married? Yes! That's why I drank myself into oblivion. I don't even remember it, but it was your brother who gave me the ride home. He was sober. I was not.

Don't forget that I stood by your side during those years when they tried to save your leg. Eight surgeries and I was there. Your decision to have the doctors amputate was difficult for me as well. Just as you needed to relearn things, so did I.

But I stumbled and fell.

Just like you.

But I helped you back up.

You left me on the ground.

Please forgive me, Finn. I love you.

I'm heading home in two weeks. I've sold everything here and I'm moving back for one reason—you. We have something so special, I believe it's worth fighting for.

With all my love always,

Karen

In shock, Annie stared down at the letter. Her heart ached for Finn and the story that she pieced together from Karen's words. She never should have read it. She'd thought it was a thank-you from Jacob and Yu. That explained why she opened it, but . . .

Annie closed her eyes and felt the tears running down her cheeks.

How can I tell Finn I read it?

A MiniMystery Series

THE ADVENTURES OF

Finn&Annie

THE CASE
OF THE
MISSING
GIFT

WALL STREET JOURNAL BESTSELLING AUTHOR
CHRISTOPHER GREYSON

A MiniMystery Series

THE ADVENTURES OF
Finn &
Annie

THE CASE OF
THE MISSING GIFT

WALL STREET JOURNAL BESTSELLING AUTHOR
CHRISTOPHER GREYSON

GREYSON MEDIA

CHAPTER 1

Annie paced in her living room, alternating between glancing out the window for Finn's car and looking down at the letter in her shaking hand.

The letter was for Finn, but she'd inadvertently opened it, thinking it was a thank-you note for helping Yu and Jacob save their restaurant, because Yu had handed the envelope to Annie, saying, "How can I ever thank you?" But she never mentioned that it had been in Finn's jacket pocket and the dry cleaner had retrieved it.

Annie figured she had a pretty good explanation for why she'd accidentally opened it. But even she didn't know why she continued reading when it was clearly private correspondence. And now Annie couldn't tell if she felt more guilty about reading it or devastated because of the message it contained: The letter was from Finn's ex-fiancée, Karen. She was moving back to town and wanted to get back together with Finn.

Annie took another turn around the living room, but it didn't help to settle her stomach. She'd never admitted it to anyone, but she was smitten with the tall ex-soldier—and it started the day she met him. He was handsome, a true gentleman, and over the next six months she'd learned that he was also smart and funny, patient and kind—not just to her but to her two children as well, and to everyone he met. She never thought that someone like him might actually be interested in her, and just when she'd started to hope . . .

The letter crumbled in her clenched fist.

Shoot!

She laid it against her stomach and tried to smooth the envelope out. The ink on the front had been so smudged it was illegible, but the letter inside looked untouched. She thought again about dumping water on it, then Finn wouldn't wonder if she had read it or not . . . but she couldn't do that. Nor could she lie to Finn.

How can I admit I read it?

Annie exhaled. It was a private letter. It even referenced a drunken night with Finn's brother, Arthur. Finn never spoke of Arthur and now she suspected the reason why. Obviously, the relationship between Karen and Finn ended badly, complete with the bitter heartache only betrayal can bring.

Movement in the driveway caught her attention and snapped her out of her stress fest. She grabbed her camera bag and headed out the door.

Finn, smiling from ear to ear, got out of his car and walked over to open the trunk. "Good morning!" He waved.

Annie couldn't help but smile back. She found herself grinning like an idiot whenever he was around. He was such a wonderful example to her. He'd lost his leg but every day he strove to make himself better, stronger. Could she do any less after losing her hearing?

"Hi, Finn. You look great." She quickly corrected herself— "Happy, I mean"—and stuffed her camera bag into his immaculate trunk.

"I'm just really excited about today." He closed the trunk and opened her door. "I've got some great news."

Annie cringed. The last thing she wanted to do was rain on Finn's fireworks display, but she had to tell him. She handed him the envelope. "This was in your jacket when it went to the dry cleaner's, and I—"

"Thanks. But that's the last thing I want to talk about." Finn opened the glove compartment and tossed the letter inside.

"But you need to know—"

Finn shook his head. "That letter doesn't mean anything to me and I don't even want to think about it until after this case is over. I've got some wonderful news."

The infectious smile on his handsome face quickly had Annie smiling and nodding, despite her pangs of guilt. "Did we get another insurance case?"

"It's not an insurance case. I was speaking to this friend of mine. I was in the service with him. He's a great guy. He used to be a police officer but he's a bounty hunter now."

Annie's eyes went wide and Finn chuckled.

"We're not going bounty hunting, although that could be quite exciting." He took a deep breath. "It's a private investigator job. The owner of Goodard's Cards and More must have spoken with Jacob about us helping them out. He wants to hire us!"

"Really? What kind of private investigation?" Annie was bouncing in her seat. She'd loved mysteries growing up, but it was Finn's exuberance that was so irresistible.

Finn took out his phone. "I wrote it all up. The owner is Sai Agrawal, and I told him I'd come over this morning. I had to google a rate, but we agreed on $2,000 to start, with a $500 deposit. I was hoping you'd agree to go in on it with me. We'll split it, fifty-fifty."

Annie gulped in so much air she felt light-headed. What she could do with that money!

"Of course I will, but . . ." She sighed. "It's not fair for me to get fifty percent. You got us the job."

Finn shook his head. "No. I've been thinking about it and, here." He reached into his pocket and took out a check. "There's no reason I should be making more than you on the insurance investigations either. You contribute just as much as I do, if not more. This check covers the difference, since the first case."

Annie looked down at the amount and tears sprung up in her eyes. She covered her mouth and shook her head. "I can't accept this, Finnian."

"You earned it." Finn smiled. "And if we're going to be partners with this private investigation business and it takes off, that's the only way it will work. Deal?" He held out his hand.

Annie wiped her eyes with the back of her hand, then shook on it. "Deal."

Smiling, Finn put the car in reverse. "I really think this could work out. Do you know why I think we make such a good team?"

Annie shook her head.

"Trust. You've been so . . . real. I can't thank you enough for that."

Annie smiled, but her thoughts were never far from the letter that was closed up for now inside the glove compartment, and she felt like the guilt was gnawing a hole inside her.

Once this case was done and she told Finn she'd read the letter, would he still feel the same way about trusting her?

CHAPTER 2

F inn parked out front of Goodard's Cards and More and shut off the engine. It was a cute little shop with purple and white awnings.

"Sai wasn't able to give me many details over the phone," Finn said, turning to Annie and speaking carefully so she could read his lips. "To tell the truth, I was so excited I didn't ask many questions. I didn't want to spoil the deal."

Finn loosened his tie. The whole truth was, he was about to short-circuit with stress, and the last thing he wanted was to have a full-blown panic attack in front of Annie. This was so big for him. Before the army, all he wanted to be was a police officer, but he'd assumed that dream was over after he lost his leg. Being a PI wasn't the same as being a cop, but it was closer than he thought he could ever get.

"Ready?" Finn asked Annie, readjusting his tie.

"I'll follow your lead, if that's okay?"

Finn signed, *A-OK*, gave Annie a quick fist-bump, and grabbed his briefcase. He got out of the car slowly and carefully, as always, and forced himself to be calm. Times like this, he felt his prosthetic leg was not completely a misfortune: it forced him to remain focused and controlled—what he'd lost in mobility he'd gained in willpower. And with Annie by his side, dressed in a turquoise silk blouse that made her eyes look like two enormous sapphires, his worry began to ebb, replaced by optimism and determination.

Sai Agrawal, a middle-aged man with hair so dark the highlights were blue, was waiting for them and held the door open as they approached. "Good afternoon. Finnian Church?" he asked.

Finn was slightly taken aback by his London accent. "Yes. This is my partner, Annie Summers."

"It is a pleasure to meet you both." Sai shook their hands. "With your name"—he looked at Finn—"I thought perhaps you were English, too."

"A few generations back." Finn smiled.

Sai nodded understandingly. "My family came from India a few generations ago. It doesn't take one long to lose the accent or develop a new one."

They walked into the brightly lit store and Sai stopped in front of a rack of hundreds of colorful gift cards emblazoned with the logos of stores, coffee shops, online businesses, and restaurants from all over the world. Sai had something for everyone.

"This is the reason that I hired you." Sai stretched both arms out toward the display. "The gift is gone!"

Annie glanced down at the speech-to-text app on her phone and raised a puzzled eyebrow.

"You said the gift is gone?" Finn repeated, enunciating as he did.

Annie gave him a little *thank you* wink.

"Exactly!" Sai held up his index finger. "But I have *no idea* how. See, a customer selects a card." He reached out and picked up a card for R. C. Classic Clothing. "They bring it to the register to activate it and put money on the card. Simple, yes?"

Finn nodded.

"No!" Sai held up his index finger again and this time stamped his foot. "I have had five complaints that when the person who receives the card goes to use it, the gift is gone! There's a zero balance on the card and when they call the company it says that the funds have been used."

"And this has happened five times?" Finn asked.

"That I know of." Sai ran his hand through his thick hair. "Every day this week someone has come in, irate, accusing me of stealing from them. I have done nothing wrong, of course, but when I call the vendors, they tell me the same thing they have been telling the gift recipients. The money is gone. My wife said I'd better get some professional help before we get a visit from the police, so I am reaching out to you."

Finn loosened his tie and cleared his throat. He was stalling for time as he attempted to organize his racing thoughts that fear was busy scattering. He wasn't ready for this; he had no idea where to start, even. "I'll need to . . ."

"Finn will want to review the computer process for activating the cards," Annie said, coming to his rescue.

He had never mentioned doing that, but it was a great idea. "Yes. It's not uncommon for software to make errors."

"Right!" Sai raised his index finger in the air again. "That is a possibility. Though we are so careful to do things right at our end."

Finn lifted one of the cards off its hook. The display case was directly in front of the doors. There was an anti-shoplifting scanner, but still . . .

"You have this display so close to the front doors," Finn said, walking toward the scanner. "Aren't you worried about someone stealing them?"

"No," Sai said.

Finn walked between the sensors of the shoplifting scanner.

Annie raised a puzzled eyebrow. "Is an alarm going off? There are no lights."

"Annie's deaf," Finn explained to Sai as he signed to Annie, *Nothing*.

"The gift cards don't set off the shoplifting alarm because it would be useless to steal them." Sai's eyes narrowed and Finn picked up the disappointment in his voice. "You have to activate the cards or they're worthless."

"You never want to rule out any possibility." Finn tried to sound confident while he really wanted to smack his own forehead for not realizing that fact. "In addition to documenting the activation procedure, we'll need a list of the people who contacted you about missing gift card money and"—he pointed at the ceiling and the security camera—"any security tapes you may have. I'm hoping your system works?"

"Does it ever!" Sai beamed. "Follow me, I'll show you."

They followed Sai to the back of the store and Finn stopped cold as he watched the man climb a narrow staircase with tall steps.

Finn felt Annie's reassuring hand on his arm. "I got your back." Her breath warmed the skin of his neck. When he glanced back, the look in her blue eyes was all the encouragement he needed. He handed her his briefcase and seized the railing with one hand, then pressed the palm of his other hand flat against the wall.

She gently held her hand against his back as he went. One tall step at a time he climbed the stairs, Annie right behind him the whole way. He reached the top and felt the urge to lift his hands over his head and cheer.

They followed Sai down the hallway and into a room on the left.

"Wow!" Annie expressed how Finn felt as they stepped into a room filled with monitors and recording equipment.

"My son-in-law started an electronics store, so I thought I

would give him a leg-up and get something out of it, too," Sai said proudly. "When I added up all the money we were losing to shoplifting, it was an easy decision."

"How far back do you keep the footage?" Finn asked.

"Three months," Sai said. "I assumed you would want to see it, so I had my son-in-law make a copy." He handed a large hard drive to Finn. "All of the store footage for the last month is on there. That's when we started selling the gift cards. Cameras three and eight cover the display rack. They're in their own separate folders on the drive."

"This is fantastic," Finn said.

"Here." Sai handed him a sheet of paper. "That is the contact information for everyone who has complained so far. Once you see the checkout procedure, do you think you will have everything you need to figure out what's going on?"

"Well, it gives me a strong start, that's for sure," Finn said, wiping the sweat from his brow.

Standing proudly at Finn's side, Annie said, "If anyone can figure this out, Finn can."

Sai grinned and shook Finn's hand again. "That's why I called you. What's our next step?"

Finn tried to keep the rising panic from showing on his face. He had no idea.

CHAPTER 3

Annie kept her eye on the glove compartment like it contained a bomb, and it might as well have, since the letter inside could blow up everything she had with Finn. Who knew how he would react when he found out she'd read the letter? And what about the letter itself? Karen was his ex-fiancée. He had planned to marry her, a decision the fastidious former soldier wouldn't have made lightly.

And she was coming back to town.

Something bad had happened between them, but Finn was such a wonderful man, would he find it in his heart to forgive her as Karen asked?

Where would Annie fit in?

Of course the job was important to her, but her relationship with Finn mattered more. It had quickly evolved from business to friendship, and the way it was growing . . .

Finn waved at her.

Annie glanced down at her speech-to-text app.

Annie?

Is everything all right?

Annie?

"Sorry." She shifted in her seat to look at him.

"I hope you don't mind getting the surveillance video setup without me," Finn said. "My father asked if I could stop by."

"No problem. I think I just have to plug it in to my computer. Are you okay with working on it at my house? The kids will be home in the afternoon."

"They're no problem."

Annie chuckled. Whenever Finn came by the kids couldn't stop talking. She knew it was because they needed the attention a father brings. But it had to be difficult for him—Tammy tugging on one arm, wanting to show him her dollhouse, while Tommy tried to drag him over to see his latest LEGO construction.

"Okey-dokey. I'm making meatloaf, special green beans, and mashed potatoes."

Annie normally relied on pasta for dinner, but since Finn was coming over, she'd switched meat night.

"Special green beans?" Finn turned down her street.

"I had to call them fast green beans when Tommy was younger to get him to eat them. I ate one *fast* green bean and told him to watch me out the window, and proceeded to do the fastest lap around the house I could. He was hooked until Tammy wanted princess green beans, but that would have triggered a boycott, so I settled on special. There's nothing special about them; I slow-roast them with a little olive oil, fresh garlic, salt, and pepper."

"They sound pretty special to me." Finn pulled into her driveway. "I can't wait. I'll be over as soon as I finish with my dad."

Annie nodded and got out of the car.

"I really think we're going to make this work!" Finn waved. He gave her a big thumbs-up and pulled away.

Annie watched him go. His excitement filled her with hope. Until she met him, she'd been praying to keep her head above water. She'd never dreamed of getting out of the sea of misery she'd been swimming in before Finnian Church threw her a life ring.

She carried the hard drive over to the mailbox, gathered up the mail, and headed inside. It would still be a couple of hours before the kids got home. That would give her a chance to tidy up the house, organize the area around her computer, and put dinner together so all she'd have to do was put it in the oven.

She set the hard drive down next to her computer and started to flip through the mail. The little stab of panic she typically felt each time she saw a bill was less sharp today. Maybe it was the check in her pocket shielding her, or perhaps it was the fact that everything had been working out lately, but the fangs of fear seemed to have lost their bite.

Until she saw the last envelope.

It had been almost a year since she'd seen a similar one—a child support payment. Camden had paid support for only a few months before the excuses started and the payments stopped. As the months stretched on she was left with two choices: go to court or let it go. She chose the latter because Camden had also dropped all demands to see the kids.

The last thing Annie would do was stand between the kids and their father, but neither Tammy nor Tommy wanted to see him. Both of them feared Camden's temper. Neither child admitted it, but Annie and the court-ordered therapist suspected that Camden had struck them. Tommy had come home once with a red cheek and a bruise on his jaw. He said he fell and he stuck to the story, but Annie didn't believe him.

She flinched. The harsh memory of her own beatings was all too real. Camden promised he'd never raise a hand to the children, but she didn't believe that either. She had then. Not now.

She opened the envelope, removed the check, and froze. It

wasn't a token gesture of money to keep her from going to the court; it was the full amount—and then some.

Camden was now current with the child support.

She opened the accompanying letter. On the page was just one handwritten sentence.

Annie stopped breathing.

I want full custody.

CHAPTER 4

F inn pulled into his parents' driveway but kept the engine running. His little sister's car was there, but neither of his parents' cars were.

It's a trap.

The muscles in Finn's jaw flexed. Amelia was the baby of the family and the peacemaker. She was the tool his parents used for interventions and to end fights.

But the fight between Finn and Arthur was out of her league. Arthur had crossed a line. Maybe someday Finn could forgive his brother, but would he ever be able to forget?

Not bloody likely.

His grandfather used to mutter that when Finn was little. His grandmother would get upset and Finn's mother would hush him, so of course Finn picked up the habit as well.

He thought about reading the letter in the glove compartment. He was certain that somehow it played into this meeting, but right now he just wanted to concentrate on this new job and not old drama.

The side door opened and his little sister leaned out. "Are you going to sit in your car all afternoon?" She smiled.

Amelia was a very petite woman but she was a little firecracker. She'd surprised everyone a few years ago and taken a secretary position at the sheriff's department. No one expected her to be able to sit still all day. But she thrived there—so much so that she'd recently made the decision to go to the police academy.

Their policeman father was proud. So was Finn, but he had to admit that part of him was jealous. It was supposed to be him, but his plans for that life had gone off the tracks.

Amelia asked Finn first. That had been an awkward conversation. Of course he said it didn't bother him, but Amelia kept pressing until he admitted that it didn't bother him *much*. That was enough for her. She signed up the next day.

He was glad she did. She'd make a good police officer because she had such a way with people. Besides, it was in their blood—their father a police officer, their eldest sister, Olivia, chief coroner, and now Amelia a rookie cop.

"Hey, Sis." Finn gave her a hug and peck on the cheek, which she returned with gusto.

"Hey yourself. What's this I hear about a new gal in your life?"

"Professional relationship," Finn said, peering inside and listening for anyone who might be waiting in the house.

"No one else is here," Amelia said.

"That's what scares me." Finn walked past her and over to the fridge. His mother always kept a pitcher of sweet tea on hand and didn't disappoint him today. He took out a glass and glanced at Amelia. "You want a cup?"

She shook her head. "I have a weigh-in coming up."

Finn smiled. "Thought you lost weight. What are you down to, ninety-five pounds?"

"Ha-ha." Amelia smiled and shut the door. "One-ten. I should be fine, but I'm trying to stay focused."

"You'll be fine. Dad said you passed his physical fitness test so well he was going to test you for steroids."

She laughed. "That's because he's Dad." Her smile faded. "Have you read the letter from Karen?"

"No."

"Why?"

"I don't want to. Simple as that." Finn poured himself a sweet tea and sipped it. "And I do need to point out that the decision to do so is mine and mine alone. I don't know why you or Mom or Dad are even involved."

"Because of Arthur."

At the mention of his brother, Finn's fingers tightened around the glass. So much so that he set it on the counter for fear of it breaking in his hand.

"What does *he* have to do with the letter?"

"I can't tell you because I haven't read it, but there could be a connection. Can you just read it?"

"What's Arthur saying now?"

"He wants to move home."

Finn shrugged. "I'm not stopping him. I won't have anything to do with him, but it's Mom and Dad's house. If they want to get taken advantage of—let them."

"He's changed, Finn. He went to rehab. He's really broken about what happened."

Finn loosened his tie. "You talked to Arthur?"

"Yes," Amelia admitted. "Yesterday."

"In person?"

"Over the phone."

"And that's what he said? He's really broken about what happened?"

Amelia's eyes softened. Maybe she thought his question was a signal that Finn was prepared to forgive his brother. "He said, 'What happened broke me.'"

The muscles in Finn's jaw flexed. "You notice Arthur said

'what happened' and not 'what I did,' right? There's no accepting personal responsibility there."

"He is, Finn. He was drunk."

"You're not accepting it either!" Finn swayed as he stepped too hard to the left on his prosthetic. "How much would you have to drink to sleep with your future brother-in-law?"

Amelia didn't say anything.

"Tell Mom and Dad they can do whatever they want, but I don't want anything to do with Arthur."

"Mom's hoping you'll forgive him."

Finn ground his teeth. "Sometimes forgiveness doesn't mean a bunch of crying, hugging and pretending nothing happened. I forgave Arthur and didn't jab a spear in his chest. Right now, that's the extent of my forgiveness, and if he was truly sorry, he'd leave me alone and tell everyone else to as well. Do you have any idea what it feels like to discuss this with my mother? My sister? The issue is dead. I'm not reading the letter. Let Karen live her life and Arthur live his. And all of you, do me a favor and let me live mine."

Finn tore the door open and grabbed the railing as he lurched down the steps. With an awkward gait, he hurried for the car—pushing away the memory of racing out of his parents' house as a boy on two legs, eager to find the day's adventure.

Slamming the car door, Finn jerked at the knot in his tie and finally yanked it loose. The tie fell on the floorboards of the passenger seat. He stared at the gift from his grandfather. To some the Christmas present would have been held in the same regard as a pair of socks. But to thirteen-year-old Finn, it was his grandfather's way of saying that Finn was now a man.

Finn hung his head. His grandfather was old-fashioned. Whenever he imparted a pearl of wisdom to his grandson it always began with the phrase, *A real man* . . . And Finn could hear his grandfather now: *A real man takes care of his things, even when he's angry.*

Finn lifted the tie off the floor and laid it on the seat, his eyes stopping on the glove compartment. He took out the letter and opened his car door. He walked over to the sewer grate that he used to drop rocks into while he waited for the bus. After folding the letter twice so it would fit, he dropped it through the slot.

As he limped back to the car, he saw Amelia watching him from the window. He couldn't see her face clearly, but from the way she was standing and the fact that she didn't wave, he deduced that she was disappointed.

Finn got in and backed out of the driveway.

She shouldn't be disappointed in him. He'd forgiven both his brother and Karen for what they'd done. He just wasn't going to be a part of their soap opera anymore.

He had his own life to live.

CHAPTER 5

F inn hurried up the steps to Annie's house. The sun was starting to set. He had told her he was just running over to his parents' while she set up the video.

He rang the doorbell and waited.

The sound of both children rushing for the door made him grin. His smile didn't last long when he saw the expression on the kids' faces. They both gave him a look that he'd seen too often as a child—*Boy, are you going to get it.*

Finn looked past them to the dinner table, which was all set up for the special meal that he'd forgotten all about.

"I'm so stupid," he muttered.

Tammy's eyes went wide. She glanced back at the kitchen as Annie walked into the room. "Finn said a bad word. It was the S word."

"Stupid," Finn blurted out. "I said I'm so stupid."

Tommy ran over to Annie's desk and lifted off a large jar filled with change. "Three times. Seventy-five cents, please." He pointed to the label: 1 X SWEAR = 25¢.

Finn took a dollar out of his pocket. "I'm sorry I'm stupid."

Tommy and Tammy chuckled and Annie cracked a little smile.

"I completely forgot and then I had to get gas on the way over." Finn said.

Annie looked like she was about to burst into tears. The expression on her face was a mix of disbelief and hurt. As Annie closed her eyes, Finn realized that he'd stopped for gas with her this morning.

He reached out and touched her arm. When she opened her eyes, the hurt was gone. She was mad.

"Can we talk privately?" Finn pointed to the back porch. Annie debated for a moment before heading out the back door.

Once the door was closed behind them, Finn decided the best course of action was to be as honest as he could tolerate. "I'm not lying about the gas. I know I filled up this morning, but I spent the morning and afternoon driving."

"Where?" Annie crossed her arms.

"All over." Finn exhaled. Right now, he didn't want to look into her blue eyes, which were blazing as hot as a welder's torch. "I went over to my parents' this morning and got ambushed by my sister. She's the official peacemaker of the family."

The fire in her eyes flickered but it didn't go out.

"I had a falling-out with my brother. She was sent to try to repair the relationship and find out . . ." Finn looked away. It was emasculating to talk about his fiancée's infidelity with his sister, and it would kill him to speak about it with Annie.

"Do you remember that letter?" Finn stared out at the forest for a moment and then realized that Annie had left her phone inside. He turned to face her, so she could read his lips, and said, "The letter that you found in my jacket was from an old girlfriend. There's a lot of drama between her and my family, and they wanted to know what it said."

Annie nodded understandingly. "Did you tell them?"

"I couldn't," Finn said. "I didn't read it."

Annie started wringing her hands. "Are you going to?"

"I can't." He shrugged. "I threw it away. The person who wrote it . . . It doesn't affect me."

Finn watched Annie's face as her eyes glistened and a tear rolled down her cheek. He didn't understand why she would be so upset, but her crying created a panic in him like the sun going out in the middle of the day.

"Annie, what's wrong?" Finn's hand hesitated next to her skin. His fingertip was so close, the tear touched his skin and rolled down his finger.

"I read it."

Finn froze. He didn't know if he had suddenly developed the ability to read lips, but Annie's words made no sound when she said them.

"I'm so sorry." Annie grabbed his shirt. "When Yu gave me your jacket, she handed me the envelope separately. I thought it was for me."

Finn started to turn away, but Annie's grip on his shirt tightened. "I'm so sorry, Finn. I didn't mean to keep reading it. I just did. It was wrong, but everything with you and me is so right that . . . Please forgive me."

"What do you know?" It hurt to ask the question. "About what happened between her and me?"

More tears ran down Annie's cheek. "She's moving back to town. She wants to get back together with you. She wrote . . . I know something happened between her and your brother. They hurt you. She didn't mention specifics but . . ."

Finn nodded as he stared at the floor. He closed his eyes, feeling like his fresh start had just died. Lifting his head, he said, "I was a fool." To his surprise, Annie nodded.

"You and me both. I married an abusive alcoholic and thought it was love. Camden wants full custody of the kids."

"What are you talking about?"

"I promised myself I wouldn't bring that up but . . . without this job he'll get it."

"Annie." Finn lifted her chin. "You have a job. Three of them, really, with your photography and being a working mother."

"Can you still work with me after I broke your trust?"

Finn stared up at the darkening sky before meeting her gaze. "You didn't break my trust. I can see why you read the letter and why you didn't want to talk about it. I don't want to talk about it either. So forget the ridiculous notion that you're going to lose your job. What's happening with Camden?"

"I can deal with Camden." She sniffed. "It's you I'm worried about." She stepped close to him, her hands on his arms. "I'd never hurt you on purpose." She said the words in a way that made him believe them. In spite of all that had happened between him and Karen, Annie's closeness didn't make him raise his defenses.

Finn started to tip his head forward.

The back door burst open and Tammy and Tommy flooded out onto the porch.

"We're *starving*," Tommy moaned.

Tammy melodramatically laid her arm across her forehead and flopped to the floor. "I'm dying of hunger."

Annie glanced up at Finn.

Finn smiled, reached down, and tickled Tammy and Tommy. "Then let's get some food in those bellies."

Giggling and squealing, both kids danced back into the kitchen.

Are we good? Annie signed.

Finn gave her a thumbs-up.

The truth was, neither of them was okay, but together they had a chance to get better.

CHAPTER 6

After dinner, over which the kids told Finn about their day, Annie finally got them to bed. Even with the specter of Camden looming in the shadows of her mind, she was happy. Finn had understood.

Annie hurried over to the computer and Finn, sitting in the copilot's chair. "Sorry about that." She reached for her still-warm tea and added a dash of honey from the bear-shaped plastic container.

"Don't be. You're a good mom. Kids need stories."

"Tammy especially," Annie said, wiggling the mouse and bringing the screen to life. "She's been having nightmares. I gave both kids a panic button that causes an alarm to vibrate under my pillow to wake me up, but she's too afraid to reach out from under the blanket to use it."

"Why don't you put it in the bed with her?"

"Because she sets it off every time she rolls over, which is about every two minutes. I put it on her nightstand, but when she wakes up, she hides underneath the blanket and won't peek out."

"What are the nightmares about? Maybe you can stop the source?" Finn said.

"She won't tell me or she doesn't remember."

"That's another problem to noodle on. I'll try to come up with something."

"I wasn't asking you to solve it. I was just venting."

"I know, but I'm a guy." Finn smiled. "We're kinda hard-wired to be problem-solvers."

"Speaking of problems . . ." Annie turned in her chair to face the monitor. "I found something but I don't understand it."

"What is it?" Finn watched as his words came up on the second monitor where Annie was running another speech-to-text app.

"It's easier to show you." She clicked the mouse and rewound the security tape until she found the correct spot, then hit play. "Watch here." She pointed at a specific place on the screen and wiggled the mouse pointer over the same place for emphasis. "They're the gift cards for R. C. Classic clothing stores."

The video was from camera 8 and showed the gift card display rack. After they watched a couple of shoppers walk past the camera, a slight man in skinny jeans and a T-shirt stopped in front of the display rack. A moment later, he turned and headed toward the right of the store and off-camera.

"Did you see that?"

Finn stared at the screen, his eyebrow rising. "Can you rewind it, please?"

Annie rewound the tape and played it again. She watched as Finn realized what had happened and his eyes widened.

"Did he *add* gift cards to the rack?" Finn sat back in his chair.

Annie nodded. "Almost a dozen."

"So they're fakes?" Finn wondered aloud. "But that won't work. They wouldn't activate."

"I don't think they're fake." Annie started to rewind the video. "Wait a second, it gets even weirder."

She went back fifty-three minutes and pressed play. The same man in skinny jeans walked through the front door and over to the rack. Just before he reached it, Annie paused the video. "Watch that same spot."

The man stopped at the rack for a minute, presumably picking out a gift card, then walked to the right of the store.

Annie paused the footage.

"Wait a minute." Finn blinked and shook his head. "There are less cards there now."

"A dozen less." Annie made a face she hoped matched her puzzlement.

"This was almost an hour earlier, correct?"

"Yes."

"So some guy comes in and steals a dozen worthless gift cards," Finn said, loosening his tie. "Then he returns them an hour later."

"But those are the cards that have been tampered with."

Finn closed his eyes and tapped his index finger against his forehead. "I'm stupid. I didn't take a gift card with me." He gasped as Annie's hand gently took his.

"Don't say that about yourself." She smiled and tapped the swear jar with her other hand. "You owe another quarter."

Finn took out another dollar bill. "It's an expensive bad habit."

Annie started to reach into the jar, but Finn shook his head. "It's a deposit for future violations. Besides, I didn't mean it."

"It doesn't matter. If you say it often enough, you may start to believe it. That's why it's a bad word."

Finn's eyes went wide and he jumped up and started down the hallway. Annie rushed to catch up. She grabbed his arm just as he reached Tammy's door.

"Sorry," he said, turning around to face her. "Tammy started screaming."

Annie hurried inside. Tammy was hidden beneath the blanket.

"Mommy's here."

When her mother sat down, Tammy sobbed, "I was calling."

"I heard you," Finn whispered. "It's okay."

Tammy continued to sob, "I wish Mommy could hear me."

Annie's heart ached. "I wish Mommy could hear you, too."

Finn walked over to the nightstand and picked up the alarm. It was nothing more than a wireless doorbell. "How come you don't ring the alarm?"

Tammy's blue eyes peeked out from beneath the fuzzy blanket. "If I get out of bed, the monsters will get me."

Annie was about to argue that there were no such things as monsters, but that fact hadn't comforted her when she was Tammy's age, so she wasn't going to use it on her now.

Finn glanced around the room and saw a stuffed tiger. "What if we have your tiger stand guard on the table?"

Annie nodded. "That's a great idea."

"No, it isn't!" Tammy looked horrified. "Then the monster would get Mr. Stripes." She grabbed the tiger and pulled him under the safety of the blanket with her.

"What about your shark?" Annie grabbed another stuffed animal. "It has such big teeth."

"Not Flipper! Flipper's a vegetarian." Tammy snatched the shark away, too.

"Hold on one second." Finn turned and left the bedroom.

"Do you want to tell me what your nightmare was about?" Annie asked.

Tammy shook her head. "No."

"It might help you feel better."

"No, it won't, Mommy." Tammy's lip trembled, so Annie just stroked her curls.

Finn came back into the room with one hand behind his back and a big smile on his face. "I've got the solution!"

From the way Tammy's shoulders jumped, Annie suspected Finn was loud.

Like a magician, he waved his hand in front of himself as he spoke. "I have found an animal that can stay on the nightstand and keep the monsters away so you can press the alarm." He started moving his hand in bigger and bigger circles and suddenly pulled his other hand forward with the plastic honey bear in his palm.

"That's honey!" Tammy said, clearly disappointed.

"No, no, no!" Finn grinned. "It's a bear *filled* with honey. He's sweet on the inside, like you." He touched Tammy's nose and she giggled. "But on the outside he's ferocious and monsters are super-duper afraid of him. Do you know why?"

Tammy shook her head, waiting with rapt attention.

"Because Beary has fangs and claws and most importantly —honey!" Finn leaned close like he was sharing a secret. "See, when a monster comes into the room, Beary squirts honey all over the floor so the monster can't get close to the bed. Then he guards the alarm until you do your part."

"What's my part?" Tammy asked.

"You need to press the button so Mommy can come in and scare that monster away. But do you know what I think? I think once the monsters see that Beary is sleeping in here now, they are going to run for the hills and never come back!"

"Never?"

"Never ever." Finn held out his fist and Tammy bumped it.

"Do you think you can get back to sleep now?" Annie asked.

Tammy nodded. "Leave Beary on the table, okay, Finn?"

"You got it." Finn set the honey bottle down and headed for

the hallway. He stopped in the doorway and gave her a little wave. "Pleasant dreams."

Tammy wiggled back under the covers. "I like Finn, Mommy."

Annie smiled. "I like him, too."

CHAPTER 7

The next morning, Finn and Annie walked through the front doors of Goodard's Cards and More. Sai noticed them and rushed over.

"Good morning, Finnian and Annie! I didn't expect to see you so soon. Don't tell me you've solved it already!"

"Not yet," Finn said. "But we're making great headway. We do have a couple of questions for you."

"Of course."

"Do you know this man?" Finn asked as Annie held up her tablet and showed a still from the security camera footage.

Sai nodded. "His name is Tom . . . Timmy, no, Jimmy. Jimmy something or other. American last name. He lives close by. Comes in every couple of days. Usually buys one of those energy drinks."

Finn typed those details into his phone. "The second question is, would it be possible for you to pull up how many R. C. Classic gift cards you've sold since last Monday?"

"Certainly. No bother. I'll be back in a jiffy."

Annie's smile turned a little melancholy.

Finn raised a curious eyebrow.

"There are some things I really miss about hearing," she said. "I used to love hearing different accents. Right now I'm wondering if Sai sounds like Mary Poppins!"

"He does." Finn smiled because of Annie's perseverance and in spite of the sadness he felt for her loss. "Sai's voice is a little deeper, though."

Annie chuckled.

Finn walked over to the gift rack and eyed the R. C. Classic cards. "So Jimmy stole a dozen cards and then put them back."

"I went through the footage again and it looks that way. From the recording that we have, which doesn't include yesterday, I think Sai has sold nine R. C. Classic gift cards."

Finn lifted four of the cards off their hook and gave Annie the last one. "So the one you're holding should be untouched." He turned the three he held over in his hand. They were plastic cards with a lively print of models wearing retro clothes. Printed on the back was a barcode, legal disclaimers, a customer service number, and a metal pull-off strip.

"Unless you take them up to the cashier, they're worthless," Annie said. "And I triple-checked the footage. Jimmy never took the cards to the register."

Finn's eyes widened as he stared down at the back of the gift cards and a smile dawned across his face.

"Nine!" Sai announced as he strode up. "We've sold nine."

"You were right." Finn gave Annie a wink.

"Is that good news?" Sai asked.

Finn smiled. "Great news. I know how Jimmy did it. Now we have to prove it."

CHAPTER 8

Annie let the wind blow through her hair as she drove across town in Finn's car. It was such a beautiful day that she'd really wanted to drive, but she was surprised Finn had said yes. She was so used to dealing with Camden and his macho pride, it was difficult for her not to let the past influence her. But Finn was so different. He didn't seem to feel threatened by her at all. And he included her. He said *we* all the time and was quick to give praise.

Annie followed the directions on the GPS as they headed to the outskirts of town. Long stretches of woods and fields were interrupted by little subdivisions and apartment complexes. She drove through the open gates of one and parked outside a little brick townhouse with a giant wooden WELCOME sign out front.

Finn shifted to face her. "This is my sister Amelia's house. She's going to the police academy. If it's all right with you, I'd like to run our information for the police through her. Maybe get her a little recognition right off the starting block."

Annie nodded. "You're a good brother."

"That depends on who you ask," he said wryly.

She cringed when she remembered his falling-out with his brother Arthur. She'd have to choose her words more carefully.

Finn climbed out of the car and Annie followed him past the two cars in the driveway. The front door opened before they reached the steps. A petite woman smiled at Finn but not with her eyes. The skin around them was tight. She looked nervous.

Why?

"Amelia, this is Annie Summers. Annie, this is my sister."

"Pleasure to meet you, Annie. Olivia said that you were lovely. She was right." Amelia shook Annie's hand and looked to Finn. "I didn't expect to see you so soon. I'm sorry about the other day."

"No worries." Finn opened his arms and gave her a hug. "Can we come in for a minute? I have something to discuss with you. Of a police nature."

"Ah . . ." She glanced back over her shoulder. "Sure." She stepped aside and Annie followed Finn inside.

The townhouse was modern country chic. Brass, glass, and wood accents gleamed in the afternoon sunlight streaming in through the glass doors out back.

"Would you like something to drink?" Amelia asked as she led them over to the living room.

"No, thank you," Annie replied.

"All set," Finn said. He looked like he was about to burst with excitement. "You'd better sit down."

"Sounds like you've got something good." Amelia's brown eyes flickered as she caught the spark of excitement in Finn's voice.

"I do. I'm sure Mom told you that I started a private investigation business."

"What?" Amelia feigned shock. "Of course Mom told me." She turned to Annie. "My mother keeping a secret works about as well as a screen door on a submarine. Don't get me wrong, I love her, but if you want someone to find something out, just let her know."

Finn laughed and nodded. "She'd kill us if she overheard this conversation, but it's true."

Amelia and Finn stared at each other for a moment. Even though they didn't speak, Annie could see that they had a mini-conversation using micro facial expressions and that secret link some siblings possessed.

"Congratulations! How's business?" Amelia said, the corner of her mouth ticking up.

"Very well." Finn reached into his briefcase, took out a folder, laid it on the coffee table, and opened it up. He told her about the missing money on the gift cards and being hired by Sai.

Amelia tapped the picture of Jimmy. "So Jimmy here stole a dozen gift cards and then put them back? How does he steal the money? Did he use fake gift cards?"

"No." Finn grinned crookedly. "It's simple yet scummily brilliant. Let me walk you through the scam." Finn took out one of the gift cards and held it up. "Jimmy goes into the store and takes a dozen gift cards off the rack. There's no security on the gift cards because they're worthless until you load them up with money, so taking the cards out of the store won't set off any alarms."

"And the display rack is right at the front of the store and accessible by anyone?" Amelia asked.

"Yes. But we have it on two cameras that Jimmy stole the cards," Annie said.

"Then Jimmy goes out to his car." Finn flipped the card over and pointed at the metal strip. "This is an original card. Untouched."

"There are two kinds of bars on gift cards," Annie explained. "One has metallic paint covering the card activation number. For that type, you have to scratch off the paint to reveal the number."

"The other kind, like this one"—Finn tapped the R. C. Classic card in his hand—"has a thin foil bar glued over the number. When you peel the bar off, it reveals the number and distorts it so you can't use it again." He peeled the metal bar off and it bent out of shape.

"If you can't use the bar again, then the gift cards became useless when Jimmy removed the bars," Amelia said.

"Not if you can order other metal bars." Finn pointed at Annie. "Annie figured that out."

Annie pulled up a page on her tablet and showed it to Amelia. "You can order a hundred of them from China for less than five dollars."

Finn sat forward on the couch. "So Jimmy pulled off the original metal bars and wrote the gift card numbers down. Then he applied new metal bars over the cards again. Look at this card. It's one he stole, tampered with, and put back."

Amelia took the card and examined it. "The bar is slightly crooked."

"Because he put it on by hand."

Amelia shook her head. "But how does Jimmy get the money?"

"Jimmy checks those numbers, waiting for someone to buy a gift card and load it with cash. He probably checks ten times a day if the card has been activated. When it is, he spends the money before the customer even gets out of the store." Finn crossed his arms and gave Annie a big wink.

"Wow." Amelia sat back. "What a scumbag. But how do we prove it?"

Finn pulled out a piece of paper on which he'd detailed everything Amelia needed to do. "You need to go to the robbery division of the police department. Take this card that Jimmy doctored. Have them put six hundred dollars on the card and activate it."

"Why six hundred?" Annie asked.

"Because if he steals over five hundred it's a felony. When the money is taken out of the account, they can get a warrant to see the IP address of the person who used it and where the merchandise was shipped."

"How do you know Jimmy will order online?" Amelia asked.

"He has to. He won't have the card." Finn smirked.

Amelia looked like she would have thrown a pillow from the loveseat at him if Annie hadn't been there. "Why don't *you* take it to the robbery division?"

"Because I'm looking out for my sister." He grinned at her. "Besides, with Annie and me going into the private investigation business, it will be good to have a friend on the force."

"You always have that." Amelia got up, leaned in, and kissed Finn on the cheek. "You are a genius."

Finn patted Annie's shoulder. "Geniuses."

Amelia smiled. "Of course. Well, kudos to both of you for solving your first case!"

"Don't go opening the champagne just yet," Finn said. "It's not closed until Jimmy is caught. You have to do your part for that to happen."

"I'll go right now."

Finn suddenly stood up and glared down the hallway. Annie followed his gaze and almost fell over. Walking down the hallway, clapping his hands, was a man who looked exactly like Finn except his hair was longer.

"Hello, big brother," the man said.

Annie could tell he was an identical twin, but she quickly processed the differences between the two men. Finn's brother's eyes were darker, and he looked older than Finn. More miles, Annie's father would have said. And they were rough miles.

Finn turned to stare at his sister.

"Arthur needed a place to stay." She shrugged and gave Finn an apologetic look.

The man stepped forward and started to hold his hand out to Annie.

Finn moved so fast, she worried he'd lose his balance, but he was rock steady as he stood nose to nose with his brother. Finn said something, but with his back to her, Annie couldn't tell what it was, and right now she didn't want to check her speech-to-text app. With both men standing with one foot slightly back and their hands balled into fists, it appeared like the pair could come to blows at any moment.

Finn turned to Amelia. "Run that information by the robbery division today."

"I will."

Finn reached back, took Annie by the hand, and kept between her and Arthur as he led her outside.

As they marched to the car, Annie glanced down at her phone to see what Finn had said to his brother. When she read it, she shivered.

"If you touch her, I'll rip your hand off and beat you to death with it."

CHAPTER 9

It had been two days since Finn had seen Annie, and he missed her. He thought of a thousand reasons he could use to stop by her house but they all seemed contrived. The last thing he wanted was for Annie to see him out of pity. Though that was probably why she put up with him in the first place; she had a heart of gold and felt sorry for him.

Finn sat in his living room with the lights off. It was dark outside and even darker in the house. He knew he was spiraling down but he couldn't seem to get off the pity train. Normally, he'd go for a drive, but with the way things were going, he was certain he'd run into either Arthur or Karen.

Maybe both of them. They're probably together again.

Finn leaned back in the chair. It was almost 8:30. Too early for bed, yet there was nothing else that he wanted to do— except see Annie.

But he didn't want her to see him like this. He rubbed his chin. He needed a shave. He wanted a beer. Or maybe twelve.

How's that going to help?

He was tempted for a moment to get wasted and forget all his problems. He glared down at his prosthetic.

Stupid thing. I probably couldn't walk after three beers. And what if Annie came over? What a sight that would be, a drunk cripple crawling around the floor of his apartment.

Finn's phone buzzed in his pocket.

"Congratulations, Finn." Amelia's voice was filled with excitement. "You just bagged Jimmy the scammer. Nice job on your business's first case!"

Finn covered the phone and roared triumphantly at the ceiling.

****

ANNIE SAT ALONE in her kitchen with the lights out. The glow from the stove clock provided ample light to see. Not for the first time, Annie found herself wondering, if she had to choose which sense to lose, would it be sight or sound? She of course hadn't had a choice in the matter, but if she had, she would have chosen to keep her sight.

She closed her eyes and said a prayer for the blind. She couldn't imagine how hard life must be for them.

No sooner had she said Amen than she added, "And please help with Camden."

She crossed her arms on the table and laid her head down.

Full custody. Why?

Camden never seemed to even want to be around the children. It didn't make any sense. Could he get it? Courts typically didn't change the custody without cause, but . . . He could say it wasn't safe for the kids to be in a house with a deaf woman. It wasn't true, but he could still claim it.

Would he stoop that low? Absolutely.

Annie's hand balled into a fist. She'd come too far to lie

down like a doormat again. There was no way she was going to let him get custody of her precious children.

She took out her phone, but before she could start a list of all the reasons why she was a fantastic mother, it buzzed with a text from Finn.

Sitting up like she'd just had a pot of coffee, she read:

I KNOW IT'S LATE BUT CAN I COME OVER TO SPEAK WITH YOU? REALLY GOOD NEWS.

Annie fired off her reply faster than a game show contestant pressing a buzzer before she realized how desperate it might seem.

YES!!!!!

She got up and hurried into the living room to see what state it was in. Between the remains of Tommy's fallen LEGO city and Tammy's canceled Barbie fashion show, the room was a disaster zone.

She closed her eyes and spoke to herself: "Deep breaths. Calm. Quiet." But when she thought about the last word, her eyes snapped open. She fired off another text.

DON'T RING THE DOORBELL—IT WILL WAKE THE KIDS!!!

Annie hit send and made a face. She sounded rude.

JUST COME IN WHEN YOU GET HERE.

She closed her eyes and pressed both her hands against her head. She felt like the Cat in the Hat and everything she was doing was just making the situation worse. She opened her eyes and Finn was standing in the open doorway.

He gave a little wave and said, "I texted from out in the driveway. Hi."

"Hi." Annie broke into a big smile until she realized how she was dressed. Pulling on the oversized T-shirt that doubled as her nightgown, she darted for the hallway—and stepped on a LEGO piece. Gritting her teeth against her rising pain and embarrassment, she tried to navigate the minefield, and her foot landed on a miniature pair of high heels that dug into her skin.

Clamping her hand over her mouth to keep from swearing, she made it into the hallway and rushed into her bedroom. Once inside her little sanctuary, she let fly with a stream of muttered, fictional swears. She'd lost so much cash to the swear jar she'd taken to making up her own oaths just in case the little ears out to make a quick buck were listening.

After throwing on a pair of jeans and a different T-shirt, Annie sheepishly headed back to the living room. Finn's excited grin wiped her lingering embarrassment away.

"They caught Jimmy red-handed!" Finn announced, holding out a check. "I stopped by Sai's and he paid the remainder of our fee."

"That's unbelievable."

"Jimmy used the gift card right away and picked expedited, two-day shipping. He had it sent to a mail pickup location and the police were waiting for him. And my sister got the credit."

Without thinking, Annie lunged forward and wrapped her arms around Finn. She squeezed him tightly, careful about his balance. As she held him, once again she was surprised by how muscular he was. He normally wore a suit that hid his physique, but with his rock-hard stomach, he had nothing to be ashamed of.

Finn hesitated a moment and then hugged her back. Annie smiled and snuggled against his chest. With all the poor man had been through, here in his moment he was thinking of others and giving a check to Annie and credit to Amelia. She gazed up at him and his hand gently moved up her back.

The lights of the living room flashed like a disco.

Tammy's panic button!

Annie rushed down the hallway with Finn following close behind. She whipped open Tammy's door, took two steps inside the room, and came to a stop as her bare feet stuck to the floor.

Tammy was sitting up in bed holding the now empty bear bottle. In spite of the tears on her cheeks, she had a huge grin on her face. "It worked! The honey kept the monsters away from my bed!"

Annie slowly turned her head to stare at Finn.

He chuckled nervously. "I didn't realize my bedtime story would . . . come true."

Annie laughed and signed to him: *Good trick. But messy.*

Tammy shook her head. "Of course it did, Finn. Don't be mad, Mommy." She lifted up her toy tiger. "Mr. Stripes can eat the honey." Tammy swung her arm and launched Mr. Stripes through the air toward the pool of honey on the floor.

Annie caught the stuffed animal an inch before it landed.

Finn placed a gentle hand on her back and warmth radiated through her. He signed, *I'll clean this up.*

Annie grinned at him and said, "We'll do it together."

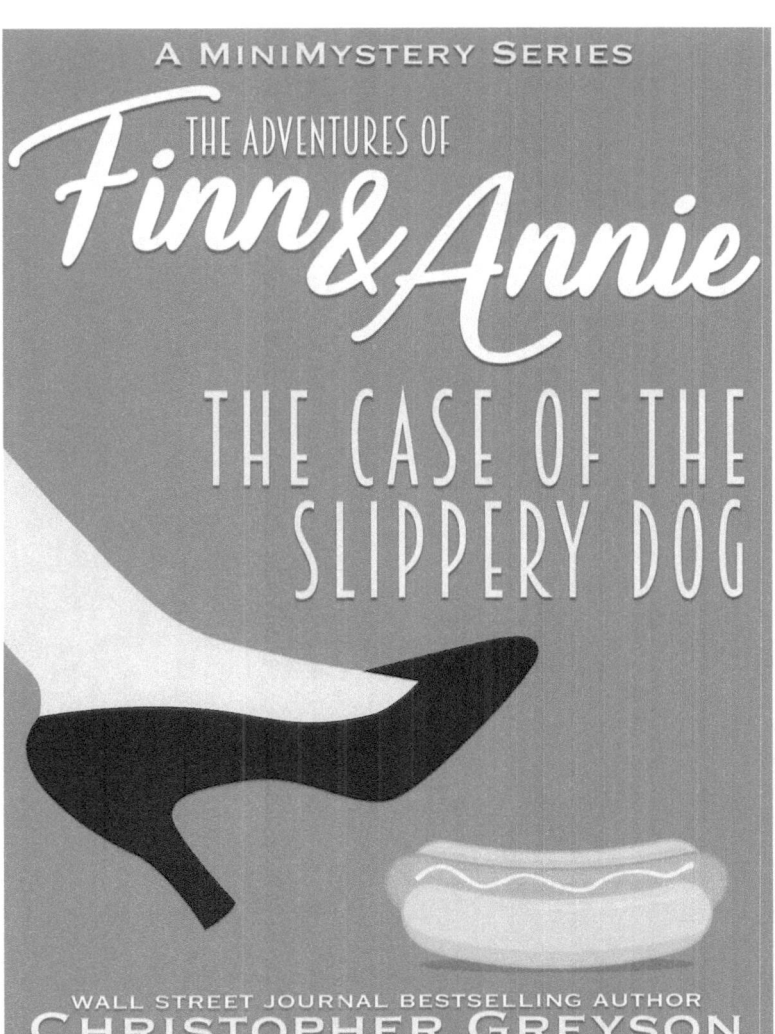

A MiniMystery Series

THE ADVENTURES OF

Finn & Annie

THE CASE OF THE
SLIPPERY DOG

WALL STREET JOURNAL BESTSELLING AUTHOR
CHRISTOPHER GREYSON

A MiniMystery Series

The Adventures of

Finn &
Annie

THE CASE OF
THE SLIPPERY DOG

WALL STREET JOURNAL BESTSELLING AUTHOR

CHRISTOPHER GREYSON

GREYSON MEDIA

CHAPTER 1

Annie brushed her hair as Tammy sat on the sink chatting happily away. Tammy was chewing gum, so the app that converted speech to text was having a difficult time understanding the little girl's rapid-fire story. Annie had a feeling that even if she could hear, she'd have a hard time understanding bubblegum-munching Tammy, who was telling her all about a dream she had last night. As usual, a lot of the words were made up, including all the names—like the unicorn she called Rainbow Dash Pinky Pie.

Satisfied that her blond hair was brushed to a golden shimmer, Annie chose lip gloss over lipstick, and added a dash of taupe eyeshadow to make her blue eyes pop.

"You look beautiful, Mommy." Tammy swung her legs.

"Thank you, princess. That was a fabulous dream."

Tammy nodded. "I need to tell Finn all about it."

At the mention of Finn's name, Tommy suddenly appeared at the bathroom door. "Finn's coming over? Did you ask him? What did he say?"

Annie sighed. "I didn't ask him, because I thought it would be best coming from you."

"Oh, come on, Mom!" Tommy whined. "Please?"

"No."

Tommy scowled and stormed down the narrow hallway.

"Why doesn't Tommy want to ask Finn to take him to Cub Scouts?" Tammy asked, her pigtails bouncing back and forth.

Annie leaned forward and did her best at what she thought was a whisper. "Sometimes it's tough to ask someone for a favor. But it's my job as your mommy to teach you to be independent and do things for yourself."

Annie reached out to lift her down off the counter, but Tammy shook her head. "I can do it. I'm in-dip-in-dent, too."

Annie thought about correcting her pronunciation, but the mangled word might have been the app's fault.

Tammy hopped down, pitched forward, and went face first toward the edge of the tub. Annie snagged her just before she smashed her nose on the porcelain.

"Thanks, Mommy," Tammy said, wide-eyed. "Maybe I'm still too little to be in-dip-in-dent."

Annie lifted her up on her hip. "Some things just take time. You're growing every day. Like a flower."

Lights flashed, signaling that someone had rung the doorbell, and Tammy wiggled like a fish in her arms. Tommy shot past the door and Tammy hopped down and chased after her brother toward the front door.

Annie took a deep breath and stood up taller. Determined not to fall apart like some love-struck teenager, she squared her shoulders as she walked into the living room—but when the kids opened the door and Finn smiled, she found herself grinning like she'd just won a two-week cruise to a tropical island.

Finn waved at her. "Good morning, Annie."

The kids were bombarding him with questions so fast the speech-to-text app was useless, and with their backs to her she had no idea what they were saying.

"Give Finn a chance to come in and have some coffee."

Annie tried to hold her miniature paparazzi back from the star in their lives.

"I want to tell Finn about my dream!" Tammy said. "I have good dreams now that you gave me Mr. Sticky Butt."

Finn's eyes went wide and Annie blushed. She texted Finn. *IT WAS MR. HAIRY BUTT OR MR. STICKY BUTT. LESSER OF 2 EVILS.*

Finn glanced at his phone and chuckled as he read the text.

Tommy pulled on his mother's sleeve and angled his head toward Finn.

"Tommy wants to ask you something," Tammy said.

Tommy scowled at his sister and rolled his eyes.

"What can I do for you, Tommy?"

Tommy looked up desperately at Annie.

The mom in her wanted to scoop her little man up and beg Finn to take him, but she shook her head. He needed to do some things on his own.

"Please?" Tommy pressed both hands together.

Tammy pulled on Finn's suit jacket and motioned for him to lean down. Annie was sure the little girl meant to whisper, but she spoke loudly enough that her app picked it up: "Mommy said we need to be in-dip-in-dent, so Tommy has to ask you *himself* to go with him to Cub Scouts."

Tommy's look of horror was replaced with hope. He stood there wringing his hands, awaiting Finn's answer.

"If it's okay with your mother, I'd be honored to go with—"

"Thank you!" Tommy did a little happy dance. "It's in two nights. Wait!" He raced down the hallway and came back a minute later holding a clear bag filled with a block of wood, metal rods, and four plastic tires. "I have to make this but I have no idea how."

"What is it supposed to be in the end?" Finn asked.

"A car."

"*That's* supposed to be a car?" Tammy made a face. "It looks like it blowed up."

Tommy swallowed.

Finn grinned. "It's a Co_2 racer!" With some effort, he squatted down in front of Tommy so he was on eye level with the little boy.

Annie was nervous about the strain Finn would feel, holding that position with his prosthetic leg, but she quickly realized two things: it would be crossing a line to intervene, and the way Finn was speaking with Tommy was exactly what the boy needed.

"I love these. I'd be glad to show you how to make the coolest racer ever!"

Tommy's whole body vibrated with energy, and when Finn held up his hand, he gave him a high-five.

Annie glanced at the clock. "Okay, you two need to get out front for the bus."

The kids kissed Annie and ran for the door, Tommy still carrying his bag with the racer parts.

"Tommy, you should leave that here."

"But I want to show my friends."

Annie was about to give in when Finn said, "If you forget it at school, we won't be able to work on it tonight."

"Oh, snap." Tommy dashed back into his room and darted right back out. "Thanks." He hugged Finn and headed for the door.

"I want a hug, too!" Tammy called out as she rushed over and claimed her hug from Finn. She kissed his cheek and said, "Thank you again for Mr. Sticky Butt."

The two kids raced out the door before Annie could even say goodbye. She hurried to the open door as the bus pulled up outside. "Tammy! Where's your bear?"

Tammy yelled something back, waved, and disappeared into the bus after her brother.

"What did she say?" Annie asked Finn, who was standing beside her waving at the kids.

"The bear is in her backpack. Tammy's taking Mr. Sticky Butt to school for show-and-tell."

Annie covered her mouth with her hand as she stifled a laugh. Tammy's teacher was a former nun. There was certain to be a note sent home today.

Deciding to change the subject, she asked, "Which kind of case do we have today? Private investigation or insurance?"

"Insurance." Finn smiled, but she knew he'd been hoping for another private investigation case since they had decided to start their own business together.

Annie was so grateful for the work—not only for the money but for the opportunity and the new skills she was developing. And now that Finn was splitting the money with her fifty-fifty, with some skimping and saving she had hopes of getting out of the red.

"If you're ready," Finn said, "we're off to the mall. Big Ben's Wholesale Club. Someone stepped on a dog and fell."

Annie's hand covered her mouth and her eyes went wide with alarm.

Finn shook his head. "No real dogs were hurt. A hot dog."

Annie exhaled loudly. "I'm glad."

"But Bridget Evans claims she was severely injured when she slipped and fell. She's already made several phone calls to the insurance agency, and they want us to go right out."

"I'll grab my bag."

Just as Annie turned to go, she saw a black Mustang with tinted windows turn on to her street. She didn't recognize the car, but as it slowly drove down the road, the hairs on the back of her neck prickled. She couldn't see the driver, but whoever it was, she sensed they were looking right at her.

CHAPTER 2

Finn and Annie walked through the doors of Big Ben's Wholesale Club and headed for the offices in the back of the store. It was just after eight, but the store was already filling and shoppers were waiting in line at the coffeeshop in the small food court.

Finn's mind was in overdrive as he noted a number of concerns for his report: a peeled-back corner of a linoleum tile, the overextended legs of a sale sign, an unsecured electrical cable snaking to a cooktop used to make samples—all hazards for tripping and falling.

Finn looked into the food court and grimaced. There were a number of poor safety practices on display there as well, but he had to concentrate on getting the facts from the manager first.

"Do you want anything to eat?" Finn asked Annie.

She gazed appreciatively at him with those big blue eyes and shook her head. Finn almost walked straight into a display stand. He managed to step aside at the last moment but wobbled precariously.

Annie grabbed his arm.

"Wasn't paying attention," Finn mumbled and kept walking.

"That display stand was too far out in the aisle," Annie said, defending him.

Finn glanced back. The stand was fine. Finn had simply been paying far too much attention to Annie to notice it.

They made their way to the far corner and stopped outside the door labeled *Office*. Finn knocked.

A harried-looking woman opened the door. She was short and shaped a little like a pear, and her green dress only added to that image.

"Good morning. We're Finnian Church and Annie Summers, from A. G. Maxwell Insurance."

"Oh, thank you." The woman stepped back into the office, motioning for them to follow. "Jan Miller, the general manager. The regular manager is out sick today. Probably over this. Poor guy is really torn up. He just got promoted and . . . I'll save you the drama. What do you need from me?" Jan sat behind a cluttered desk and motioned to the two mismatched chairs positioned in front of it.

Annie scooted over to the far one, for which Finn was grateful, because it saved him from having to navigate around a tall pile of papers on the floor. Finn made a note of it as yet another hazard.

"Do you have a report on the incident?" Finn asked, taking his seat.

"I just put it down here someplace." Jan looked distracted, touching the tops of the piles and setting off a mini-avalanche of paper. "Here it is!" She triumphantly plucked a manila folder off the tippy pile. "All the information is right here. Names, dates, times, DNA samples . . ." Jan laughed at her own joke.

Finn chuckled. "Were you here yesterday?"

"I was. This is actually my main office."

Finn did his best not to chastise her about her apparent complete lack of organizational skills. "Can you talk me through what happened, just as far as you're concerned?"

"I was in here when I heard the call over the intercom system. We use certain codes for incidents so as not to worry the shoppers. This call said we had a Code 88 in jewelry. That means someone was injured."

Finn jotted down notes as she spoke. "And the time of the call is listed in the report?"

Jan hesitated a moment, then nodded.

Sitting beside Finn, Annie opened the folder that Jan had given them.

"So I hurried—" Jan started to say, but Annie cut her off.

"I'm sorry to interrupt, but this isn't the accident report."

"What?" Jan's eyebrows traveled in different directions. "I'm sure it is."

Annie shook her head and handed the folder back to Jan. "It's inventory related."

"Oh, *that's* where I put that." Jan made a face and laughed. "I'd lose my head if it wasn't attached."

Finn believed her.

Jan went back to scanning the pile, and after two attempts at opening folders and scowling, she opened one and then handed it to Annie. "That's it."

"Thank you." Annie checked the folder and nodded.

Finn kept his hand low so Jan couldn't see it and signed, *No, thank you.*

Annie smiled.

"Now, where was I?" Jan took a sip of coffee and started speaking rapidly. "Oh, yes. So I hurried over to the jewelry department and there was a small crowd gathered around a woman lying on the floor. Three employees and a couple of shoppers were there. I shooed the shoppers away, but one man stayed. He said he saw the whole thing and was too upset to leave the poor injured woman."

"Kenny Draker?"

"Yes." Jan stared down into her coffee cup for a moment and

sighed. "There was a smushed hot dog on the floor. It had a lot of mustard."

"Was it just the hot dog? No roll?" Finn asked.

Jan's eyelids fluttered as she thought about it. "I didn't see any; nor did I pick one up." She leaned over, opened a drawer, and handed a clear plastic bag to Annie.

Annie's lip curled as she looked at the brown, greasy, squished contents of the plastic bag, which was bulging from the gases building up inside.

Jan smiled proudly. "I saved it as evidence. I also took photos." Once again, she started to search the mountain of papers on her desk until she located another folder.

Finn leaned over as Annie opened it and took a look. There were several photographs of the floor and the hot dog. Someone had placed numbered, folded-over index cards next to the hot dog and spots of mustard on the floor.

"I thought numbering would help," Jan said. "I'm a big fan of *Crime Scene Investigators.* I watch it every Tuesday night."

"So you think Bridget Evans is lying?"

"No." Jan shook her head. "I think she's telling the truth."

CHAPTER 3

Annie held her front door open for Finn. With the kids at school, they had the house to themselves, and Annie felt a bit of a flush rising up inside her at the prospect of being alone with Finn. As he smiled at her, she was tempted to kiss him then and there. The thought of throwing caution to the wind filled her with the same hopeful excitement as cresting the first hill on a roller coaster, but that feeling came shooting down as she considered the consequences.

What if he doesn't feel the same way I do? How awkward would that be?

Annie hurried over to the computer area. In addition to the report and pictures, Jan Miller had given them a flash drive with all the security footage for two weeks. Annie plugged the drive in and turned to Finn.

"Why did you ask Jan to give you two weeks of footage?" Annie asked. When he had made the request, she hadn't said anything because she would never undercut Finn in front of anyone.

"Because I doubt Bridget Evans's story," Finn said, pulling

up a chair beside her. "And if they did stage this accident, then they most likely performed recon of the target location."

Annie chuckled. "Recon. You sound like a soldier."

Finn blushed. "Is that a bad thing?"

"Not at all," Annie said. "You just never talk about it."

Finn stared at her for a moment like he was debating something. "It's hard to talk about. It's complex. Part of me really misses it. I felt like I was doing a lot of good. And there was so much to think about—it was like my mind was on full throttle all the time and I loved it."

"You're the same way about these investigations," Annie said. "We get a case and you light up like a little boy on Christmas morning."

Finn nodded. "I've always liked solving puzzles. I guess these cases remind me of puzzles with a lot of missing pieces."

Annie pointed at the contents list for the flash drive. "I just found twelve pieces. That's how many security cameras are in the store."

Finn frowned. "A store that size should have twice that many cameras. Can you please tile them on the screen?"

Annie arranged the security footage by camera number, moving them around so that all twelve were arranged on the monitor in a grid of four by three.

"I learned a new trick. Watch." Annie worked the mouse and clicked. "Synchronized scrolling!" She rewound the timeline and the footage in all twelve windows rolled back at the same time.

"That's going to make this so much simpler to do. Great job. Can you rewind until we reach around eleven o'clock?" Finn asked.

Annie scrolled back until just when Bridget fell.

"She's much younger than I thought," Finn noted as a young woman pushing a shopping cart came into view in the jewelry section. Bridget made one loop around the jewelry case, but as she reached the main aisle, she fell backward and landed on the linoleum floor.

"The display stand for Sylvester Stallone is in the way of the camera," Finn grumbled and he searched the other videos for a better angle.

Annie frowned. The cardboard cutout of Stallone flanked by two muscular men blocked the view of the floor exactly where Bridget fell, and none of the other cameras captured the fall.

"None of the other cameras are focused on the jewelry department." Annie shook her head. "That's our best shot."

"That's a problem." Finn rubbed his chin.

"I agree." Annie crossed her arms. "That shot stinks. You can't really see anything."

"Actually, you can see a lot. I want to see more, though."

Annie made a face. "What do you mean you can see a lot? All I saw was Bridget shopping and then falling."

Finn pulled his chair closer to hers. "Do you mind if I rewind?"

He smelled like cedar with a touch of mint. She blinked twice and stared into his amber eyes. "Ah . . . sure."

Like a magnet, Annie was drawn to him. She jammed her arm against the side of her chair to keep from leaning closer. She was even starting to sweat.

Finn rewound the footage a few minutes and pressed play. "Watch Bridget as she comes over to the jewelry counter."

Annie stared at the screen as Bridget pushed her cart and made her way around the jewelry case.

Finn paused the video. "See how her head is angled?"

"She's looking at the floor!" Annie patted Finn on the back, but in her excitement she hit him harder than she'd meant to—in fact, her hand was stinging. "Sorry!"

Finn grimaced and arched his back. "Boy, you really pack a wallop."

"I'm so sorry! Did it really hurt?" She started rubbing his back.

Finn made a face. "I'm just joking. I'm fine."

Annie kept rubbing and Finn kept staring at her. The muscles in his back were as hard as rock. As she made small circles with her hand, she pressed with her thumb, but it was like pushing against marble.

"Wow, you're really jacked," she blurted out. Blushing from ear to ear, she put her hands in her lap.

"Thanks. I traded my love of cardio for weight training," Finn said. He cleared his throat and pointed back at the screen. "Watch Bridget as she goes around the counter."

He pressed play again. Bridget casually strolled around the display case. Every time she reached a corner, she leaned forward and glanced ahead at the floor.

"Oh, she's totally checking out the floor."

"That's what it looks like to me," Finn said. "Now watch as she reaches the last corner."

Bridget repeated her actions of leaning forward and peering at the floor, and when she reached the last corner, she straightened up and looked around the whole store.

"Is she checking to see who's around?" Annie asked.

"I think that's exactly what she's doing."

"Oh, she just sees the hot dog now! She couldn't see it before because of the display case." Annie raised her hand to give Finn a high-five, but he leaned away from her.

She knew she was blushing again. "I wasn't going to pat your back again."

Finn laughed. "I'm teasing you." He high-fived her waiting hand.

"Wait a second. Did you solve this already?"

"Not even close," Finn said. "We may need more than this. A good lawyer could argue that she was just shopping."

Annie shook her head. "That's ridiculous."

"That's why insurance is so expensive," Finn said.

"Maybe if we rewind the footage, we can see how the hot dog got on the floor in the first place."

Finn smiled, his eyes dancing with hers. He seemed overjoyed that his business partner's instincts were so on point. He signed, *Go, Annie!*

She expertly rewound the footage until a tall, youngish man came into view, holding a hot dog in one hand and pushing a shopping cart with the other. As he walked down the aisle, the Stallone cutout blocked him from view. He paused for a moment and then kept going.

"We can't see anything because of Rainbow!" Annie frowned.

Finn chuckled. "What? You mean Rambo?"

Annie's blue eyes sparkled. "You're right." She blushed. "I don't know what I was thinking."

"Can you rewind it ten minutes and switch over to the food court cameras?"

"Sure. Why?"

"If he paid with a credit card for the hot dog, we can figure out who he is."

"You're brilliant."

A couple of minutes later, Finn's theory was confirmed. The man had paid with a card. Annie wrote down the time and printed out a still picture of the man. She was reaching for the printer when Finn suddenly leapt to his feet and turned around.

He had to grab the edge of the desk to steady himself and Annie took hold of his other arm.

"Easy there," Camden said to Finn from the doorway. "I didn't mean to scare you. I'm here to talk to my wife."

CHAPTER 4

"Ex-wife," Annie said, feeling in her chest how loudly she spoke. She stood up and marched over to the front door. "And you can't just walk into my house."

"Our house." Camden held up his hand with his index finger tipped slightly toward her, like a teacher correcting a child. "It's still fifty percent mine."

Annie's hands balled into fists. After the divorce she couldn't afford a mortgage on her own, and she'd been a stay-at-home mom. The judge ordered that they keep the house in both names, keeping both on the hook for six years. This would give Annie time to establish a work history, save some money, and apply for a mortgage on her own. If she did not secure a mortgage within six years, the house would be sold and they would split any proceeds after satisfaction of the mortgage. It seemed like a good plan at the time. The kids got to stay in the only home they had ever known and be near their friends and school. In hindsight, she should have burned that bridge and gotten a small apartment for her and the kids.

Annie stuck her chin out in defiance towards her former oppressor. "That doesn't mean you can come in here whenever you want." She could feel her leg shaking. The ex-professional baseball player liked to fight. Would Camden try something with Finn right there?

"Actually, I can." Camden crossed his arms and smiled smugly at Finn, almost daring him to do something.

"Sorry, but actually you can't." Finn met his gaze unflinchingly. "Pursuant to Article 57B of the Equity and Fair Housing Act, since Annie and the children are living here full-time and you are not, you legally have to get her permission to enter."

Annie crossed her arms and nodded vigorously. "So leave. Now."

"Hold on a second." Camden pulled an envelope from his pocket. "This is the formal notification that I'm seeking full custody." His snake-oil salesman smile returned. "And I'm selling the house."

"What? You can't—"

"According to the lawyer I consulted, I sure can. I'm putting it on the market next week. I got a new job in the city. I'm moving out of this dung pile of a town." He waved the envelope under her nose.

Annie felt like the floor shifted beneath her. How could he do this? She gazed up at Camden, ready to beg him not to sell the house out from under her, but one look at his smug face hardened her resolve. "Get out."

"You can't stop it, Ann." Camden flicked the letter and it bounced off Annie's chest.

She flinched and her eyes welled with tears.

"Let's go have a talk outside, Camden," Finn said, his voice steady but firm.

Camden scoffed. "You're gonna fight me?" He looked down at Finn's leg.

"No one said anything about fighting. I just want a conversation with you outside."

Annie moved between the two men. She was all ready to

burst into tears and now she was filled with terror at the thought of Camden taking his anger out on Finn.

"Finn, no. Please."

"Don't be so dramatic, Ann. I'm not going to fight a cripple." Camden made sure every mean word was clear on his lips for Annie to read.

The muscles in Finn's jaw flexed.

Annie wanted to kick Camden in the groin and knock him down to size, but Finn placed a restraining hand on Annie's arm.

"I was trying to treat you like a man and speak with you privately," Finn said. "But if you want to have the discussion here and now, that's fine. Your new job is with WXLM sports radio."

Camden raised an eyebrow. "You've been checking up on me?"

"I'm an investigator. That's what I do. But I'm not sure that you looked into WXLM besides listening to the broadcast. Did you?"

"Of course I did." Camden pulled at his ear, a sure sign he was lying.

"Then you are aware that the owner, Tracy Marinarti, was a single mom who raised two kids on her own."

Camden's smile started to fade.

"And I'm *sure* that you know she's deaf. How do you think she'll feel about one of her employees putting the deaf mother of his children out on the street? I can tell you what Tracy said about her own abusive ex-husband. She felt he should be chemically castrated. I wonder what results a meeting with her and Annie would produce?"

Annie wanted to clap. Finn had just given Camden a verbal smackdown that left him looking like the one about to cry.

"I'll hold off on selling the house until I get full custody."

Camden stormed over to the door and turned around to glare at Annie. "But this isn't over."

"One more thing." Finn strode over to stand nose to nose with Camden. "You need to get permission before you come by here. If you try to just walk into the house again, you'll be arrested for breaking and entering."

Camden glared at Finn. "I tried to be civil about all of this. But if you keep getting in my face, we're going to have a problem."

"Leave, now." Annie held up her phone. "Or I'm calling the police."

"I'm going." Camden yanked open the door and stormed down the steps.

Annie breathed a sigh of relief, but it caught in her throat when he turned back around.

"Hey, crip." Camden smirked at Finn. "Tell you what, if you do want to come out here and get in my face, I'll only use one hand." He tucked his left hand behind his back. "Or did you lose more than your leg in the war?"

Finn started forward, but Annie slammed the door shut.

"Open the door, please," Finn said as Annie blocked his way.

"Why? Do you really want to explain to Tommy and Tammy that you beat their father up because he called you names?"

Finn's amber eyes blazed and his nostrils flared. He stared down at Annie and his face softened. "I apologize. When I get around you, I start acting like a hormonally challenged teenager." He shook his head. "Some jerk calling me names wouldn't normally bother me, but in front of you, I, uh . . ." He put both hands on the back of his neck. "I'm going to stop talking now."

Annie grinned. "Not before I thank you. I don't recall anyone ever standing up to Camden. Did you research that Fair Housing code?"

Finn smiled lopsidedly. "It is a law, but I made up the

number. I just wanted to get him to shut up and get out. So I made up the specific code. I apologize."

"Don't." Annie laughed. "It worked." Her smile trailed off as she recalled Finn talking about Camden's new job. "Why did you research Camden?"

Finn crossed his arms. For some reason that action didn't come off as threatening to Annie. With Finn, it seemed more like a defense.

"From what you've shared about him and how he behaved at Tommy's T-ball game, Camden seemed like bad news that wasn't going away." Finn shrugged. "The soldier in me always says be prepared. I hope I didn't overstep."

Annie's stomach tightened as she thought about her next question. "Did you research me?"

Finn shook his head. "I was tempted, but . . . that was clearly crossing a line. Besides, I figure you'll tell me what you want to about yourself. Anything else is private."

Annie started breathing normally again. Camden had posted horrible, vindictive things about her on the internet after the divorce. They were blatantly untrue, but the thought of Finn encountering any of it made her sick to her stomach. She already knew that Finn was a gentleman, but his assurance that he hadn't read those terrible things about her made her embarrassment begin to face. "Thank you."

Finn glanced over her shoulder, and she felt the pounding of the children's feet up the back steps and the door slamming. A second later, the kids raced into the room and stood before her, trembling.

"Is he gone?" Tommy asked.

"We saw his car." Tammy wrapped her arms around Annie's leg.

Finn's eyes widened in understanding and a look of shock and disgust spread across his face. He stepped closer to Annie.

"He's gone. Everything's fine," Annie said, stroking their hair and hugging them.

Finn waved his hand to get her attention and mouthed, *I'm going to get going.*

"You can't leave," Tommy said. "You were going to help me with my car."

Finn raised an eyebrow. "How did you know what I said?"

Tommy grinned impishly.

"Can you read lips, too?" Finn asked.

"Mom's teaching me."

"I can, too!" Tammy said. "Say something."

Hello, Finn mouthed.

Tammy wrinkled her nose. "Candy?"

Tommy laughed and she shot him a dirty look.

"Let's try again," Finn said. He mouthed *Hi,* and gave a little wave.

"Hi!" Tammy lit up.

"You cheated!" Tommy started to point, but Annie wrapped a hand over his. She smiled at Finn. "So, you're staying."

"Are you sure you don't need a break?" Finn asked.

Annie nodded. "I do, but I don't want you to leave. How about you and Tommy work on the car and I make you supper after?"

Finn nodded. "But do you mind if we change the deal a little? I'll help Tommy with the car, and then I'll take everyone to Big Ben's Wholesale Club for hot dogs and pizza."

Tammy and Tommy broke into a little jig and Annie melted. Finn's offer meant more than a dozen roses to her. And the fact that he read her emotional needs so clearly made her want to wrap her arms around him and lay her head on his chest.

Tammy poked Annie's side. "Say yes, Mommy."

"That would be wonderful."

CHAPTER 5

After working for almost two hours on Tommy's racer and getting the block of wood down to the rough shape of the car, they all headed over to Big Ben's Wholesale Club. As they pulled into the parking lot in Finn's car, with Annie beside him and Tommy and Tammy giggling and peering out the windows in the back, Finn felt . . . whole. He couldn't put his finger on exactly what it was, but he was calmer than he ever remembered feeling. He didn't have much experience with children, or even dating, for that matter, but for some reason he felt like he could not only handle this but excel at it.

He parked in a space near the sidewalk that led directly to the store. Annie glanced over her shoulder at the empty spaces closer to the front of the store. Finn's confidence took a direct hit as he second-guessed his parking decision.

"I parked here because of the sidewalk. Tammy seems pretty excited and I didn't want her crossing the street."

"I am excited!" Tammy tapped her feet on the floorboards.

Annie stared at Finn like he was from Mars. She suddenly leaned forward and kissed his cheek. "You are the most thoughtful man in the world."

In the back seat, the kids froze. They looked back and forth between themselves and Finn and Annie, before Tammy giggled.

"Mommy, you—"

"Who wants hot dogs and pizza?" Annie almost shouted, her face flushed.

"Me!" both kids screamed in unison and struggled with their seat belts.

Finn was surprised when they got out of the car and Tammy took his right hand, but when Tommy took his left, he was truly shocked.

Annie mouthed, *Wow*, and gave him a thumbs-up as they walked between the large glass doors and headed for the food court.

Finn turned to Annie. "I'd like to walk around after we eat. I also need to speak with the manager and see if she can pull the credit card receipt for the man who bought the hot dog."

Annie nodded.

Tammy and Tommy looked like they were about to explode with excitement when they reached the food counter. Finn smiled down at the kids. "What do you guys want?"

Tommy started chewing his bottom lip. "I don't know! I can't decide between pizza or a hot dog."

"Why don't you get both?" Finn offered.

Tommy's mouth fell open and Tammy grabbed his arm. "Seriously?" Tommy asked.

Finn nodded. "And pick out a drink. Those icy, slushy things look good."

"We can have our own drink?" Tammy's eyes went wide.

"We usually all split one," Tommy said.

Finn looked at Annie and she shrugged. "I try to give them treats once in a while, but eating out is expensive."

"Well, today they get their own drinks, and as far as dessert is concerned—"

"Let's hold off on a dessert discussion until we've eaten and walked around the store to digest a bit," Annie suggested.

With the prospect of slushies, pizza, and hot dogs, the kids didn't argue. Finn ordered the food, and after they were done eating, he headed for the manager's office while Annie and the kids walked around the store.

Jan had gone home for the day, but after making a couple of phone calls seeking permission, the covering manager pulled the receipt records. Finn couldn't help making a fist pump when he read the name of the man who bought the hot dog—Kenny Draker.

Finn marched out of the office and forced himself to slow down. With the prosthetic, he found that if his stride was too wide, it would throw off his balance. As he walked down the aisle, a child's wailing tugged on his heart. In spite of his fear of falling, he sped up.

Annie was carrying Tammy and the little girl was sobbing in her mother's arms.

Tommy noticed Finn and walked over. "She saw Mr. Feather Face," he said simply, like that was all the clarification Finn needed.

"Who is Mr. Feather Face?"

Tommy pointed to a large stuffed chicken on a shelf. "It's not really *her* Mr. Feather Face. He threw that out the car window."

"Your dad?"

Tommy scowled but nodded. "Yeah. Tammy kept playing with it in the backseat after he told her to stop."

"So he threw it out the window?"

Tommy nodded. "Mom wasn't there, so he wouldn't go back for it."

"If Tammy found it, why is she crying?"

"It costs seven ninety-nine." Tommy pointed at the sign. "That's a lot of money."

Finn grabbed the chicken off the shelf and marched over to Annie and Tammy. He handed the stuffed animal to the little girl, but she shook her head.

"No, thank you." She wiped away tears. "We can't afford it."

Annie closed her eyes until Finn touched her arm. "You actually earned it. Your mom and I are working a case, and since you're here with us, you should get paid, too."

Tammy gasped. "Really?"

Finn nodded. "How does ten dollars sound?"

Tammy looked at Tommy. "Is that enough to buy Mr. Feather Face?"

He nodded.

Tammy cheered, but just as soon as her arms shot up, they started to droop down. "But what about Tommy? Does he get paid, too?"

"Of course." Finn grinned.

The kids cheered. Tammy wiggled around until Annie set her down.

"Can I get a puzzle?" Tommy asked.

"Anything under ten dollars," Finn said.

"We'll be in the jewelry section right over there." Annie pointed. "Stay together."

"Sure!" Both kids disappeared into the toy section.

"Usually when they ask for toys while we're shopping, I tell them to put it on their birthday or Christmas list, whichever one is coming up sooner. It keeps me from saying no all the time. But it's been a long time since my budget has allowed me to say yes. So, thank you."

"A workman is worthy of their due," Finn said, remembering his grandfather, who frequently quoted the Bible. "Besides, seeing them happy is worth it."

"You're too sweet," Annie said.

Finn tried to smile but felt himself making a face. "I don't know if that's a compliment for a guy."

"It's one of the most important qualities to me in . . ." Annie's voice trailed off. She changed the subject: "There's that Stallone cutout." She pointed at the cardboard display that had obscured some of the view from the video cameras. "She must have slipped right here."

Finn stopped at the other side of the display and pointed down. "There's still a faint mustard stain on the floor." He scanned the ceiling. "I don't see any other cameras."

"Neither do I." Annie frowned.

Tommy and Tammy came racing down the aisle toward them.

"Don't run," Annie cautioned as she held up a hand.

"That was fast," Finn said.

"Look what I got!" Tommy held up a robot warrior that flashed its eyes and opened its wings when he pressed a button. "It was in clearance for nine ninety-nine. Can I get it?"

"It's less than ten dollars!" Tammy pranced around in a circle, rocking her stuffed chicken back and forth and singing to it.

"Sure you can." Finn grinned.

"Hey!" Tammy pointed into the electronics section. "Look! Mr. Feather Face and I are on TV!"

Finn turned around. A camera on sale was pointed in their direction and the image of all four of them was being broadcast on the largest television on the wall. Tammy waved and danced about while Tommy started sticking out his tongue and making faces.

Finn's mouth dropped open. He rushed over to the counter and flagged down a salesman, hope rising in his chest. "Does that camera record video?"

"Over two hundred hours with the extra memory drive."

"Is it recording now?"

The man checked the camera and nodded.

"I need that footage!" Finn handed the man his insurance card. "It's evidence."

The kids and Annie laughed as Finn did a happy dance.

CHAPTER 6

Annie plugged the memory stick from the electronics department into her computer as Finn pulled up the chair next to her. Tammy was busy playing with Mr. Feather Face and Tommy was getting dressed for Cub Scouts.

Finn watched the monitor with all the excitement of Jacques Cousteau scanning the ocean floor for mysterious creatures of the deep. The file loaded and Annie rewound the video until she saw the three of them laughing while Finn danced. She pointed at the date and time stamp on the corner of the screen.

"You're ingenious!" Finn patted her leg and a thrill raced through her body. Not just at his touch, although that was a large part of it, but also at his words. She wasn't used to being complimented.

She rewound the video until just before the time of the slip and fall written in the report. Kenny Draker pushed his cart down the aisle. As he passed the Stallone cutout, he stopped, looked around, and flicked the hot dog, slick with mustard, out of the bun and onto the floor.

"Got him!" Annie held up her hand and Finn returned her

high-five, but he wasn't grinning as broadly as she thought he would. "What's wrong?"

"Nothing." He forced a smile on his face.

She raised an eyebrow to convey her doubt.

Finn exhaled. "Proving fraud is incredibly difficult. His lawyer could come up with some fanciful excuse and they walk." He took out his phone and checked his email. "I requested background checks on Kenny and Bridget, but they haven't come through yet."

"They have to be in on it together." Annie frowned.

"Don't get upset." Finn turned to face her. "The evidence we have right now might be enough for a conviction, and who knows what the background checks will produce?"

Tommy ran out of his room, carrying his race car and dressed in his Cub Scout uniform. He stood at attention and smiled proudly as he held his car out. "Do you like my car, Mom?"

Annie looked at the slightly lopsided block of wood that had been painted blue, with what she thought were supposed to be red flames.

"I wanted to do most of it myself, but Finn helped me with the tough parts."

Annie brushed Tommy's hair out of his eyes and resisted the urge to scoop her little guy up into her arms. "It's fabulous. Really cool."

"I bet it's the fastest car there!" Tommy made racing sounds and zoomed the car down an imaginary race track only he could see. "Are you sure you want to go?" he asked Finn, his voice cracking.

"Are you kidding? And miss seeing you race this car? I am so going!" Finn smiled and turned to Annie. "We'll be back in a few hours."

When Tommy turned his back to her, Annie signed, *Thank you.*

Finn winked.

Annie watched as they headed down the steps toward Finn's car. Tommy was talking a mile a minute. She couldn't tell what he was saying, but it didn't matter. Finn was listening to him. Finn was giving Tommy his undivided attention, and right now that was what her son needed most.

****

Annie paced back and forth in front of the window, peering down the road each time a car's headlights lit up the street. It had been almost three hours since they left. She was dying to find out what had happened.

She glanced down at her phone again. There was no message from Finn.

Tammy walked past Annie, placed her hand against the window, and stared out at the darkness. Another car appeared and the little girl started to wiggle like a puppy excited to go for a walk. When the headlights turned in at their driveway, both Tammy and Annie cheered.

"We don't know how it went," Annie said, suddenly panicked, as she imagined Tommy teary-eyed after losing the race, rushing in and heading straight for his bedroom.

That would be the case if he had gone with Camden. Her ex-husband wouldn't have comforted him the way Finn would.

Annie sat down on the couch and picked up a photography book. She pointed at Tammy. "Act casual."

Tammy nodded, grabbed a magazine off the table, and climbed to the other side of the couch.

Annie glanced over at her and stifled a laugh. Her five-year-old partner in crime was pretending to read an old copy of *TIME* upside down.

The front door whipped open and Tommy rushed in clutching two little gold trophies, one in each hand.

Tammy threw the magazine high into the air. "You won! Tommy won!"

Annie clapped and Tommy barreled into her with a huge hug. His cheeks were rosy red and he was trying to catch his breath.

"I lost the race," he said with a big smile on his face.

Finn appeared and both Tammy and Annie turned to him for an explanation.

"I'll let Tommy tell you what happened," Finn said, closing the door behind him.

"It was awesome!" Tommy moved to the center of the living room like it was a stage. "Everybody loved my car. It got voted *most coolest!*" He set the trophy in his left hand down on the coffee table and Tammy scooped it up.

"It's so pretty," she said, admiring the shiny gold car affixed on top of the winner's cup.

"It's cool," Tommy corrected her. "I came in fourth in the race, but that's because the wheel wobbled, so it's totally okay." He winked at Finn and gave him a thumbs-up.

Finn returned the gesture to Tommy, but glanced at Annie and gave her a wink.

Her heart soared. He was so different to Camden. Instead of berating Tommy for making the car wrong and bringing disgrace to his legacy, Finn had made the loss a teachable moment.

"What's the other trophy for?" Tammy asked.

"The car race wasn't the only race tonight. They had a race for the boys and the guys who took them."

"What kind of race?" Annie asked, once again panicking inside, this time about how Finn would feel with his prosthetic.

"A three-legged running race!" Tommy grinned broadly.

Annie wanted to throw up. Here Finn had volunteered to take her son to Cub Scouts and found out that it involved a foot race. She mouthed, *I'm so sorry.*

Finn signed, *It's OK. You'll see.*

Tammy asked what Annie was thinking. "How did you get a trophy? Finn can't run with the metal leg, can you, Finn?"

"I'll let Tommy tell you." Finn grinned impishly.

"That's what I thought," Tommy said, "and I told Finn we didn't have to do it, Mom. But when Bobby said I was chickening out, Finn said he'd do it and we were going to win!"

"Is Bobby Martinez still bullying you?" Annie fumed. "I'll call the Cubmaster and—"

"It's all cool now, Mom. Bobby and I are friends."

Annie raised an eyebrow. Bobby had been mean to Tommy for almost a year.

What brought on the sudden about-face?

"Tell me about the race already!" Tammy clamped both hands to the sides of her head. "I'm gonna die!"

"Finn and I went up to the starting line. They tied a rope to one of my legs and Finn's metal one. I was thinking, this is a bad idea and Mom's gonna kill me—"

Tammy laughed and Annie nodded.

"But Finn said, 'Don't worry.' Then he started doing stuff with the straps on his metal leg. And he said, 'Whatever happens, just listen to me and run. We'll win, okay?'"

Annie found that her own heart was racing as she raptly listened to the story.

"So the starter says, 'On your mark. Get set. GO!'" Tommy's smile was so big it hurt Annie's cheeks. "And then Finn yanked off his leg!"

Tammy screamed.

"The metal one!" Tommy rolled his eyes.

"Oh!" Tammy giggled.

"Finn handed me his leg and yelled, 'RUN!' So I did. I ran and ran. Everyone was looking at me really weirdly until they figured out what was going on. Then all the kids and their dads were cheering me on. I won!"

Annie gazed at Finn with newfound respect. She was well aware of how nervous he was about anyone staring at him because of the prosthetic. But he'd faced that fear for her son.

Annie walked over and kissed Finn on the cheek. Her mouth brushed his lips but she didn't care. As Tammy and Tommy cheered in the background, Annie gazed into Finn's eyes and realized that she'd fallen in love.

CHAPTER 7

F inn pulled his car over across the street from Bridget Evans's apartment. The background checks on her and Kenny had come back while he was at the race with Tommy. Neither of them revealed a connection between Bridget and Kenny. If they were going to prove fraud beyond a reasonable doubt, Finn needed to find the connection.

In spite of his frustration, Finn smiled as he inhaled the faint scent of lily of the valley. Annie's perfume still clung to his shirt. He closed his eyes. She'd hugged him for a long time tonight and her kiss had brushed his mouth.

He picked up his phone, tempted to call her and ask her out right now, but . . . why would she want . . . less?

Finn opened his eyes and his reflection glared back at him. He had to stop thinking about himself like that, but like a playlist stuck on repeat, self-loathing was on a constant loop. The encounter with Camden certainly hadn't helped things. He had a few four-letter words besides *jerk* for that piece of work.

The door to the apartment across the way opened and Bridget appeared, followed a moment later by Kenny. Finn started taking pictures with his phone as the couple descended the steps and got into a car parked at the curb. Once inside, Kenny leaned over and kissed Bridget.

Finn's excitement was short-lived. *What if they say that they met at the scene of the accident?*

Finn scowled as he watched them drive off. He needed to prove they knew each other before the slip and fall. Kenny and Bridget had each entered Big Ben's Warehouse Club separately and they left that way, too—Bridget by ambulance. Both had also denied knowing the other in the insurance claim.

They can say they just met. How am I going to disprove that?

The door to the apartment next to Bridget's opened and a man carrying a trash bag came out and trotted down the steps. Finn shoved open his car door and hurried as fast as he could across the street.

"Excuse me!" Finn called out as the man set the bag down on the curb and started back around. "Sir, I just need to ask you a quick question."

The man eyed Finn suspiciously.

"Are you a neighbor of Bridget Evans?"

"I am. Why?"

"My name is Finnian Church." He handed the man his card. "I'm with A. G. Maxwell Insurance." He took out his phone and opened the picture of Kenny. "Have you seen this man before?"

"I wish I hadn't! He's Bridget's rock-star-wannabe boyfriend. Plays the guitar to one o'clock in the morning." A stream of oaths and curses flowed from the man's mouth, followed by him spitting on the sidewalk.

Finn tried to push down his rising excitement. "Are you saying that you've seen this man before the beginning of this week?"

"He's been living next door for almost a year! I've

complained to the supervisor plenty of times. He'll back me up."

"Can I get you to put that in writing?"

"In a heartbeat. That is the rudest couple that ever walked the face of the earth." The man let loose with a long stream of swears again. "Just bring by whatever you want me to sign to Unit 16B."

"I will. And thank you!" Finn headed back to his car feeling like he was on top of the world—but when he saw who was waiting for him, his world came crashing back down.

Standing next to his car, wearing his favorite blue dress and looking like a million bucks, was his former fiancée, Karen. The time apart had been good to her. She lived for CrossFit, and it showed in her toned muscles and shapely curves. She'd gotten her breasts enhanced two years ago. Finn preferred the natural look she had before, but they still drew the eye.

He marched forward, determined to take the high road.

"Karen." He nodded as he stepped up on the curb.

"Finn." She said his name and the memory of their old love flickered somewhere inside him like wind stirring a day-old campfire. "I've missed you." She stood blocking the driver's door.

"I never read your letters." Finn decided to lay it all out honestly. No games. No agenda. "What we had is done. Let it stay dead."

Karen shook her head. "I can't believe that. Not what we had. Do you remember Acapulco?"

How could he forget? It was the vacation they took right before he went into the service. They made love like rabbits and ran along the beach like wild horses before making love there, too.

"I was a different man then."

Karen shook her head again. "That's where you're wrong. You keep thinking you're different because you lost your leg, but you're not. You're the same man. And with the right training, you can do everything we used to do together."

Finn smiled. He almost laughed. *Training. She makes me sound like a pet on a leash.* Karen hadn't changed at all. She still wanted the old Finn back. What she didn't understand was that even if he hadn't lost his leg in the war, the war had changed him. And the old Finn was as gone as his leg.

"I'm sorry, Karen." Finn inhaled. "It's over."

Karen stepped closer to him. "It will never be over, Finn—"

A baby's cry filled the night air. Karen rushed to the car parked in front of Finn's, reached inside the open window, and popped a pacifier into the mouth of the wailing infant. Finn peered over her shoulder into the backseat and into a pair of very familiar eyes—his own.

THE ADVENTURES OF

Finn & Annie

THE CASE OF LIGHTNING STRIKES TWICE

WALL STREET JOURNAL BESTSELLING AUTHOR

CHRISTOPHER GREYSON

A MiniMystery Series

THE ADVENTURES OF
Finn & Annie

THE CASE OF LIGHTNING STRIKES TWICE

WALL STREET JOURNAL BESTSELLING AUTHOR
CHRISTOPHER GREYSON

GREYSON MEDIA

CHAPTER 1

Finnian Church ran his hand through his hair and stared into the bathroom mirror. He felt the heartburn he'd tried to snuff out with a handful of pastel-colored tablets an hour ago still smoldering. "I should rethink this, Dad."

"Don't be silly." Howard Church smiled as he leaned against the doorframe of the bathroom. "You're going to have a nice time. I'm sure of it, Finn."

"I hope you're right. It's upstate, so it makes sense to stay overnight . . . and it is work, after all."

"Exactly." Howard nodded patiently. "Not a big deal."

"I shouldn't complicate it by inviting Annie to the wedding. That's what's bothering me. You always told me never to date someone I work with."

"So it is a date."

Finn could hear the excitement in his Howard's voice. "Not officially." Finn splashed on some aftershave and dried his hands as he spoke. "But it's a step in that direction."

Howard nodded again. "It is. But it's also a baby step."

Finn cringed at the last words and so did Howard. Finn stared back into the mirror.

Karen's baby has my eyes.

Is he mine?

"Not to change the subject, and I don't know quite how to say this . . . Your mother is going to reach out to Karen."

Finn's hand came down hard on the counter top. "Why?"

Howard placed a comforting hand on Finn's shoulder. "Because that baby is her grandchild. I'm not saying he's your son, but if he isn't, he's Arthur's. Karen wouldn't—"

"Wouldn't what, Dad?" Finn marched out of the bathroom and into the living room with Howard following after him. "She slept with my brother. I never thought that would happen, so I'm not ruling anything out."

"Don't they have paternity tests that give results pretty quickly?"

"They do, but not if the father's a twin." Finn grabbed his shirt off the chair and started to put it on. "Karen agreed to the testing and we've already submitted one. The problem is, the test can't differentiate between the DNA of identical twins. As far as the test is concerned, there's no difference between Arthur and me. This test will either rule both of us in or rule us both out. If there's a match . . . we won't know who's the father and who's the uncle."

Howard made a face and blew out a breath. "I'm sorry, Finn. How did Karen react to that?"

"She cried. She insists that the child is mine and that I'm being horrible to think so poorly of her." Finn grabbed his tie off the chair and started putting it on.

Howard crossed his arms. The retired policeman looked even older as the weight of the drama between his two sons got even heavier on his shoulders. "Karen made a mistake, Finn. It was one night. She was drunk. Who knows what Arthur was on?"

Finn tightened his tie and had to immediately loosen it a little. "I'm through with having my life be an open discussion in the family. I've done my best not to sully Arthur's name because of you and Mom. But it *wasn't* a one-night, drunken thing." Finn vainly tried to block out the memory of fixing Karen's computer and finding the emails. "They got together when I was in the hospital. They had an affair for over a month."

Howard stared at him in disbelief that slowly simmered into anger. "Arthur lied straight to my face. Are you certain?"

Now it was Finn's turn to scowl.

Howard glared at the wall. "I haven't wanted to put my fist through a wall since I was your age, but I'm certainly tempted right now."

"It's not worth breaking your hand over, Dad."

"I'm glad you take after your mother."

Finn shook his head. "I just got tired of patching the holes."

Howard smiled and changed the painful subject. "Where is the next case taking you?"

"Marshfield. It's right next to Darrington."

"Someday I have to meet this Jack Stratton and thank him for saving my son's life."

"Do you want to come with me to the wedding? Annie might say no to my invitation and you can be my plus-one."

"I'd be a terrible date. Besides, I don't do weddings." Howard laughed. "My own or my kids', that's it. Now stop worrying about what you don't have control over. Try to relax and go with the flow, buddy."

He hadn't called Finn his buddy in a long time. Finn felt a wave of gratitude wash through him. He was blessed with a wonderful, loving father, an amazing example of how to walk this earth as a man of integrity.

Finn walked past Howard and into the living room. He sat down in his favorite chair and began putting his socks and shoes on. He preferred a prosthetic that allowed him to wear two shoes.

His dad entered the living room looking tense. The muscles

in his father's jaw flexed, and Finn cautiously studied his face. "What's on your mind, Dad? You didn't drive over here to just say hi."

"No, I didn't."

"If you'd give me a call first, you wouldn't keep catching me getting ready for work, Dad."

"You're right. Maybe I've gotten a little too comfortable with the freedom of retirement and my drop-in visits." Howard nodded as he spoke. "Your mother said I should call you first so it wouldn't be a surprise. But this isn't a talk you can have on the phone." He glanced down at the floor before slowly, almost painfully, making eye contact with Finn. "This is tough stuff, Finn. Arthur insists the child isn't his. But if it is, he wants nothing to do with the boy."

"That's not a surprise and it's not my problem."

"No matter what, that child is family, son."

"It's not the kid. It's Karen. I don't want anything to do with *her*."

"You should have thought of that before you slept with her."

The words were a slap in the face. Howard might as well have added *I told you so*. He'd always warned his children about the possible consequences of premarital sex and now it certainly looked like Finn was reaping what he sowed.

"If the child is mine, I'll do the right thing, Dad. But if the boy is his, he's his responsibility."

"Arthur and responsibility have never gone together," Howard snapped. "He made it clear. He wants absolutely nothing to do with the child."

"What do you want me to do?"

"Talk with Karen." Howard wrung his hands. "Your mother wants you to let her know that we'd take the little guy in."

"What? Do you think Karen would ever—"

"You said yourself that you don't know what Karen would

do. If there's a possibility that raising him on her own is not in her plans, your mother wants Karen to know we are an option."

Finn ground his teeth. His ex-fiancée continued to crush his spirit even though they weren't together any longer. But what now? Howard was right. Chances are the child was family. It wasn't the boy's fault his paternity was in question.

And like it or not, he might be Finn's son.

CHAPTER 2

As Annie sat in her favorite reading chair by the window and watched the road for Finn's car, she felt like a lovesick teenager. She recognized the fluttering in her stomach and the giddy dreams circling in her head—and this was just because he'd texted her and asked if he could "come over for a minute to run an idea past her."

She laid her head down on the comfy chair but kept her eyes open. Some things about losing her hearing were harder to deal with than others. One was that she could almost never relax and close her eyes; her eyes had to work double duty now. When she closed them, she entered a void, a truly frightening place to be, like one of those sensory deprivation chambers she'd read about.

But Annie's biggest concern wasn't the darkness or the silence, it was the isolation from her children. What if they needed her? She peered over her shoulder into the empty living room. Both of the kids were playing in their rooms. She was so grateful they'd let her know they were coming up behind her by flicking the lights on or stamping on the floor so she could feel the vibrations. Camden used to take a cruel delight in scaring her. He'd laugh and say that making her scream was all in fun, but she was sure it was some kind of bullying power play. Picking on her for her disability made her feel weak ... and he knew it.

She peered at Camden's Facebook page again on her phone. Her ex-husband was now engaged to a former model whose biggest claim to fame was walking around a boxing ring in a bikini holding up a numbered card at heavyweight fights. Crystal Amedee.

Now it made sense to Annie why Camden was suddenly seeking full custody of the kids. Instant family. It was clear from Crystal's Facebook page that the silicone stunner wanted a child, but didn't want to chance ruining her "fabulous figure." Before she'd met Camden, which was only two months ago, she was looking to adopt. She even started a GoFundMe page asking for people to donate so that a needy child could be raised by a beautiful woman. To date the page had one $50 donation, which Annie suspected was from Crystal herself. The thought of losing custody and having Tammy and Tommy raised by her abusive ex-husband and that narcissist made Annie burn with righteous indignation. Over my dead body, or someone's dead body . . . Camden was her first choice, with Crystal a close second.

Movement in the driveway caught her eye.

He's here!

She'd been so preoccupied with her thoughts she hadn't noticed that Finn had pulled in and parked. She quickly closed the Facebook page and put her phone in her pocket.

One look at the tall, fit former soldier dressed in gray slacks, a neatly ironed white shirt, and a silvery-blue tie made her whole body tingle. She raced to the door and yanked it open, before realizing how desperate she must appear. She didn't have any experience dating. Camden was her high-school sweetheart . . . from Hell. But from what she saw on TV, playing hard to get was sometimes the best tactic.

She pretended to look down the walkway, then glanced up and smiled at Finn as if noticing him for the first time. "Ah, hello. I . . . was checking for the newspaper."

His face lit up. "You read a paper newspaper? I thought I was the only one left."

Guilt punched her in the gut. "Actually, no. I, ah . . . that was a poor attempt at a joke." She flushed and shook her head from side to side, sending her blond hair dancing on her shoulders. "No. I'm fibbing all over the place." She inhaled and then confessed in one long stream. "I was excited to see you, so I was sitting by the window waiting for you to come down the road, and then I got distracted, and when I looked again . . . there you were! So I whipped open the door, but then thought I should play it cool, so I pretended to look for a newspaper, and then I felt guilty after you said you read the paper, so I said I was joking, but I wasn't. I was fibbing." Annie's cheeks were nearing cherry red. "I'm not cool, Finn. I was sitting at the window waiting for you. It feels so much better telling the truth, even if I'm totally embarrassed."

She was glad to see that Finn's smile had remained in place and his eyes twinkled as he said, "I think I followed that. Is now a good time to talk?"

Something barreled into the back of Annie's legs and she pitched forward. Letting out a startled cry, she stumbled down the steps and into Finn's outstretched arms. Finn was so toned that smashing into his chest actually hurt a bit, but as his arms wrapped around her, she didn't care.

Tammy and Tommy appeared at either side of her.

"Sorry, Mommy," Tammy said. "I told my feet to stop but they didn't listen."

"Is now a good time for what?" Tommy asked Finn.

The tips of Finn's ears turned red as he gazed down at

Annie. Thank you, she mouthed, and forced herself to let go of him. Finn had arrived starched and pressed, military neat; his shirt now resembled crepe paper, and his pants were no better.

"What were you going to ask Mommy?" Tammy asked.

Finn ran his hands down the front of his shirt in a lame attempt to smooth it. "It's about our next case. It's an insurance case. A house fire."

"A house burned up?" Tommy asked, wide-eyed.

"It burned down," Annie corrected him.

Tammy shook her head. "Fire doesn't burn down, Mommy. It burns up."

Finn was grinning, and between his smile and Tammy's sparkling eyes, Annie completely forgot what they were talking about.

"Can we come?" Tommy asked. "I want to see the house."

"Me too."

"Not this time," Finn said apologetically. "It's all the way in Marshfield."

"That's a long drive," Annie said.

"Which is why the insurance company said it would put us up in a hotel. I think the investigation would take at least two days and, ah . . ."

Annie watched his lips carefully, not wanting to miss a word.

"A friend of mine is getting married this Saturday in the next town over, Darrington. Since we'll be up there, I was wondering if you'd accompany me."

Tammy and Tommy grinned impishly at each other, but Annie started to panic. What would she do with the kids? "I don't know if I could get a babysitter in time."

"I spoke to my parents and they said they'd be glad to watch the children. My father is a former policeman and my mother was a librarian. They love kids! We can run a background check on them if it makes you feel better."

Annie laughed. "On your parents?"

"I know how protective you are of the kids, and since you don't know my folks . . ." Finn put one hand on the back of his neck and loosened his tie with the other. "Maybe this is a bad idea."

"No!" Annie blurted out. "Let me ask the kids if—"

"Yeah!" Tommy and Tammy grabbed hands and danced in a circle. "Sleepover at Finn's."

"My parents' house," Finn clarified.

They stopped dancing. "Are they nice?" Tammy asked.

"Super-duper nice. My mom is already baking cookies."

"I love cookies!" Tammy hugged herself.

"Me too!" Tommy patted his belly. "When do we go?"

"First thing tomorrow morning, if everybody's ready." Finn smiled at Annie.

Annie, suddenly in a game of mental whack-a-mole, fought back the reasons that popped up like groundhogs begging her to back out. What if Tammy had a night terror? What outfit could Annie possibly slap together to wear to a wedding? A thousand fears and hesitations floated through her mind, but one look at Finn, so handsome and tall, waiting for her answer with hope in his eyes as the children danced around him, blew away all her doubts. "We'll be ready."

"Great!" Finn beamed. "I'll let my parents know."

The kids gave another cheer and rushed inside.

"I appreciate your lining up your folks to watch the kids. They're clearly excited."

"Happy to do it. I'm going to head out now. I'll see you in the morning." He signed, Eight o'clock OK? and Annie nodded eagerly.

Finn headed to his car, stopped, and turned back to face Annie. "One more thing. Just for the record . . . there's no one else I'd rather take to the wedding as my date." When the words hit Finn's own ears, he blushed and quickly got into his car.

Annie gave him a quick wave and bounded up the steps. She felt she could fly. Not only was she going on the road with Finn on another case, but she was going to a wedding with this wonderful man.

What could possibly go wrong?

CHAPTER 3

"You must be Annie." Finn's mother shook her hand and then leaned in to give her a big hug. "It's so nice to finally meet you in person."

"Thank you for recommending me for the job, Mrs. Church." Annie smiled.

"Please, call me Grace. It was Emily Thomson who thought you would be perfect for the position, and she was right." Grace smiled. "And now who might these two be?"

"I'm Tommy." Tommy stuck out his hand for a shake, but Tammy clung to Annie's leg and hid her face.

Annie said, "This is Tammy. She's sometimes a little shy."

"Oh, that's too bad." Grace shook her head. "I needed a big girl to help me with that big plate of chocolate chip cookies I just made."

Tammy looked up. "I can help!"

"Me too!" Tommy raised his hand.

"You're not a girl. She said she needed a big *girl* to help," Tammy said.

"I need a big girl *and* boy to help. There are lots of cookies."

Tommy and Tammy grinned.

"The kitchen is right through there." Grace pointed. "Why don't you two go in and wash your hands?"

"Give me a kiss first," Annie said.

Tommy and Tammy quickly hugged and kissed her and then darted down the hallway.

Grace smiled at Annie. "Finny said that you'd be gone four days with the travel. If it's okay with you, I arranged a couple of play dates with Finn's brother's and sister's children. Liam has three kids and Olivia has two. They're close to the same age as Tommy and Tammy, so I think they'll get along well."

"That sounds wonderful. I really appreciate you and your husband doing this."

"We appreciate all the help you've given to Finny."

Annie was tempted to check her speech-to-text app, but it looked like Grace had referred to Finn as Finny. The thought made the corners of her mouth tick up.

"Did you say Finny?" she asked.

Grace's smile widened. "I must say, your gift of reading lips is quite remarkable. I'm the only one in the family who refers to him that way. Habit. I've called him Finny since he was a baby."

"It's endearing."

"Is there anything I should know about the children?"

Annie ran down a long list of the likes, dislikes, fears, and quirks of the kids, before handing Grace two sheets of paper and Mr. Sticky Butt, the bear-shaped honey bottle that Tammy was convinced had the power to ward off monsters in the night. "Everything I've explained and my contact information is on there."

"You are thorough." Grace smiled. "And either your children are either extremely well behaved or my Howard is up to no good."

Annie followed Grace down the hallway and Finn's mother pushed open the first door on the right. Like three raccoons caught rooting through a trash bin, Tommy, Tammy, and Finn's dad stared up at them, wide eyed. Each sat in front of a plate of cookies and held a glass of milk in their hand.

"I was going to say that the children could have one cookie before lunch."

Finn's dad shrugged and grinned impishly. "I thought this was lunch."

The kids giggled.

"Annie, meet my other child, Howard," said Grace.

"Nice to meet you," Howard said—at least that was what Annie thought he said; his mouth was full of food, so it was difficult to be sure.

"It's a pleasure." Annie shook his hand.

"As you can see," Grace said, "the kids will have fun since my husband is the original Peter Pan."

Tammy's eyes went wide.

"That's right!" Howard gave a big laugh and grabbed his plate of cookies and milk. "Follow me to Neverland. Grab what you can."

Tommy and Tammy grabbed their plates of cookies and milk and chased after him, calling out, "Bye, Mommy. Love you!" before disappearing through the door.

"I hope you don't mind." Grace frowned. "I'll make sure they get an extra-healthy dinner. My big baby is probably showing them the tree fort he built for the other grandkids. It's perfectly safe. He installed railings all around it and even put in that outdoor rubberized playground padding below."

"I see where Finn gets his thoughtfulness."

Grace tilted her head slightly and gazed thoughtfully at Annie until she got the feeling that somehow Grace was looking straight inside her, examining what kind of person she was. Seemingly satisfied, Grace gently placed a hand on Annie's arm. "Thank you for helping Finn."

"I can assure you, Mrs.—Grace—it's the other way around.

Finn has done so much for me and the kids. I'm in his debt. And they love him."

Grace didn't say anything, but one eyebrow rose almost imperceptibly higher.

Annie cleared her throat. "I'm really looking forward to the wedding, too."

"Finny is over the moon about it. The groom—" Grace suddenly choked up. "I'm sorry," she said, turning her back to Annie.

Annie reached for her phone. It was clear Grace was not only crying but saying something, but her back was turned and Annie couldn't read her lips. The speech-to-text app wasn't perfect, though, and would delay Annie's reaction.

Laying her hand on Grace's elbow, Annie moved around to try to face her. "Can you say that again?"

"I'm sorry," Grace said, looking up at her. "You can't read my lips if I bury my face in my hands." She smiled, but it was tinged with pain. "The groom saved Finnian's life. I owe him a debt I can never repay."

Annie waited for Grace to continue, but instead she squeezed Annie's hand and shook her head. "It's not my place to tell you that story."

"What story?" Finn asked as he walked into the room.

Grace covertly wiped her eyes and smiled. "Oh, the one where you were a little boy and Dad had a piece of paper with a penny inside in his pocket—"

"Not that one." Finn shook his head. "Never." He leaned closer to his mother, a mock scowl on his face.

Grace kissed his cheek. "You'd better get going."

"Thanks a million, Mom." Finn kissed her back and turned to Annie. "I'd better get you out of here before she starts showing you my baby pictures."

Annie thanked Grace again and followed Finn out to the car.

Once they were on their way and Annie's butterflies of excitement had died down a little, she asked, "So what is this case about?"

"Patrick and Caroline Gallagher have submitted a claim for a house fire started by a lightning strike."

"Really? That's bad luck."

"I'd say so." Finn held up two fingers. "This is the second house owned by Mr. Gallagher that burned down after a lightning strike."

CHAPTER 4

Finn drove past the bed-and-breakfast where he and Annie would be staying, eager to look over the Gallagher case before checking in.

"That's where we're staying." He pointed at the former farmhouse.

Annie said, "Oh, look, it has a gazebo and a pond!" Her blue eyes sparkled. "I thought that the insurance company would put us up in . . . more modest accommodations."

Finn held his tongue. The truth was, A. G. Maxwell Insurance had only authorized enough to stay in the cheapest hotel in town, but Finn was covering the difference in cost out of his own pocket. Seeing Annie's smile was well worth it.

He headed down the main road and through the center of town until he reached an upscale lakeside community. There was no missing Patrick Gallagher's place. The once-grand home stood out like a black eye. One side of the charred house was almost completely destroyed and a blue tarp covered the roof. Plywood blocked up the windows and the lawn was churned into deep ruts—from the fire trucks, Finn presumed.

"I hope no one was home at the time of the fire," Annie said.

"They weren't here. This is their summer house."

"How bad is the damage?"

"The house has been declared a complete loss, but the Gallaghers also submitted a contents insurance claim for the personal property inside that was damaged or destroyed."

Finn turned down the driveway and parked. "The fire department has confirmed the fire was started by a lightning strike."

Annie raised an eyebrow. "Then why are we here? You can't *make* lightning hit your house. Are we just documenting what was destroyed?"

"We need to confirm that what Patrick claims was destroyed was actually destroyed. One common insurance fraud is the old bait-and-switch. Say you insure an entertainment system. You buy an old entertainment system and burn that one, and then you get the insurance money for the expensive entertainment system that you can continue to enjoy or sell."

"That's just plain wrong," Annie said.

Finn nodded. "It happens a lot. That's why insurance companies need investigators like us. False claims drive up everyone's insurance."

"Let's just hope that Patrick is one unlucky guy."

"Tell me about it. I order for that to happen, he has to be one of the unluckiest guys on the planet.

"We need to suit up for this," Finn said, reaching for a tote bag on the backseat. "When things burn, the residue left is loaded with toxins. I have Tyvek cover-up suits and booties for our shoes. If it's really bad, I have some wellies, too."

Annie stepped into her suit and zipped up the front. Finn stood shakily attempting to don his. Without a word, Annie reached out her hand and steadied him as he pulled the pant leg up and over his prosthetic. Grateful for her awareness of his needs and her gentle show of support, Finn smiled his thanks.

Annie looked at Finn's handsome face, the only part of him visible in the white suit, put her hands on her hips, and burst out laughing. "Oh, Finn. Do you know what we look like?"

"Oompa Loompas?"

Annie looked at Finn, puzzled. She took out her phone to use the speech-to-text app. "Like what?"

"Oompa Loompas. You know, the candy makers in *Charlie and the Chocolate Factory.*"

"Oh, ha, ha, ha. I was going to say we look like house painters, but I like Oompa Loompas better. We should take a picture to show the kids!"

Finn and Annie laughed and made silly faces, mugging for the phone's camera. It was Finn's first selfie, Annie's first fire investigation, their first trip together—and happiness and hope shone on both their faces.

While Annie got her video equipment out of the car, Finn inputted the entry code into the keypad affixed to the front door. They stepped inside together and took a first look around. The house still reeked of burnt material. In the foyer, it smelled like burnt carpet mixed with mold.

Finn pointed to the walls. "Please be sure to record all the water damage, too. A number of electronic items were ruined when the firefighters tried to save the house."

Annie gave him a thumbs-up and her bright smile. As she went to work, Finn found it hard to focus on the task at hand. In some ways, this house was like his own life. His once-promising career in the military and the one in law enforcement that he was so certain would follow had been set on fire in a bomb blast. His relationship with Karen had been collateral damage. Because of all of the surgeries, hospital stays, and rehab in the futile effort to save his leg, they spent more time apart than together. Karen had said she stayed away because it was too upsetting for her to see him in the hospital.

But distance hadn't made either of their hearts grow fonder. If Finn was being truthful with himself, he had realized during that time that their relationship was as unsalvageable as his leg. He had once been as shallow as Karen, but literally getting his legs taken out from beneath him had taught him a lesson he'd never known—humility. Karen had not been able to go down that road with him.

Now he had interesting work, and he was working with a woman who gave without being asked, and when asked gave double; who thought of her children's or his needs before she thought of her own; who made him laugh and feel hopes he'd forgotten he had ... Why did Karen have to show up now, when things were going so well, and try to drag him back into the past, or into a future with a baby he could never be sure was his? He was beginning to feel like Patrick Gallagher, struck twice by lightning.

As Annie hummed and methodically took pictures of the grim interior, Finn forced himself to refocus his attention. He made his way through the burned-out shell of a house, taking careful notes and following behind Annie from room to room, checking off items on the claims list.

It took almost two hours to meticulously make the rounds inside before Annie said, "I should get some shots of the outside, too."

Finn nodded, still lost in thoughts of the past clashing in an epic battle with his present. He shut and locked the front door before following Annie around the outside of the house.

This was his fault. It was wounded pride that had made him sleep with Karen that last time, after he came home from the hospital without his leg. If it weren't for his father, Finn would have let his pride kill him. He couldn't let go of his leg. He'd refused to let the doctors amputate, but when the infection spread and he slipped into a coma, Howard made the decision Finn was unable to make.

Karen was furious. She wept harder and longer than Finn. Crying about how this would affect *her* life. And when she questioned if he'd be able to perform as a man, he led her to the bed and gave the performance of a lifetime.

Still a fool.

And now what? Whose child is it? Mine? My own brother's?

"Watch your step." Annie's words made him look down.

Preoccupied, he'd almost stepped into some tire tracks next to the burnt chimney. Something glimmered in the mud at his feet. Awkwardly, he squatted down and picked up a long strand of wire, spiderweb thin. It looked like copper and was quite strong.

He pulled on the wire, plucking it out of the mud. The wire ran up the side of the house to a charred bracket.

"Annie, please turn on the video." Finn gave a slight tug. The wire broke free and dropped to the ground.

After getting the footage and taking some stills, Annie asked, "Is that a TV wire?"

"No." Finn shook his head. "I've seen it before. I just can't remember where."

"What's it doing on the side of the house?"

That was the question on Finn's mind, too.

CHAPTER 5

Annie sank into the down comforter on the four-poster bed with her arms out to the sides like a little girl making snow angels. The last time she'd been without the kids at a hotel was her honeymoon. Camden had gotten so drunk at the wedding that he passed out, needing his best man and ushers had to carry him up to the bridal suite like pallbearers and toss him onto the bed. She spent the next day nursing his hangover before driving him home. Some honeymoon.

Casting the memory of that horrid day aside, she closed her eyes and inhaled the scent of freshly cut flowers from the nightstand.

Here she was now. A professional photographer on a business trip! The kids were having a ball at the Church's. Tammy was making a pie with Grace today, and Tommy and Howard were making a birdhouse. It was like summer camp for them, and a paid vacation for her. She made fists with her hands and excitedly kicked her legs. She was doing this. She was making her way in a world where everyone told her she would fail.

But Finn believed in her. His trust and her kids' love sent a surge of confidence racing through her. She felt like she could rip open her shirt like Superman and there would be a giant purple *A* there. Awesome Annie!

Laughing, she sprang off the bed, threw her arms wide, and twirled in a circle like Julie Andrews in *The Sound of Music*.

She stopped and stared at Finn standing in the doorway. Her mouth opened and closed like Tammy's Hungry, Hungry Hippos game.

"Sorry." Finn waved. "I knocked, but I knew you couldn't hear it. I tried to text, too."

Annie shrugged and laughed again. She was so happy she didn't care who saw her dancing, even Finn. "This place is fabulous."

Finn smiled. "I'm glad you like it. I want to drive over to Norwood and get Mrs. Gallagher to sign off on the itemized sheet before dinner. Is that all right with you?"

"Sure. I feel so much better having showered off that awful smell. Let me grab my camera gear."

Annie gathered her equipment and followed close behind Finn as he walked out to the car. He smelled of soap and aftershave. They drove for several miles with Finn looking like he wanted to ask her something, but each time he glanced her way, he quickly looked straight ahead again.

After the fifth time, while they were waiting at a red light, Annie held up her hand like a school traffic guard. "What do you want to ask me?"

Finn pressed his lips together. "Sometimes I think you can read my mind."

"I can." Annie grinned playfully. "But that would be rude, so I thought I should ask."

Finn laughed. "It's a little awkward. And you can say no. The bachelor party for my friend who's getting married is tomorrow night, and so is the bachelorette party for his soon-to-be bride. They invited you too. They're pretty conservative, so I don't think the parties will be anything too wild . . ."

Annie inhaled. The thought of going to a party where she knew absolutely no one would normally terrify her, but this was the new Annie. Awesome Annie, or maybe Adventure Annie? "I'd love to. I'll have to pick up a present, though."

"I hadn't thought of that."

The light changed and Finn started to drive.

"How do you know Jack?" Annie asked.

Finn grinned crookedly. "He saved my life. He and his foster brother, Chandler."

"I can't wait to meet them."

Finn's face turned somber. "Chandler didn't make it."

Annie nodded. She wanted to reach out and comfort him, but instead she sat there, waiting to see if Finn wanted to discuss something so heartbreaking.

"It was in Iraq. I got hit with an RPG. Rocket-propelled grenade. It hit the sand in front of me and disappeared. It was so fast. I remember thinking it hadn't gone off. But it did. Blasted me like an out-of-control astronaut, feet over head, twirling through the air, until I made a crash landing."

Finn pushed back in his seat. The strong muscles in his forearms flexed as he gripped the steering wheel. "Then all hell broke loose. Thirty men opened up on us. Everyone was pinned down and I was bleeding out. I didn't call for help."

Annie had always been an easy crier. Even now, when she watched *Bambi*, it was Tammy consoling her and not the other way around. And right now, she strained against the tears to keep from weeping, but she forced her voice to get through her question without breaking. "Why didn't you call for help?"

"Because it would've just got someone else killed when they came to get me."

"But Jack did?"

"And Chandler. They disobeyed an order to do it." Finn chuckled. "Jack still says that he never heard the platoon sergeant, but ... I was lying there and I saw this big metal panel moving toward me. Bullets were dinging off it, and behind the panel I heard these two guys yelling at each other."

"Jack and Chandler?"

"Yeah. They were griping like some old married couple. Chandler was enormous, just a mountain of a man. And he held this armored panel off a Humvee up like a shield while Jack put a tourniquet on my leg. Jack dragged me out of there while Chandler held up that panel and bullets rained down on us."

Finn grinned.

"What?"

"They dragged me back to cover and Stratton was just cracking up. He was laughing so hard it looked like it hurt. Chandler asked him what was so funny, and Jack looked at him and said, 'I had no idea that would actually work.'"

Finn laughed. "Chandler pushed Jack so hard he rolled over three times in the sand. But he kept laughing."

"Why was he laughing? All of you could have died right there."

"That's one of the crazy parts of war." Finn shook his head. "You just reach this point where you're so scared and then . . . nothing. It's like moving into the eye of a hurricane. I was laughing, too."

"And Jack is the one getting married? What is his fiancée like?"

"Alice is Chandler's foster sister. I haven't met her, but they talked about her a lot." Finn smiled mischievously.

"What aren't you telling me?"

"Chandler always said that she was crazier than Jack." Finn chuckled. "I can't wait to meet her."

"Oh, great!" Annie rolled her eyes. "And I'm going to her bachelorette party?"

"You don't have to go." Finn slowed down and turned onto a pretty cul-de-sac. He frowned. "Do you find it odd that the

Gallaghers' vacation home is only two towns away from their permanent residence?"

"Maybe he's an avid fisherman." Annie shrugged.

Finn parked at the end of a herringbone-patterned brick driveway. The Gallaghers' house filled up the entire lot.

"Wow!" They exclaimed in unison.

"Should I bring my gear?" Annie asked.

Finn grabbed his briefcase. "I'll take notes. We're just going to have her go over the list and sign some forms."

Annie exhaled. She was fine videotaping inanimate objects, but when it came to recording people, she felt less confident. She absolutely dreaded the thought of recording a deposition. It wasn't the video that intimidated her, it was the audio. She could see the meters moving, so she could tell if the audio levels were too low or high, but what about background noise or static? The truth was, she didn't know how it would go, and it was going to be a learning experience.

Shoving her worries aside, she thought about her super-hero persona and followed Finn into the unknown with a smile.

Finn nudged her to get her attention and said, "I'm surprised there isn't a drawbridge or a moat."

Annie smiled and rang the bell.

After a moment, a middle-aged woman answered the ornate door. "You must be the insurance investigators." She extended a bejeweled hand toward Finn. "I'm Caroline Gallagher. It's a pleasure."

Annie eyed the three gold bangles and diamond tennis bracelet on her wrist and the several expensive-looking rings on her fingers. Between that and her glossy inch-and-a-half nails, Annie wondered how Caroline had managed to punch the numbers into a phone to call the insurance company. "Annie Summers."

"Please come in." Caroline led them into an opulent living

room. "My apologies, but my husband took our boys to the game. I can sign whatever you need, though."

"We stopped by your summer residence at 361 Sandy Beach Lane to photograph the damage. I need you to confirm the itemized list," Finn said, taking a seat by the coffee table.

"When can we expect due compensation for our loss?" Mrs. Gallagher settled onto the sofa and crossed her legs daintily.

"I'm afraid that's something that's handled by the corporate office."

"Of course." Caroline picked up a piece of paper from the coffee table. "One of my sons realized that he'd brought his laptop and a game station to the lake house. My apologies, he'd forgotten about them and we left them off our initial claim."

Finn handed the sheet to Annie. "We'll be certain to add them."

Annie sat there while Finn and Caroline ran down the list and she signed several forms. The longer it went on, the more Annie's thoughts wandered, and so did her eyes, stopping on the pictures of the family on the wall. They were mostly vacation photos of places Annie could only dream of taking Tommy and Tammy. Tropical islands with blue water and snowcapped peaks. Oh, how she'd love to head off one day and photograph this breathtaking planet!

After nearly an hour, Caroline signed the last of the pages and Finn placed them back in his briefcase. He stood and shook Caroline's hand. "I'm sorry for your loss."

Caroline shrugged. "When life hands you limes, you make margaritas. We've been through this before, you know. All of my friends are making jokes about broken mirrors and black cats, but you know what? Who cares? We'll build an even bigger house!"

Annie smiled. "That's the way to look at it."

Caroline took cut her phone and glanced at the number. "I'm sorry, but it's the fire cleanup service. I have to take this."

"Of course," Finn said. "We'll see ourselves out."

As they made their way to the front door, Annie noticed that though the photographs were ordinary, all the frames were unique and artfully designed, which made the pictures seem even more interesting. She took out her phone and snapped a quick shot of one of the family photos for a frame idea.

Meanwhile, Finn stared at a picture of the Gallaghers in front of the Sydney Opera House in Australia. It was taken at night with fireworks going off in the background. On the frame was written, CELEBRATING NEW YEAR'S!

The muscles in Finn's jaw flexed. Annie watched as he leaned closer and stared at the multicolored explosions and his chest began to rise and fall rapidly.

He grabbed her by the wrist and hurried out the front door. She was starting to wonder if he was having a PTSD flashback. Maybe the sight of the fireworks triggered memories of the grenade that cost him his leg.

"Are you okay, Finn? Do you want me to drive?" she asked.

"I'm fine." He grinned but his eyes were wild. "Great, actually, but I don't think that fire was an accident," he said, starting up the car.

"But that's impossible." Annie clicked her seat belt. "The arson investigator said it was lightning and the weather station confirmed that a lightning bolt hit that area."

Finn nodded but his smile widened. "Too much of a coincidence. I was sure of it from the beginning, but now we need to prove it. Can you do me a favor? Get directions to the nearest army-navy store between here and the lake."

Annie raised a skeptical eyebrow. If Finn was experiencing PTSD right now, she wasn't sure how to handle it. She decided to try for humor. "Are you telling me that Patrick Gallagher somehow obtained Thor's hammer and figured out how to call down lightning?" She chuckled.

Finn laughed. "That's exactly what I'm saying."

CHAPTER 6

Annie pulled up in front of the only army-navy store within a hundred miles. Finn had ridden in the passenger seat, frantically searching the internet on his phone, but so far he hadn't filled Annie in on whatever had gotten him so excited.

"You're still not ready to tell me your theory?" she asked as he started to get out of the car.

Finn stopped with the door partially open. He gazed at her for a moment, then lowered his eyes. "It's kinda out there, and if I'm wrong, I'll feel pretty foolish."

Annie squeezed his hand. "A fool is the last thing you'd ever be to me."

Finn reached into his pocket and pulled out a piece of the fine wire he'd found in the tire ruts at the scene. "This could be the proverbial smoking gun."

Annie could hardly wait to hear what he was thinking.

"There's only one reason to have a wire like this running up the side of a house and clamped at the top. I knew I'd seen this wire before, but I didn't remember where until I saw the photograph of the fireworks. Then it all made sense."

"Not to me." Annie smiled sheepishly. "You lost me at fireworks."

"This is a tow wire. It's used by the military on wire-guided missiles. The missile is controlled by signals sent to it via these thin wires that spool out behind it after it's launched." He gazed at her hopefully.

"And?" Annie still couldn't figure out where Finn was going with this.

"I think it's possible that Patrick Gallagher attached a tow wire to a rocket and fired it during a lightning storm."

"A rocket-rocket?" Annie stared at the store. "You can't buy those things here, can you?"

"You can buy model rockets at hobby stores and online. They can go high enough if you know what you're doing, and there's a chance he bought the wire here."

Annie closed one eye as she tried to take in what he was saying. "So you think Patrick was like a space-age Ben Franklin and his kite?"

"Exactly."

Annie found herself smiling to match Finn's wide grin. "It's not that crazy a theory," she said. "Tommy told me about a university in Florida that did something like that. Florida is the lightning capital of the world and . . . " She scrunched up her face. "I should have paid more attention when he was telling me."

"I figure it's worth a shot," Finn said.

Annie nodded and they got out of the car.

The army-navy store was stacked floor-to-ceiling with an eclectic mix of old and new military gear. Bright-yellow and orange SALE signs were everywhere. A large older man wearing a cowboy hat eyed them from behind the counter. "How ya doin'?"

"Exceptional." Finn made his way around several tables

covered with merchandise and Annie followed close behind. "I was wondering if you sell tow wire."

The man eyed Finn up and down. "You were army."

Finn nodded.

"Marines." The corner of the man's mouth ticked up and he placed both hands on the counter like he was going to challenge Finn to an arm-wrestling contest right then and there. "You serve overseas?"

"Iraq."

The man nodded. "'Nam."

Finn returned the gesture.

"Name's Nate."

"Finn." They shook hands.

"What you planning to do with tow wire?"

"Why's that suspicious?"

"You didn't answer my question, son." The man crossed his arms, flexing his faded tattoos.

Finn looked like he was debating what to tell the man. As the staring contest continued, Annie thought about interjecting, but then Finn said, "I'm an insurance investigator. I think someone might have bought tow wire to start a fire."

Nate scoffed. "I don't know nothing about starting a fire with it, but tow wire's perfectly legal."

"I'm certain it is," Finn said. "Do you sell it?"

"Sold out last week, matter o' fact."

Finn glanced at Annie, his eyes wide and hopeful. "Did the person pay by credit card?"

"Nope. Cash only." Nate pointed at a sign in front of the register.

"Do you have security cameras?" Finn asked.

Nate pointed at his own eyes. "I have security in spades. Got a gun on a magnet every ten feet along the counter."

"Wait!" Annie took out her phone. She held it out and

showed Nate the Gallagher family photo she'd snapped. He nodded.

"That's the fella. He bought the whole spool."

"Would you sign an affidavit to that effect?" Finn asked.

"Is this gonna come back to bite me on the butt?"

"Not at all. And you'd be helping a good cause."

"If you were a customer, I suppose I'd have to sign. That's just good business."

"Then I am in need of a few things." Finn shook Nate's hand. "Did the man who bought the wire buy anything else?"

"Nope." Nate rolled his eyes.

Annie held up her hand and Nate chuckled. "This ain't school, miss. If ya got a question, shout it out."

"After Finn asked if the man bought anything else, you said no but then rolled your eyes and made a face. Why?"

"Because that guy was a yahoo. He comes in here asking for tow wire and then asks me if I sell any rockets. I was ready to hold him until the cops came, but he said he was only looking for the model kind. I gave him directions to the hobby store in the center of town."

Finn turned to Annie and his eyes sparkled. "I guess I'm not a fool after all!"

Annie hugged Finn, but his arms stayed out at his sides like she was measuring him for a suit jacket.

Nate leaned over the counter and said, "If you don't hug that pretty lady back, I'd say you're the biggest fool I ever met!"

Finn wrapped his arms around Annie and they all laughed.

***

ANNIE BARRELED across town to reach All Ages Toys and Hobbies before it closed. The rental car had great pickup compared to her bruised banana-mobile, as they called her speckled yellow car, and with new shocks and brakes, she loved the way it hugged the road. She powered into a turn, the speed pressing her into the seat and the wind whipping her hair back. Exhilaration coursed through her—until she glanced over at Finn. He was holding onto the crash handle with a white-knuckled grip.

Annie slowed down. "Sorry. I like to drive fast."

"I could tell." Finn loosened his tie. "There it is!"

Annie jerked the wheel, slightly clipping the curb. The front end rose about a foot and a half in the air. She locked up the brakes, cut the wheel, and skidded to a stop directly in front of the hobby store.

A father and young son stood, wide-eyed, on the sidewalk.

"That was awesome!" The boy gave Annie a double thumbs-up before turning to his father. "Dad, can you do that?"

His father frowned at Annie, then unlocked the minivan parked in the next space. Annie bounded out of the car and forced herself to slow down for Finn.

Finn shook his head and pointed at the store. "Go! Go! Go!"

Annie rushed over to the door and yanked it open. A startled clerk stood there, keys in his hand like he was about to lock the door. "We're closed."

"Not yet." Annie smiled, pointing at the open door. "This will only take a minute of your time and we'd really appreciate it."

Finn waved and smiled at the clerk. "We just have a quick question."

Annie took out her phone. "Did this man buy any model rockets here last week?" She pointed to Patrick Gallagher in the photograph.

The teen shrugged and held up his index finger, then he turned and yelled something inside the store.

"He's getting his father," Finn explained to Annie.

The teenager looked at them and pointed at his right ear. "I'm deaf."

Annie signed, *Me too!*

The boy's eyes lit up and he started signing so fast Annie had a hard time keeping up.

Annie and Finn spent almost an hour at the hobby store. The boy, Michael, and his father, Matt, provided Finn and Annie with a virtual treasure trove—a list of model rocket engines that Patrick Gallagher had purchased, as well as credit card receipts and security footage proving it was Patrick doing the buying. He had all the equipment he needed to take advantage of a lightning storm to start a fire.

"You're a genius!" Annie hugged Finn and patted his back in admiration. This time he pulled her close to his broad chest and wrapped his strong arms around her.

Michael signed something and Annie's breath caught in her throat.

"What did he say?" Finn asked.

"He said that when he gets married, he hopes he and his wife get to work together, too."

CHAPTER 7

Finn set his fork down, picked up his water glass, and raised it in a toast. "To Annie Summers and Finnian Church. An investigative team for the ages."

Annie blushed as red as her wine. "To the adventures of Finn and Annie!" she proclaimed quite loudly.

Far from embarrassed, Finn ignored the sidelong looks from the other diners. They would have no idea that Annie was deaf and that regulating her voice's volume was difficult for her.

Let them stare.

"I noticed you looking at that little gazebo out by the pond when we came in," Finn said. "Would you like to take a walk before going to bed?"

Annie finished off her wine and nodded. When they'd finished dinner, they stepped outside and headed toward the little pond and the gazebo. The spring night air had a bit of a chill to it and Annie shivered. Finn peeled off his suit jacket and held it out. "Do you want to go back inside?"

Annie shook her head and pointed. Two rows of lights lit up a narrow path leading to the gazebo and reached up to circle its roof. The fairy lights cast golden reflections in the water that danced as a fountain sent ripples across the pond.

The two walked slowly along the gravel path. Inside the gazebo, speakers hung from the ceiling and "*That's Amore*" was playing. Finn started to hum along with Dean Martin before he realized that Annie wouldn't be able to hear it.

"Sorry."

Her brows knit together. He pointed at the speakers. "Music."

"Oh." She rushed over to the railing and stood on the bottom rung. Reaching up, she held her fingertips to a speaker and smiled forlornly. He watched a tear roll down her cheek.

"What's wrong?" He stared at the speaker, and felt a sudden, completely irrational urge to rip the wires out for causing this beautiful woman pain.

But Annie smiled and wiped away the tear. "Music. I miss it. I can feel the vibrations, but it's not the same. When I was a little girl, I wanted to be a dancer."

Finn felt like his heart was being squeezed inside his chest. He pictured Annie as a child, dressed like a ballerina and standing in a silent music hall. "I'm so sorry."

Annie shrugged.

"Do you mind if I ask what happened to your hearing?"

Annie recoiled like he'd raised a hand to slap her.

"I'm sorry. You don't have to explain. I completely understand."

She exhaled and seemed to relax again somewhat. "It's still hard." She lifted her hand up to the speaker again. "The song changed?"

Finn nodded and smiled. "Now it's Elvis. My father is a big Elvis fan. We used to all dance together when we were kids. We still do at weddings . . . Oh, the stupid wedding!"

"What?" Annie stepped down from the railing.

Finn forced himself to look at her. "Everybody dances at weddings and I can't dance anymore."

Annie nodded and her smile faded.

Anger washed over him. They had both lost so many little things, but this felt like the proverbial straw breaking the camel's back. How many joys had they been robbed of? Now this, too?

Finn reached out and Annie took his hand. But when he stepped close and placed his other hand on her waist, she stepped away.

"I can't." Annie mashed her lips together. "I can't hear the music."

"I only have one leg." Finn grinned. "We should practice before the wedding."

She gasped. "I couldn't. We couldn't. Everyone will look at us!"

Finn stepped forward and held out his hand once again. "Frankly, my dear, I don't give a damn."

Annie grabbed him and didn't let go. Together they danced, holding onto each other beneath the stars. Annie swayed to the rhythm of Finn's body and Finn was supported by her firm hold. The lights twinkled along the ripples of the water, but all Finn saw was their glittering reflection in Annie's gorgeous eyes.

At the beginning of their third dance, Finn pulled away a little so she could read his lips. "If we help each other, we can both learn to dance again." He smiled crookedly.

Annie nodded. "What song is this?"

"'I Can't Help Falling in Love with You.'"

And they kissed.

ALSO BY
CHRISTOPHER GREYSON

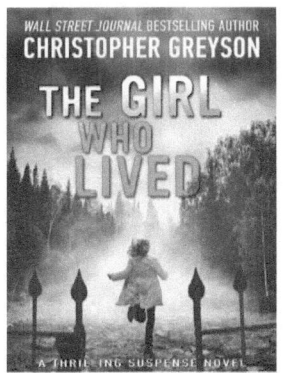

THE GIRL WHO LIVED

Ten years ago, four people were brutally murdered. One girl lived. As the anniversary of the murders approaches, Faith Winters is released from the psychiatric hospital and yanked back to the last spot on earth she wants to be—her hometown where the slayings took place. Wracked by the lingering echoes of survivor's guilt, Faith spirals into a black hole of alcoholism and wanton self-destruction. Finding no solace at the bottom of a bottle, Faith decides to track down her sister's killer—and then discovers that she's the one being hunted.

ONE LITTLE LIE

A LIE IS A WELCOME MAT FOR THE DEVIL...

Kate had high hopes when she moved to her husband's hometown, but her domestic bliss was short-lived. Blindsided by her spouse's public affair with his high school sweetheart, everything she worked for begins to unravel, along with her sanity. Confused, alone, and afraid, can Kate untangle the web of lies and unmask her stalker, or will she lose everything—including her life?

One Little Lie is a riveting suspense novel set in an idyllic town where money talks, gossip flows, and the court of public opinion rules. Jump on for a fun, fast-paced ride with a book you can't put down!

The Detective Jack Stratton Mystery-Thriller Series, authored by *Wall Street Journal* bestselling writer Christopher Greyson, has 5,000+ five-star reviews and over a million readers and counting. If you'd love to read another page-turning thriller with mystery, humor, and a dash of romance, pick up the next book in the highly acclaimed series today:

And Then She Was GONE

A hometown hero with a heart of gold, Jack Stratton was raised in a whorehouse by his prostitute mother. When his foster mother asks him to look into a missing girl's disappearance, Jack quickly gets drawn into a baffling mystery. As Jack digs deeper, everyone becomes a suspect—including himself.

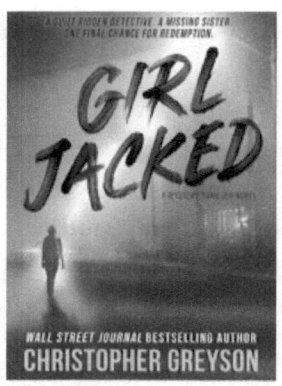

GIRL JACKED

They say a dangerous man is the one who had it all and lost it. But they're wrong, it's the one who lost everything but has a chance to get it back...

Guilt has driven a wedge between Jack and the family he loves. When Jack, now a police officer, hears the news that his foster sister Michelle is missing, it cuts straight to his core. The police think she just took off, but Jack knows Michelle would never leave her loved ones behind—like he did. Forced to confront the demons from his past, Jack must take action, find Michelle, and bring her home... or die trying.

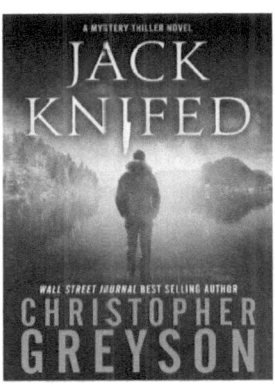

JACK KNIFED

How far would you go to uncover the truth of your past?

Constant nightmares have forced Jack to seek answers about his rough childhood and the dark secrets hidden there. The mystery surrounding Jack's birth father leads Jack to investigate the twenty-seven-year-old murder case in Hope Falls.

A heart-rending mystery-thriller about lost love, betrayal, and murder that will keep you on the edge of your seat.

JACKS ARE WILD

As the body count rises, the stakes are life and death—with no rules except one—Jacks are Wild.

When Jack's sexy old flame disappears, no one thinks it's suspicious except Jack and one unbalanced witness. Jack feels in his gut that something is wrong. He knows that Marisa has a past, and if it ever caught up with her—it would be deadly. The trail leads him into all sorts of trouble—landing him smack in the middle of an all-out mob war between the Italian Mafia and the Japanese Yakuza.

A strong hero, smart women sleuths, and more twists and turns than a piece of licorice.

JACK AND THE GIANT KILLER

A serial killer is stalking Jack's town--and no one's safe. But they don't know Jack.

Rogue hero Jack Stratton is back in another action-packed, thrilling adventure. While recovering from a gunshot wound, Jack gets a seemingly harmless private investigation job— locate the owner of a lost dog—Jack begrudgingly assists. Little does he know it will place him directly in the crosshairs of a merciless serial killer.

An action-packed thrill ride until the very end!

DATA JACK

Can Jack and Alice stop a pack of ruthless criminals before they can Data Jack?

Jack Stratton's back is up against the wall. He's broke, kicked off the force, and his new bounty hunting business has slowed to a trickle. He thinks things are turning around when Alice gets a lucrative job setting up a home data network.When the computer program the CEO invented becomes the key tool in an international data heist, things turn deadly. In this digital age of hackers, spyware, and cyber terrorism--data is more valuable than gold. The thieves plan to steal the keys to the digital kingdom and with this much money at stake, they'll kill for it. Can Jack and Alice stop the pack of ruthless criminals before they can *Data Jack*?

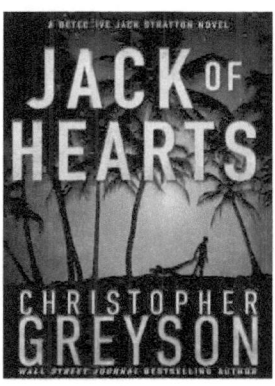

JACK OF HEARTS

Jack Stratton is heading south for some fun in the sun. Already nervous about introducing his girlfriend, Alice, to his parents, the last thing Jack needed was for the dog-sitter to cancel, forcing him to bring Lady, their 120-pound King Shepherd, on the plane with them. The dog holds Jack responsible and wants payback. On top of everything, Jack is still waiting for Alice's answer to his marriage proposal.

When his mother and the members of her neighborhood book club ask him to catch the "Orange Blossom Cove Bandit," a small-time thief who's stealing garden gnomes and peace of mind from their quiet retirement community, how can Jack refuse?

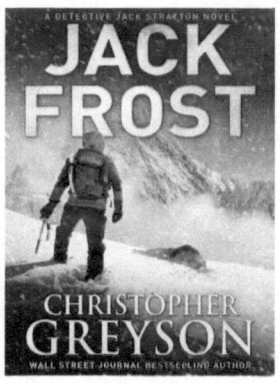

JACK FROST

What do you get when you mix the blockbuster television show Survivor with Agatha Christie's masterpiece And Then There Were None...

Jack has a new assignment: to investigate the suspicious death of a soundman on the hit TV show *Planet Survival*. Jack goes undercover as a security agent where the show is filming on nearby Mount Minuit. Soon trapped on the treacherous peak by a blizzard, a mysterious killer continues to stalk the cast and crew of *Planet Survival*. What started out as a game is now a deadly competition for survival. As the temperature drops and the body count rises, what will get them first? The mountain or the killer?

JACK OF DIAMONDS

All Jack Stratton wants to do is get married to the woman he loves—and make it through the wedding. It seems like he is finally getting his wish until he responds to a police distress call and discovers his old partner unconscious in an abandoned house. Investigators insist it was just an accident, but Jack fears there may be more to it. Sketches of women cover the walls, and among them is one sketch that makes Jack's blood run cold —a sketch of Alice, pinned up beside an invitation to a very special wedding—his own.

This time, "till death do us part"
might just be a bit too accurate!

CAPTAIN JACK

Looking forward to some fun in the surf and sand, newlyweds Jack and Alice Stratton are determined not to let something like a hurricane upset their honeymoon plans. But the storm's winds and churning tides unearthed a secret long hidden beneath the turquoise waters of the island paradise.

A local tour boat captain discovers a lost submarine and offers to sell the location to a man known only as the Dyab—the Devil. When the captain is murdered, the police suspect Jack and Alice and confiscate their passports. Trapped between the Devil and the deep blue sea, the handsome young detective and his blushing bride have nowhere to turn and everything to lose as they set out to prove their innocence and find the real killer.

Hear your favorite characters
come to life in audio versions of
the Detective Jack Stratton
Mystery-Thriller Series!
Audio Books now available on Audible!
Listen Now

Fantasy Adventure
PURE OF HEART

Orphaned and alone, rogue-teen Dean Walker has learned how to take care of himself on the rough city streets. Unjustly wanted by the police, he takes refuge within the shadows of the city. When Dean stumbles upon an old man being mugged, he tries to help—only to discover that the victim is anything but helpless and far more than he appears. Together with three friends, he sets out on an epic quest where only the pure of heart will prevail.

You could win a brand new
HD KINDLE FIRE TABLET
when you go to
ChristopherGreyson.com
Enter as many times as you'd like.
No purchase necessary.
It's just my way of thanking my loyal readers.

THE ADVENTURES OF FINN & ANNIE — MINIMYSTERY SERIES

In these heartwarming short stories, join Finn and Annie as they investigate their way through murder, arson, theft, embezzlement, and maybe even love, seeking to distinguish between truth and lies, scammers and victims. A MiniMystery series that will touch your heart and leave you craving more!

ACKNOWLEDGMENTS

I would like to thank all the wonderful readers out there. It is you who make the literary world what it is today—a place of dreams filled with tales of adventure! Word of mouth is crucial for any author to succeed. If you enjoyed the novel, please consider leaving a review at Amazon, even if it is only a line or two; it would make all the difference and I would appreciate it very much.

I would also like to thank my amazing wife for standing beside me every step of the way on this journey. My thanks also go out to my two awesome kids—Laura and Christopher, my dear mother and the rest of my family. Finally, thank you to my wonderful team, Anne Cherry, Maia McViney, Michael Mishoe, Charlie Wilson of The Book Specialist, David Gatewood of Lone Trout Editing, and the unbelievably helpful beta readers!

ABOUT THE AUTHOR

My name is Christopher Greyson, and I am a storyteller. Since I was a little boy, I have dreamt of what mystery was around the next corner, or what quest lay over the hill. If I couldn't find an adventure, one usually found me, and now I weave those tales into my stories.

My love for tales of mystery and adventure began with my grandfather, a decorated World War I hero. I will never forget being introduced to his friend, a WWI pilot who flew across the skies at the same time as the feared, legendary Red Baron. I love to hear from my readers. Please go to Christopher-Greyson.com and sign up for my mailing list to receive periodic updates on new book releases. Thank you for reading my novels. I hope my stories have brightened your day.

Sincerely,

V.I.I2.22